NYPD RED 3

JAMES PATTERSON is one of the best-known and biggest-selling writers of all time. Since winning the Edgar™ Award for Best First Novel with *The Thomas Berryman Number*, his books have sold in excess of 300 million copies worldwide and he has been the most borrowed author in UK libraries for the past eight years in a row. He is the author of some of the most popular series of the past two decades – the Alex Cross, Women's Murder Club, Detective Michael Bennett and Private novels – and he has written many other number one bestsellers including romance novels and stand-alone thrillers. He lives in Florida with his wife and son.

James is passionate about encouraging children to read. Inspired by his own son who was a reluctant reader, he also writes a range of books specifically for young readers. James is a founding partner of Booktrust's Children's Reading Fund in the UK.

Also by James Patterson

NYPD RED SERIES

NYPD Red (*with Marshall Karp*)
NYPD Red 2 (*with Marshall Karp*)

A list of more titles by James Patterson is printed
at the back of this book

NYPD RED 3

JAMES PATTERSON
& MARSHALL KARP

arrow books

1 3 5 7 9 10 8 6 4 2

Arrow Books
20 Vauxhall Bridge Road
London SW1V 2SA

Arrow Books is part of the Penguin Random House group of companies
whose addresses can be found at global.penguinrandomhouse.com.

Penguin
Random House
UK

First published by Century in 2015
First published in paperback by Arrow Books in 2015

www.randomhouse.co.uk

A CIP catalogue record for this book is
available from the British Library.

Typeset in Berkeley Oldstyle (11/15.5pt) by SX Composing DTP, Rayleigh, Essex
Printed and bound in Great Britain by Clays Ltd, St Ives Plc

MIX
Paper from
responsible sources
FSC
www.fsc.org   FSC® C018179

Penguin Random House is committed to a sustainable future
for our business, our readers and our planet. This book is
made from Forest Stewardship Council® certified paper.

For Gerri and Victor Gomperts, who helped me find what I was looking for

Prologue

"THERE'S MONEY TO BE MADE"

One

EVERY DECEMBER 31, Hunter Hutchinson Alden Jr. made the same two New Year's resolutions.

1. Be worth X dollars by the end of next year.
2. Quit drinking.

This year's goal was five billion, and considering the fact that his current net worth was 4.86 billion, getting there was a slam dunk. But forty-five minutes and three glasses of Pellegrino into his father's New Year's Day party, he knew that number two was doomed to failure. Again.

He crammed himself into the corner of a blue calfskin Himmel settee at the east end of the Great Room so he could avoid eye contact with the swarm of well-heeled narcissists who were strutting around

Hutch Alden's Fifth Avenue triplex, flaunting their glorious Christmas-in-Saint-Barts tans.

It was the same crowd every year—the A-list of the Rich and Shallow—and Hunter was there for only one reason. He was duty-bound to charm the hell out of his old man's guests.

But not yet. Right now he was too pissed to be charming.

He glared at his iPhone, willing it to vibrate, beep, chirp, or in any way show some sign of life. One of them would call eventually, and he was willing to bet it wouldn't be his son. The kid wouldn't have the balls to man up, so he'd pass the buck to Peter, who would apologize profusely and blame himself for Tripp's bad behavior.

The first note of his ringtone erupted from the phone, and he hit the green Accept button the instant it blossomed onto the screen. "Where the hell are you?" he growled, not even knowing if he was dealing with Tripp or Peter.

"Is that any way to talk to a lady?" a sexy female voice drawled.

"Sorry. I was expecting a call from the most irresponsible eighteen-year-old on the planet. Or at least from the driver I sent hours ago to bail him out of trouble."

"I'm none of those, but I'm blonde, I'm hot, and you seem to be extremely agitated. Perhaps I can do something to calm you down."

"I'm sure you could."

"Are you available?"

"Technically I'm married, but I'm not a fanatic about it."

"Good," the blonde said. "Ditch her. You're exactly the kind of man I've been looking for."

"What kind is that?"

"A lifelong challenge."

"But worth the effort," he said. "Where can I find you?"

"The same place Romeo found Juliet."

Hunter looked up at the sweeping balcony on the west side of the room. There was his wife, Janelle, waving. "Stay where you are, Romeo."

Hunter hung up and watched as the former Miss Alabama sashayed down the marble staircase and breezed across the room, a natural-born ambassador, greeting guests on the fly, a flurry of blonde hair and pink silk.

Pink was Janelle's color. She wore it often in honor of her sister Chelsea, who survived breast cancer at the age of twenty-six, only to die at thirty when the Twin Towers fell.

Hunter met Janelle a year later—September 11, 2002. He was one of the thousands of mourners who filed into the gaping hole at Ground Zero to remember the dead. And there, in the middle of the sea of somber gray and funereal black, was this golden-haired, angel-faced vision in pink.

She was the polar opposite of his late wife. Marjorie had been Yankee-bred, Harvard Business School–trained, and Wall Street ruthless. Janelle was heart of Dixie to the core and had never taken a business course in her life, yet she had raised millions for charity simply by using her abundant charm.

She sat down on the settee and rested a hand on Hunter's knee. "I'm going home. Early day tomorrow."

"I'll go with you. We haven't had sex all year."

"Not so fast, cowboy. You're wanted up top," she said, pointing toward the balcony. "Hutch has someone he wants you to shake hands with."

"He's got a house full of people he wants me to shake hands with."

"But only one is the new mayor of New York, which is why she's having a drink with Hutch in his private sanctuary while the rest of them are forced to wander aimlessly around the castle. I'll see you at home."

"How are you getting there? Peter is still off the grid."

"I'm sure he's busy fixing Tripp's car."

"He's not a damn mechanic, Janelle. He's our driver. I specifically told him to leave Tripp's car where it is and just bring the kid home. Not keeping in touch is Tripp's MO. Now he's got Peter doing it."

"Sweetie, Tripp *did* keep in touch," Janelle said. "He texted to say he needed help; you sent help, end of story. Now stop micromanaging and don't worry about me. Hutch already arranged for Findley to drive me home. Now why don't you practice what you preach?"

"What's that supposed to mean?"

"Be a good boy and don't disappoint *your* father. He expects you to go upstairs and make nice to our new mayor. Do it." She gave him a quick kiss and headed for the door.

Hunter stood up and took a deep breath. The room smelled of money: *publishing* money, *cosmetics* money, and, of course, *money* money—the kind that comes from making canny investments when the rest of the world is betting the other way. He downed his fourth glass of imported water, turned on his handcrafted smile, and glided into the clowder of fat cats.

"Hunter!" It was Damon Parker, the despicable TV journalist who once described Hutch Alden as a folksy

Warren Buffett who had tragically spawned a son as ruthless as Rupert Murdoch.

Parker advanced on him, all smiles, hand outstretched, but Hunter bounded up the stairs to hallowed ground—Hutch's five-million-dollar command center, where none could go unless summoned.

"There you are," his father said, striding toward him next to Muriel Sykes, the tall, athletic-looking woman whose face had been on page one of every newspaper in New York that morning. "Say hello to our guest of honor."

"Madam Mayor," Hunter said. "I'd shake your hand, but you don't have a free one."

It was Hutch's standing tradition at his New Year's parties to provide his guests with a taste of old New York, and the mayor had a half-eaten hot dog in one hand and a chocolate egg cream in the other.

She turned one cheek, and Hunter planted a kiss. "Happy New Year, and happy new administration," he said. "How's it going so far?"

"Crazy day, but I'll give you the highlights. This morning the president called to wish me well, and tonight your father treated me to the single best New York hot dog I've ever had in my life."

"That's my dad," Hunter said. "True to his roots."

"I hate to eat and run," Sykes said, "but they've spent the entire day moving me into Gracie Mansion, and I'm dying to kick off my shoes and stretch out in my new digs. Happy New Year."

"You've been checking your phone all night," Hutch said as soon as Sykes was out of earshot. "What's so important?"

"It's Tripp. He had car trouble—up in Harlem, of all places. Peter went to rescue him, and I haven't heard from either of them in hours."

"Relax. Harlem is Peter's stomping ground. He's probably showing Tripp a good time. Those Haitian boys sure know how to party . . . if you catch my drift."

"*Haitian boys?* Yes, Dad, I catch your extremely politically incorrect drift."

"What are you talking about? I'm as politically correct as they come. Hell, I just spent a small fortune helping that goddamn broad get elected mayor."

Hunter laughed. "That's fiscally correct. I'm sure she'll come in handy if you ever need her."

The strapping white-haired man put one arm around his son's shoulder. "If *we* ever need her," he corrected. "As they say in *español,* '*Mi mayor, su mayor.*' Now are you ready to go downstairs and show these rich old farts how charming you can be?"

"Dad, there's nothing I'd rather do than go

downstairs, rub a couple of elbows, and shake a couple of hands," Hunter said, putting on his game face. "Except maybe track down Tripp and Peter and wring a couple of necks."

Two

HUNTER HAD HATED his father's New Year's Day soirees ever since he was a kid, but if this bullshit made the old man happy, what the hell? It was part of his birthright.

He spent the next two hours working his way through the crowd, clasping hands, bussing cheeks, and tossing off honey-voiced banalities. They were nothing more than empty platitudes, but personalized just enough to give people on the receiving end the impression that he actually gave a shit. What they didn't know was how much he actually knew about them.

Hunter Alden's entire financial engine was fueled by information. He spent millions putting eyes and ears in place around the globe. His intelligence network had infiltrated governments, businesses, and regulatory bodies. And because the rich have more dirty little secrets than most, he made it his business to dig deep into the personal lives of almost everyone in the room. He was willing to use whatever dirt he dug up against them, and he had.

By 10:00 p.m., his glad-handing done, he slipped quietly out the door and took Hutch's private elevator to the lobby.

Nils, the short, squat night doorman, was on duty. "Pretty nippy out there, Mr. Alden," he said. "Nineteen degrees. Twelve with the windchill factor. You sure you don't need a coat?"

Why the hell would I need a coat? Hunter thought. His world was climate controlled. Even the canopy outside the building had been outfitted with heat lamps to warm the wealthy as they walked the twenty feet from the lobby door to their waiting limos.

"Don't worry, Nils. I'll be fine," he said.

His father's black Cadillac was idling at the curb. Findley St. John, Hutch's longtime driver, saw him and spread both arms wide.

Findley was one of the few people to penetrate the wall that Hunter had built around himself. He had sung songs with Hunter when he drove the boy to his first day of kindergarten; he had pummeled three young thugs who mugged Hunter in middle school; and he'd almost gotten himself fired when he swore that the vodka bottle in the back of the Caddy belonged to him and not Hutch's fourteen-year-old son.

"Happy New Year, sport," he boomed, wrapping his arms around Hunter.

"Same to you, old man. I see you're still driving this piece of shit American car."

Findley put a gloved hand on the rear door handle, swung open the door, and shut it as soon as Hunter was in, leaving almost no time for the preheated air to escape into the cold night.

"Piece of shit car?" Findley said, getting behind the wheel. "You know what your daddy says. 'If it's good enough for the president of the United States, it's good enough for me.'"

"My father is too old and too rich to settle for 'good enough.' Nothing is more reliable than German engineering."

The mano a mano verbal sparring between the two men had been going on for decades, and Findley was thrilled to have another go at it. "And yet," he said, looking over his shoulder at Hunter, "that reliable German car of yours had to be bailed out by this piece of shit from Detroit."

"It wasn't the car that caused the problem," Hunter said. "It was my unreliable Haitian driver."

Findley let out a throaty laugh. He was from the same village as Peter. "I just drove Ms. Janelle home, and she didn't say nothing about no unreliable Haitians. Sounded more like the problem was that footloose teenager of yours. The apple sure don't fall far from the tree."

The ride up Madison gave them less than five minutes to catch up before Findley turned left on 81st Street. "Good news," he said as he pulled the Cadillac up to Hunter's four-story Beaux Arts limestone town house. "Light's on in the garage, so it looks like Peter is home."

"Son of a bitch," Hunter said, jumping out of the car before Findley could get to the door. "Why the hell didn't he call me?"

"I'm not hanging around to find out," Findley said, putting the limo in gear. "Don't be too hard on him, sport. It's New Year's."

Hunter headed straight for the garage. He flipped the keypad cover and tapped in the code, more excited to see his dream car than to confront Peter.

His Maybach 62 S had been built at the Center of Excellence in Sindelfingen, Germany. It was, in the words of the personal adviser who had worked with Hunter during the entire fourteen-month period from commission to delivery, "a one-of-a-kind automotive masterpiece, thoughtfully designed and flawlessly handcrafted to mirror the style and personality of its owner." And to Hunter, it was worth every penny of the 1.1 million it had cost to build it.

The garage door opened, and the room lit up even brighter. The space was wide and deep and empty. Hunter sucked in a lungful of the crisp January air. His car wasn't there. The only thing on the silver-pearl and slate-gray Swisstrax floor was the bright yellow molded polyethylene box that sat in the middle— Tripp's camera case. For Hunter, it was a bit of a relief. At least his son was home.

And then he saw it. At first it looked like random red markings on the yellow case. He got closer. The brownish-red lines were not from a marker. It was dried blood. And the haphazard strokes were actually letters: **HHA III**—Hunter Hutchinson Alden III. Tripp's initials.

Hunter dropped to his knees, snapped the stainless steel butterfly latches, and opened the case. Nestled on top was a Ziploc bag with a cell phone inside. He removed the bag and jerked back in horror at what was underneath: a severed head, cushioned by the case's thick foam lining, blood-soaked viscera hanging from the stump of its neck, the whites of its eyes staring up at Hunter.

It was Peter.

A single piece of paper was wedged between his lips. Hunter unfolded it and stared at the message. Five words, neatly typed.

There's money to be made.

Hunter's chest clenched, and he could barely fill his lungs with air. It was impossible, inconceivable, but there it was. Somebody somewhere had found out about Project Gutenberg.

Shaking, Hunter Alden closed the garage door and headed upstairs to pour his first drink of the new year.

Part One

THE SINS OF THE FATHER

Chapter 1

I HAD JUST had the best New Year's Day of my life, and when I opened my eyes on the morning of January second, the euphoria continued.

In front of me was a captivating panoramic view of Central Park, still dotted with patches of last week's white Christmas. Above me, the ceiling was adorned with handpainted cherubs and half-naked women frolicking in a wooded glade. And curled up next to me on our zillion-thread-count sheets was a totally naked woman who could put every one of those Roman goddesses in that bacchanalian fresco to shame.

"I could get used to this, Zach," Cheryl said. "You definitely should start taking more bribes."

Two nights ago, Cheryl and I had checked into the Steele Towers on Central Park South for a mini New

Year's vacation. The room I booked was something I could afford on a cop's salary, but when we got there, the desk clerk apologized. There was a maintenance problem in our room.

He waited just long enough to register the look on our faces, and then he said, "But don't worry, Detective Jordan. We'll upgrade you to a slightly better accommodation."

His version of "slightly better" was an eighteen-hundred-square-foot penthouse suite, the top of the line in this world-class, five-star hotel.

"Oh my God," Cheryl said when the floor concierge escorted us to our new digs. She looked at the pricing chart on the back of the door. "And only sixty-five hundred dollars a night."

"Happy accidents happen to the nicest people," the concierge said.

Not for a second did I think this was an accident. I knew exactly what it was: a silent gesture of gratitude from Jason Steele, the man who owned the hotel. His wife had been murdered a few months ago, and my partner, Kylie MacDonald, and I had cracked the case.

I stood in the doorway of the suite, called my boss, Captain Cates, and explained the problem.

"It's not a problem," she said. "You're there as a private citizen, not a cop."

"But the desk clerk called me Detective Jordan. He knew I was a cop."

"Zach, you're one of a handful of detectives assigned to NYPD Red. You've made two front-page arrests in the past six months. You better get used to the fact that people are going to recognize you. Now, you called me for a ruling. Here it is. Hotels upgrade all the time. Shut up, take it, and you and Cheryl have a happy New Year."

Boy did we ever. But now it was time to go back to reality. I got out of bed. "I'm going to take a shower," I said.

Cheryl stretched like a cat in the summer sun, and the sheets slipped below her breasts.

"On second thought," I said, "I'm hopping back in bed."

She smiled. "Just hop to the shower. I'll be right behind you."

"Behind me, in front of me . . . I'm sure we can work out the best arrangement once we're all wet and slippery," I said.

Cheryl's cell rang. "It's probably my parents wishing me a happy New Year," she said. "We played phone tag all day yesterday. I kept missing them. I'll be right there."

There were three bathrooms, and Cheryl and I had

experimented with shower gymnastics in every one of them. I headed for our favorite.

I dimmed the lights, dialed up some slow jazz, stepped into the green granite-tiled double shower, and turned on the water. It was heaven.

Despite the fact that my job keeps me in daily contact with New York City's wealthiest citizens, rarely do I get to live like one. I lost myself in the pulsating rhythms of the six perfect-pressure showerheads, closed my eyes, and thought about the dark-haired, caramel-skinned, drop-dead beautiful, kick-ass smart Latina I was rapidly falling in love with.

I'd met Cheryl Robinson four years ago. She was an NYPD psychologist, and I was a candidate for the department's most elite unit. It took her three hours to evaluate me. I, on the other hand, needed only three seconds to evaluate her. I'd never seen a cop or a shrink this desirable, and if it weren't for that gold band on her left hand, and the fact that she stood between me and the best job in the department, I would have thrown myself at her feet.

I got the job, and six months ago, shortly after her wedding ring came off forever, I got Cheryl. I'd only been in love once before. Eleven years ago I had a torrid twenty-eight-day affair with a fellow recruit at the police academy: Kylie MacDonald. But she dumped me and went back to her old boyfriend. A year after that, she married him.

Ten years later, the Department of Let's-See-If-We-Can-Drive-Zach-Jordan-Crazy decided to test my emotional resilience and put Kylie back in my life. Not as my girlfriend, but as my partner in crime solving. And for the past six months, Kylie and I have been inseparable—except for the part where she goes home to her husband, Spence Harrington, every night.

Fifteen minutes into my bathroom reverie, Cheryl still hadn't made an appearance, and I was starting to shrivel up in more ways than one.

I toweled off, put on a thick white terry robe, and went back to the master bedroom.

She was still on the phone.

"Be strong," she said. "I'll be there as soon as I can. Tell her to feel better and give her my love."

She hung up. "Zach, I'm sorry. Family emergency."

"Is your mother sick?" I asked.

"No. It's Fred's mother."

Fred? Fred was Cheryl's ex-husband. "That was Fred who called?"

She nodded. "He's devastated."

"I thought Fred was out of the picture."

"He is. But his mother is dying. I told you I was planning to drive up to Bedford next weekend for

Mildred's birthday. It looks like she's not going to make it till then. I'm going to run into the office, wrap up a few things, and catch a train up to Northern Westchester Hospital as soon as I can."

She got out of bed and threw on a robe. "I'm sorry, sweetie, but I'm going to shower, and it's going to be short and solo." She headed for the bathroom. "Oh, I almost forgot. Your cell rang while I was on the phone with Fred. I saw it was Kylie, so I picked up and told her you'd call right back."

Kylie wanted me, which meant work. Fred wanted Cheryl, which meant I would have something to obsess about all day besides work.

I called Kylie. "Happy New Year," I said.

"Not for everybody," she said. "We have a headless body in Riverside Park."

Decapitations were standard fare for Mexican drug cartels, but rare in New York—even rarer for our unit. "Are you sure it's for Red?" I asked.

"The body is wearing a chauffeur's uniform," Kylie said, "and there's a big-ass black limo in the parking lot. License plate ALDEN 2. Which means this homicide is about as Red as you can get. Where are you?"

I told her, and she said she'd pick me up outside the hotel in ten minutes.

My New Year's euphoria was officially over.

Chapter 2

NOT TOO MANY New Yorkers know it, but Riverside Park was conceived by the same guy who designed Central Park. And while it's not Frederick Law Olmsted's most famous work, the four-mile strip that hugs the Hudson River from 72nd to 158th Streets is the most spectacular stretch of natural beauty and recreational possibilities in the city.

Kylie took the Henry Hudson Parkway north, swung around under the George Washington Bridge, and headed back south on the parkway until we spotted the 151st Street entrance to Riverside Park.

The parking lot was empty except for a dozen assorted police vehicles and one shiny black limo that looked as out of place as a debutante at a biker rally.

We spotted the one guy we were looking for: Chuck Dryden. Chuck is a brilliant criminalist with all the charisma of a wet bath mat. He'd been dubbed Cut And Dryden because he was all business, no small talk. His emotional content ranged from ho to hum, but I'd discovered that there was one defibrillator that could jump-start his dispassionate heart. Like a lot of men before him, he was totally smitten with Kylie. So as soon as we saw him, my partner took the reins.

"We're in luck, Zach. It's our favorite CSI. Happy New Year, Chuck," Kylie said, tantalizingly putting on a pair of latex gloves as if she had something in mind other than preventing the contamination of a crime scene.

He looked down, muttered a quiet "Same to you," and immediately went into his observations. "The victim appears to be Peter Chevalier, age fifty-five, from Cité Soleil, Haiti. American citizen since 1988, resides on East 81st Street."

"*Appears* to be?" Kylie asked.

"There was a wallet in the victim's pocket," Dryden said. "Normally the head shot on his license would help me get a positive ID, but as you can see, this man's head is nowhere in sight."

He peeled back the tarp that covered the body, gave us ten seconds to take in the mutilation, and then discreetly covered it back up.

"As the vanity license plates would suggest, the

vehicle is registered to Alden Investments, which is owned by Hunter Hutchinson Alden Jr. There's no evidence of a struggle inside the car. Judging by this pool of blood, Mr. Chevalier was standing outside when he was decapitated."

"Time of death?" I asked.

"Somewhere between 7:52 and 8:11 last night."

"How the hell did you come up with such a narrow window?" I said.

Dryden almost smiled. "It was well below freezing last night," he said. "Even colder here at the river's edge than in the rest of the city, so I can't give you a definitive time frame till I get him to the lab and run a thorough check on blood pooling, stomach contents, rigor—the usual indicators. However, we retrieved a cell phone from the ground under the driver's side door, and it appears that the victim was composing a text to Mr. Alden when the killer came up behind him."

He held it up so we could read it.

Cant find Tripp. Do you want me to

"The text is unfinished and unsent, so I can't tell exactly when he wrote it," Dryden said. "But then there's a flood of incoming texts, all from Alden, all basically saying 'Call me—where the hell are you?' Since all of Alden's previous texts were answered promptly, a logical conclusion would be that the time of death was somewhere between Mr. Chevalier's last reply, at 7:52, and Mr. Alden's text that followed at 8:11."

"Cause of death?" Kylie asked.

"Excellent question, Detective," Dryden said. "Many cops would hesitate to ask what killed a headless man, and they'd be wrong. There are no bullet wounds or puncture marks on the body, but there is a fresh bruise on his lower back consistent with the classic knee strike delivered in conjunction with a garrote attack. However, since his head was removed with a rope saw, which is quite messy, I can't find any visible ligature marks in the field, so a garrote is only an educated guess. It's also possible that he was strangled with the rope saw, and then the killer kept cutting. Either way, decapitation was postmortem."

"I'm a city girl," Kylie said. "What in the world is a rope saw?"

We knew that Dryden had a treasure trove of weaponry in his cerebrum, and we'd always suspected that he might have quite a few of them in his basement.

"A rope saw is a jagged-toothed carbon steel chain

attached to two handles. It affords the user all the benefits of a chain saw without the noise."

"Thank you, Chuck," Kylie said. "You are, as usual, incredibly thorough."

He nodded. "I'll call you from the lab once I have further findings. And needless to say, if you come across *la tête de Monsieur Chevalier*, make sure you send it my way."

"Sure thing," Kylie said. She waited till we were twenty feet away before she whispered out of the side of her mouth, "He probably needs it to complete his collection."

Chapter 3

"I HAD MATT Smith run Peter Chevalier's name through the system," Kylie said. "Over the years he's picked up hundreds of parking violations for Alden Investments, which is no surprise. People who ride in the back of limos would rather pay a fine than walk half a block. Otherwise, he was an upstanding citizen."

"Upstanding citizens don't usually have many enemies," I said. "His boss, on the other hand, is one of the richest, most ruthless bastards on Wall Street."

"And as good fortune would have it," Kylie said, "rich, ruthless bastards are our specialty. Let's go have a chat with Mr. Alden."

We double-parked on East 81st Street and were about to get out of the car when the weathered-bronze front door opened. Hunter Alden was standing there with another man, who was about to leave.

"Holy shit," Kylie said. "The short one in the coat is Silas David Blackstone."

"You know him?"

"Oh yeah—smarmy little bastard. He's the head of SDB Investigative Services. If you have a legal matter you want done, Silas Blackstone will do it. If it's illegal, he'll do it for more money. Let's find out what he's doing here."

We got out of the car. The two men saw us immediately.

"Kylie?" Blackstone said. "Kylie MacDonald?"

He bounded down the steps and let us in the front gate.

"What a pleasant surprise," Blackstone said. "I've been following your career, and you are just burning up a trail at NYPD, aren't you?"

"This is my partner," she said, ignoring the question. "Detective Zach Jordan."

"Silas David Blackstone," he said. "Jordan, you are one lucky devil. I'd kill to ride around town all day with this woman. Only with me, it would be a much better car."

He extended his arm, and it was hate at first handshake.

He turned back to Kylie. "How is your husband doing these days? I heard he was ill."

Smarmy was an understatement. He must have known that Spence was in rehab because he put air quotes around the word *ill*.

"He's on the mend, thank you," Kylie said. She pulled out her shield and held it up. "NYPD. Hunter Alden?"

"That's me," Alden said. "Come on up."

Kylie and I walked up to the doorway with Blackstone right behind. "Detectives Kylie MacDonald and Zach Jordan," she said. "If you've been consulting with Mr. Blackstone, you must know why we're here."

"Yes, Peter's been missing since last night. I was concerned and called Silas."

"And I picked up the one eight seven on the scanner. I came here to break the bad news to Mr. Alden."

"How did you pick it up?" I asked. "The victim's name wasn't on the air."

Blackstone's lips curled, transforming his phony plastic smile into a genuine contemptuous sneer. "Yes, Detective, but there was a description of the car. Not many Maybachs on the road. They start at about four hundred grand. Plus, this one is tricked out with armor plate, bulletproof windows, and a complete—"

"That's enough, Silas." It was Alden.

"I just want them to know that's a million-dollar

car they've impounded, and we'd appreciate it if they returned it to you sooner rather than later. By the way," Silas said, turning back to me and Kylie, "it's pronounced *Mybock,* not *Mayback.* I guess your dispatcher is more used to Hondas and Toyotas."

Alden raised his voice. "Enough, damn it."

"I was just leaving," Blackstone said. "Wonderful to see you again, Kylie. Remember, there's always a job opening for you at SDB."

He took the first three steps and then turned back to his boss. "You're in excellent hands, Mr. Alden. These two cops are not just NYPD: they're with NYPD Red, which is as good as you're going to get"—he arched his eyebrows and shrugged—"from the public sector."

Chapter 4

HUNTER ALDEN ESCORTED us into one of those grand foyers that most people see only in movies. I've learned enough to know that directly ahead of us was what they call a butterfly staircase. Or as us poor folks say, the curved kind where you can walk upstairs from either side.

I could see by the grain that the floor was wood, but it gleamed like the ebony keys on a piano. Overhead was a crystal chandelier suspended from an intricately carved paneled ceiling. To the left was a pair of ebonized wooden doors inset with silver grillwork and beveled mirrors.

The only contrast to the monochromatic tones of black and gray was a glorious Christmas tree that was the seasonal focal point of the room. It towered past the iron-forged balcony railing on the second floor and looked like it would be as at home in the White House as it was here on 81st Street. It was like stepping into the holiday edition of *Architectural Digest.*

"Sorry about Blackstone," Alden said as he closed the front door. "He's a bit of an abrasive little asshole, but he's good at what he does."

"And what exactly is that?" Kylie asked.

If there had been a tour of the Alden estate in our future, it was abruptly canceled. Hunter Alden stopped right there in the entryway.

"And what the hell business is that of yours, Detective? My family is in the middle of a devastating tragedy. Peter had been with us for twenty-three years. I'm told you're the best cops the department has to offer, and you lead off with an irresponsible question that is nothing more than a breach of my privacy."

Some cops might have apologized, but Kylie was born with a seriously defective "I'm sorry" gene. She came right back at him. "Mr. Alden, that wasn't my intended opening question, but when I see an *'abrasive little asshole'* like Blackstone at the home of a murder victim, I want to know what he's doing here. Now, I'm sorry for your loss, but since we'd both like to know who killed Peter Chevalier, let me start off with a different question."

"I have a few questions of my own." He turned

away from her and looked squarely at me. "Tell me," he said, adjusting his voice to the more respectful tone reserved for the guy who plays good cop. "Was it a robbery? I hope he didn't get killed trying to protect my car. Was he shot? Stabbed?"

"No, sir," I said. "It appears Mr. Chevalier was choked to death and then decapitated."

That was something Blackstone couldn't have told him, and Alden took a step back. "De . . . I . . . I don't know what to say."

"You can start by telling us about Peter. Did he have any enemies?"

"He had a reputation for being a bit of a skirt chaser. He probably pissed off more than a few husbands and boyfriends in his life."

"Enough to kill him?"

"Detective, I'm his employer, not his drinking buddy. All I know is what I just told you."

"Did he ever borrow your car for his own personal use?"

He looked at me like I'd spat in the punch bowl. Clearly he thought I was clueless about the boundaries between upstairs and downstairs. "Absolutely not," he snapped.

"Then he was working for you when he was murdered. Can you tell us what he was doing all alone in an empty parking lot off the West Side Highway at that hour of the night?"

Alden repeated the question, a sure tell that he'd rather not answer it. But I'd painted him into a corner. "I have no idea" was not an option.

"Simple explanation," he said. "Around six thirty last night I got a text from my son, Tripp, saying that his car broke down, so I sent Peter to pick him up."

"Then Tripp must have been one of the last people to see Peter alive," Kylie said now that she could smell that Alden was on the defensive.

"No, they never connected," he said quickly. "Tripp called me late last night and said Peter never found him. He eventually got one of his friends to pick him up and spent the night at the kid's house."

"What kind of car does your son drive?" Kylie asked.

"One of those useless hybrids. A Prius. Blue, maybe green—I don't really remember."

"There was no car matching that description in the area," I said.

"Have you been to Riverside Park?" Alden said. "It's huge. I'm sure it'll turn up. Is that all, Detectives? I'm rather pressed for time."

"That's all we have right now," I said. "But we'd like to talk to your son."

"You can't reach him now. He's a senior at Barnaby Prep, and the school has a strict no-cell-phones rule. But I'll be glad to leave him a message."

He took a cell from his pocket. "I realize Silas didn't broach the subject with any tact," he said as he tapped his speed dial, "but I really do need my car back as soon as possible. Can I count on you to expedite—hold on, I got his voice mail. Hello, Tripp. Something happened to Peter last night, and the police are here to discuss it. They have a few questions they'd like to ask you. Call me when you can, and I'll arrange a meeting with them."

He hung up. "If you leave me your number, I'll contact you as soon as I hear from him."

I gave him my card. "One last question. You said your son first called you about his car problems at six thirty. At that hour, the park was dark, empty, and bitter cold. What was he doing there so late?"

"Tripp is a film nut," Alden said. "So I hired him to make a surprise video for my father, who is turning seventy in March. I think he decided to go get some footage of the old neighborhood where my father grew up."

"Exactly where is that?" I asked.

Alden hesitated.

"Think hard," I said. "If your father is anything

like mine, he dragged you there more than once to show you where he lived as a kid."

His memory came back fast. "You're right. It's 530 West 136th Street."

"That's in Harlem."

"I know," Alden said. "Your rags-to-riches story doesn't get any better than that. I can't wait to see the look on my father's face when he sees this video."

He opened the front door. "Give me a buzz and let me know the status of my car. It's not just transportation. It's my mobile office. I'm lost without it."

He smiled as he saw us out. He seemed to have bounced back nicely from his family's devastating tragedy.

Chapter 5

KYLIE GOT BEHIND the wheel of our car and gunned it. "What an asshole," she blurted out. She shot up 81st Street, ran a red light, and hung a hard left on Fifth. "His teenage son texts him for help, the driver he sends is murdered, and he can't wait for his father to see a home movie?"

The post-holiday traffic was light, and I buckled my seat belt when I saw the speedometer creep toward sixty. "It seems like Peter getting his head lopped off was more of an inconvenience than a family crisis," I said. "And on a completely different subject, would you mind slowing down?"

She didn't. "And what the hell was that smarmshark Blackstone doing there?"

"You tell me, K-Mac. You're the one who has a history with him."

She took one hand off the wheel and flipped me the finger. "No, Zach. *You and I* have a history. Blackstone is just some dude with a hard-on for me. Nice of him to tell Alden that we're NYPD Red—that special breed of cop trained to serve and protect the insensitive wealthy."

"Hey, at least now Alden knows that we're as good as he's ever going to get—from the public sector."

"That pompous ass wouldn't care if we were NYPD Platinum. He's not about to cough up anything. He didn't even want to tell us where his father grew up. Nice move squeezing it out of him."

"Thanks, but he only gave up what he knows we can find out on our own. His story was full of holes, but I'm pretty sure he was telling the truth when he said that Peter and Tripp never connected. That was the gist of the text Dryden showed us. But I'd still like to make sure."

She came to a screeching stop at the corner of 72nd and Fifth, jumped out of the car, and moved the sawhorse that was blocking the entrance to Central Park. She ran back to the car, turned it into the park, then got out and put the sawhorse back in place.

"I don't know why they close the park to cars on a day like this," she said as we sped west. "There are no joggers, no bikers . . ."

"Just crazy drivers," I said. "I gather we're not going back to the office."

"You're starting to get good at this cop stuff, Zach. No, we are definitely not going back to the office."

"So we're either going to Barnaby Prep to talk to Tripp, or we're headed up to Harlem to check out Grandpa's old neighborhood."

She smiled. "Both. But we can catch Tripp when school lets out. First let's hit 530 West 136th Street and see if anyone saw him wandering around with a camera yesterday."

We had the park all to ourselves, so Kylie drove with complete disregard for red lights, the twenty-five-mile-an-hour speed limit, and the patches of ice on the roadway.

"And don't forget," I said, "if we survive this trip, we have to call Chuck Dryden and get Alden's *Mybock* back to him in a big hurry. From what I gather, the poor guy is lost without it."

"Absolutely," she said, hurtling around the curves of East Drive. "Getting Alden's precious mobile office back to him is at the top of my list—right after we find the person who killed Alden's driver."

Chapter 6

KYLIE BARRELED THROUGH to the north end of the park, took 110th Street to Broadway, and made the turn onto 136th Street in a record-breaking eight minutes. Then she slowed down to a crawl and headed east toward Amsterdam Avenue.

"Keep an eye out for one of those useless hybrids. Blue, maybe green."

Halfway up the block, I spotted it. "Green Prius," I said, pointing to a car that was directly in front of number 530. We ran the plates. The car was registered to Alden Investments.

We got out and tried the doors. They were locked.

"Jimmy it," Kylie said.

"It's in a valid parking space, and we have no reason to think it was involved in a crime," I said. "Or did the NYPD recently drop that whole grounds-for-breaking-into-a-legally-parked-car thing?"

"Why would Tripp text his father and say he's broken down in Riverside Park if his car is here?" Kylie said.

"I'm just guessing," I said, "but one possibility is, if you're planning to slice through someone's spinal column with a rope saw, you figure if you do it in the middle of 136th Street on New Year's Day, you're going to draw a crowd. The park, on the other hand, is deserted. No witnesses."

"You like Tripp for killing Chevalier?" Kylie asked.

"No, but he has to at least be on our list. And if he didn't do it, then somebody used Tripp's phone, sent the text, and lured Peter to the park."

"Somebody like who?"

"I don't know," I said. "Let's ask around."

"Who are we supposed to ask? It's freezing out here. The street isn't exactly teeming with witnesses."

"Let's go find the widow in the window."

She looked at me. "Who?"

Kylie and I have two histories. The first is as lovers, and even though it lasted only a month, I'm sure I bared my soul to her, told her my best-kept secrets. The second history is as partners, but that relationship is so new that there are still a few things I haven't shared with her.

"The widow in the window," I repeated. "Lots of neighborhoods have one. She's a white-haired old lady who usually lives on the first floor facing front. Her kids are grown and gone, her husband is dead, and her life is about sitting by the window and taking it all in. These days she may have a cell phone in her hand so that when she sees something interesting she can spread the news to anyone on her speed dial who might remotely give a rat's ass. Maybe they didn't have people like that where you grew up, but trust me, in this part of the city, in neighborhoods like this, there's one on every block. They see everything."

"That is the dumbest theory I ever heard," Kylie said.

"Maybe, but right now it's the only one we've got. Humor me. Let's walk around and look for her."

We did. We covered the entire block from Broadway to Amsterdam, but there were no widows looking out of any windows.

"Maybe her shift starts later in the day," Kylie said. "Or maybe she has a second job as the widow in the rocking chair watching daytime TV. Or wait, here's a thought: maybe it's just the dumbest theory any cop ever came up with."

"Fine," I said. "You have a better idea?"

"Yeah," she said. "It's my sergeant-at-the-front-desk theory. Come on—get back in the car. Humor me."

Chapter 7

MOST NYPD COPS don't get to spend much time outside the clearly defined boundaries of their precincts. One of the best things about my job is that Red has no borders, so I get to soak up the entire multicultural, geographically diversified melting pot called New York City.

The Sugar Hill section of Harlem is one of our grandest, most overlooked neighborhoods. It got its name back in the 1920s, when wealthy African Americans moved there to live the sweet life during the Harlem Renaissance.

We headed uptown and drove past stately row houses that had been homes to many of the leading black writers, musicians, athletes, and political leaders of the twentieth century. It's so spectacular that not only has it been designated a municipal historic district by the Landmarks Preservation Commission, but Kylie actually slowed down so we could take it all in.

The 30th Precinct is on West 151st Street, a tree-lined block just east of Convent Garden. We entered the building and ID'd ourselves to the front desk sergeant. One look and you knew he was a seasoned pro. Close-cropped silver hair, rugged jaw, piercing eyes, and even sitting down he had the bearing of someone who'd served his country in the military.

"Steve Norcia," he said. "What brings you to the Three Oh, Detectives?"

"We're looking for a civilian," Kylie said. "Probably an older woman who calls the precinct on a regular basis, maybe with noise complaints, double-parked cars she sees from her window, people who don't pick up after their dogs—"

Sergeant Norcia interrupted. "Say no more, Detective. I know the type. What they really want is a cop to drive by so they can talk, maybe offer him a cup of coffee and some cookies. We've got a bunch of regulars. We call it the Lonely Hearts Club. You looking for anyone in particular, or should I just tell you who makes the best chocolate chip?"

"I can narrow it down for you," Kylie said. "She'd have called yesterday—possibly complaining about a kid with a movie camera. Maybe she said he was a Peeping Tom or wanted to know if he had a permit."

"I know exactly who you're talking about. I took the call myself," Norcia said, and went to his computer. "Just give me a minute."

"Take your time, Sergeant," Kylie said. "This is a lot easier than going door-to-door." She grinned at me. "Or window to window."

"Bingo," Norcia said in much less than a minute. "I knew it was her."

"Who?" Kylie said, taking out a pen and pad.

"Fannie Gittleman. Lives at 530 West 136th, apartment 2A. She called yesterday at 3:35 p.m. Except it wasn't one of those lonely-widow-with-free-baked-goods calls I was talking about. Gittleman is a bit of a troublemaker—a community activist. Always ready to drag the cops in if it'll help whatever cause she's harping on that day. Yesterday she reported seeing two terrorists filming the building next door. She was pretty sure they were plotting to blow it up."

"Terrorists?" Kylie said. "Who'd you send to answer the call?"

"Detective, it was January first. Nine guys phoned in sick. It's our annual epidemic of post–New Year's Eve Brown Bottle Flu. Hell, I can't blame them. I did the same thing when I was their age."

"So you didn't send anyone?"

"I would have—eventually." He grinned. "Handling these old ladies is a balancing act. You start jumping too fast, and they'll call you ten times a day. I was short-handed, so it wasn't at the top of my list. I would have sent out the first available RMP, but Gittleman called back ten minutes later to thank me."

"For what?"

"Beats the heck out of me, but according to her, the guy I sent did an excellent job. Problem solved."

"Didn't that seem a little strange to you?" Kylie asked.

Norcia looked down at us from his desk on high. "Detective, do you have any idea how many calls I juggle a day? So, no, I don't think it's particularly strange if some wacky old broad calls to thank me for sending an imaginary cop to arrest a couple of imaginary terrorists."

"On the other hand," he added with a shit-eating grin that is rare among front desk sergeants, "two NYPD Red detectives investigating said imaginary crime—now *that* is pretty goddamn bizarre."

Chapter 8

ONE OF THE life skills that Kylie has never seemed to master is the ability to not gloat. Humility has never been her strong suit, and she took her most recent triumph as yet another opportunity to remind me that she finished first in our class at the academy, while I came in sixth.

We drove back to 136th Street and rang Mrs. Gittleman's bell. She was not exactly the little old white-haired lady I had pictured. I'd gotten the "old" part right: she was somewhere north of eighty. But her hair was more of a high-octane orange, and she was dressed, bejeweled, and made up as if she was expecting company. Apparently she was: us.

She blocked the doorway while she inspected our IDs. "Jordan and MacDonald," she said. "You're new to the precinct. Are you here for a follow-up on yesterday's incident?"

"Yes, ma'am," Kylie said, running with it. "We just need to clear up a few facts."

"Come in," she said, opening the door. "Careful. It's a little messy."

Messy was putting it mildly. The apartment was a pack rat's paradise. It was like she had started decorating sixty years ago and never got around to stopping. Every inch of wall space was covered with framed artwork, many pieces of which she told us she had painted herself. Three sofas were crammed into the tiny living room, one a launching pad for her abundant pillow collection, another a catchall for assorted leaflets, flyers, and brochures. The third one had a cat curled up in the corner.

"Sit there," Gittleman said. "She's deaf. You won't bother her."

Kylie sat. I stood. Gittleman sat on the edge of a cluttered coffee table. As promised, she was all business. No coffee, no cookies. "So, was I right?" she asked. "Were they terrorists?"

"It's an ongoing investigation," Kylie said, "so we can't say much just now. But we're trying to wrap it up. If it's not too much trouble, could you take us through what you saw?"

She cleared her throat. "It was three thirty. I see two boys with a movie camera. One is tall; he's white. The other is darker—I'm not saying Arab, but who knows? They're filming the building next door, pointing their camera at Mrs. Glantz's window. Some people would say 'Not my business,' but I'm a firm believer in 'If you see something, say something.' Let me tell you, this was definitely something. So I called Steve—"

"Steve?" Kylie said.

"Sergeant Norcia. I thought you work for him. Anyway, I don't bother with 911. I called Steve direct at the precinct, and he sends over an undercover cop."

"How did you know the cop was undercover?"

"Oh please. With that red wig and the fake red beard? Of course he was undercover. Anyway, he walks over to the white boy, handcuffs him, no questions asked."

We had pulled up Tripp Alden's driver's license photo from the DMV. I showed it to her.

"Yeah, that's the one," she said. "As I was saying, the cop put the cuffs on him, and then, out of the blue, the other one—the Arab kid—he comes at him with a box cutter. Cut him—you could see the blood soaking into the sleeve on his jacket."

"What kind of jacket?" I asked.

"One of those hooded sweatshirts they all wear. It was gray with navy-blue trim, and it said Yankees in blue on the front. Anyway, the cop pulls out his stun gun, and zap—the boy goes down. Then he takes the white kid to the paddy wagon, comes back, and drags off the other one."

"Did you notice which paddy wagon he was driving?" Kylie asked.

"A blue van, unmarked. Anyway, he opens the back doors and tosses the two of them in. And then— get this—he had to tie the doors shut with one of those stretchy cords. I'm not going to tell you how to run the police department, but if you're going to put prisoners in there, you'd think the city could spend a few bucks on a lock that works." She paused. "So is there a reward?"

Kylie looked at me, but before either of us could answer, Gittleman fielded her own question. "Don't worry. I'll check with Steve."

Chapter 9

HIS NEW YEAR'S resolutions officially on hold, Hunter Alden opened a bottle of Johnnie Walker Blue to help him think.

Peter's head was a problem. It was too late to turn it over to the cops. *Oh, I'm sorry, Detectives. This morning, when you told me my driver was decapitated, I completely forgot to mention that I found his head in my son's camera case last night. But I'm sure there's no need for you to talk to Tripp. He's busy with schoolwork.*

Hunter's only choice was to keep it hidden until the cops stopped coming around. Blackstone had suggested the twenty-cubic-foot chest freezer in the basement, so Peter was currently resting peacefully under a hundred pounds of Kobe beef Wagyu steaks, Canadian lobster tails, and premium pulled pork.

Hunter sat down at his desk, poured a splash of

the Scotch into his coffee, and stared at the cell phone that the murderer had sent the night before. Then his gaze shifted to the piece of paper he had removed from Peter Chevalier's lips.

There's money to be made.

The five words haunted Hunter. He closed his eyes and drifted back fourteen years to Grace Bay, a strip of beach on Providenciales in the Turks and Caicos Islands.

He'd been flown to Turks by private jet, whisked through customs and immigration, driven to a hotel that was closed for its annual September upgrades, and escorted to a conference room.

The man inside was not dressed for the islands. He was wearing a dark suit and tie, the official uniform of the Swiss lawyer. He stood. "Samuel Joost," he said crisply.

There is only one way that large sums of money can change hands between two people who don't trust each other. A third party—one beyond reproach—has to be brought in. Joost was a senior partner in a Zurich law firm that had been acting as go-between for wealthy clients and Swiss banks since the 1930s.

He opened a leather attaché and took out a small calculator, an assortment of pens, and a thick binder marked Project Gutenberg. If he had a personality, he had failed to bring it with him.

Documents were signed, funds were moved, and every detail of his involvement was spelled out and agreed upon. Joost assigned him a code name: Leviticus.

Within minutes of Joost's departure, a second man arrived. He was a tall, gaunt, androgynous presence with slicked-back shoulder-length blond hair.

"There's money to be made," he said in a measured, conspiratorial whisper. "You know the risks, the rewards, and the consequences of violating any of the rules. Do you have any questions?"

"Who else is along for the ride?"

"The identities of the other participants are as closely guarded as your own. This is not a social club. Secrecy is paramount to the success or failure of this operation."

Hunter laughed. "Secrecy and a shitload of money."

"Mr. Alden," the nameless blond man said. "In my world, billionaires are as common as fig trees. Do not think you have been invited to this meeting because of your assets. You have been handpicked because of your ideology."

"And what ideology is that?" Hunter asked.

"Greed."

It was a day that had changed Hunter Alden's life. A secret he had thought impossible to unearth. And yet . . .

He opened his eyes, and his gaze settled on the silver framed picture of Marjorie sitting on his desk. Tripp, then only four, was on her lap. The weekend before she died, Marjorie had told him she was pregnant, and there were so many times that he wished they'd had that second child.

His phone rang, jolting him back to the present. It was Silas Blackstone.

And then there were times like this, Hunter thought, picking up the phone, when he knew his life would have been so much easier if he'd had no children at all.

"Those two cops found the Prius," Blackstone said. "It was on 136th Street. I went straight there as soon as I left your house. They were still with you, but by the time I got uptown they were already there. How the hell did they find it so fast?"

"I gave them the address."

"Why would you do that?"

"Why do you think? They pressed me. I had to give them something. It doesn't matter. What happened after they found the car?"

"They did a quick scan from the outside, then they

left. I had Tripp's keys, so I searched the car. Nothing. I was about to leave when the cops came back. I thought maybe they picked up a warrant to search the car, but no—they went straight to one of the buildings and interviewed a tenant."

"Who?"

"Some old lady. She came to the window a couple of times while the cops were there. She was pointing and yakking away, so I figured she must have seen what went down with Tripp, and she was filling them in."

"Talk to her. Find out what she saw."

"Done," Blackstone said. "As soon as they left, I rang her bell. At first, she didn't want to let me in, so I told her I was a PI looking for a missing kid. I showed her Tripp's picture, and she wigged out. Said he was a terrorist, and the cops arrested him yesterday."

"Son of a bitch," Hunter said, taking a swig of his eighty-proof coffee. "The cops never told me they arrested him."

"They didn't," Blackstone said. "It's all in her head. She saw some guy with a red beard drag Tripp off in a blue van. She told Jordan and MacDonald that he was an undercover cop, but I'm sure they know better."

"I knew the kid was taken. The package I got last night made that abundantly clear. The problem is,

now the cops know it. Find Tripp before they do—
that's all I care about."

"Whoever took Tripp took his buddy too. Do you
care about him?"

"What buddy?"

"A short dark kid. They were shooting a movie
together. The old lady says he's an Arab terrorist."

"Arab? Is she nuts? He's Puerto Rican. Lonnie
Martinez—he's helping Tripp with the movie for my
father. Why would anyone take him? He's a dirt-poor
hood rat, lives with his grandmother—not worth a
nickel to a kidnapper."

"Then he's in on it," Blackstone said. "Whoever is
behind this knows they can't get close to you and your
family, so they recruited this Lonnie kid to be the
inside man. Who knew where they were going to be
filming?"

"Just me . . . and Lonnie."

"Looks like he set Tripp up."

"Little bastard. I'd send you to his house, but I
have no idea where he lives."

"No worries, boss. I scrolled through Tripp's GPS.
The name Lonnie is at the top of the list."

"Then get your ass over there and see what you
can find out from the grandmother."

He hung up the phone, dumped what was left of

his coffee into a large potted plant, and refilled the cup with straight Johnnie Walker Blue.

He sat back in his chair and picked up the note delivered by his dead driver. *There's money to be made.*

He took a long swallow of Scotch and sneered. "We'll see about that, motherfucker."

Chapter 10

"MRS. GITTLEMAN WASN'T the most credible witness," I said. "She thought Tripp was a terrorist, and she was positive that the guy with the paddy wagon that could only be locked with a stretchy cord was one of New York's Finest."

"I liked her," Kylie said. "She was feisty."

"I'm not too keen on feisty women," I said. "Usually they try to hog all the glory, and they drive too fast."

She punched me in the shoulder.

"However," I said, "her whole story about Red Beard and the stun gun, and the other kid using a box cutter to try to get away, helps explain why Tripp Alden is nowhere to be found. "We can't call him, but I'm not about to sit around and wait till school lets out to find out if he's been abducted or not."

"Finally," Kylie said, "we agree on something."

She turned on the lights and siren, shot down Amsterdam, hung a hard left at 110th, careened around the traffic circle at the north end of the park doing fifty, and ran the lights along Central Park West until we got to 88th Street.

"Was that too feisty for you?" she asked, parking in a crosswalk in front of the imposing six-story building that had been the home of Barnaby Prep since the early nineteenth century.

The first two students we passed in the hall were talking about Tripp's driver's murder.

"I guess the strict cell phone rules Alden told us about aren't being enforced today," Kylie said. "And if those two know, everybody knows."

"You're right," I said. "If Peter Chevalier had been an ordinary citizen, his murder might have gone unnoticed in a city of eight million people. But he was a billionaire's chauffeur in a car that cost more than a house."

"It's not just that," Kylie said. "The New York press loves body parts, and whether a torso washes up on Rockaway Beach or a head goes missing in Riverside Park, it's going to be fodder for every media outlet from tabloids to prime time. I'll bet you by now the text messages, Twitter feeds, and Facebook updates have spread through this school like a virus."

We found the headmaster's office and were escorted right in. G. Martin Anderson was young, preppy, and totally tuned in. I had barely gotten my shield out of my pocket when he said, "Terrible thing about Mr. Chevalier. Everyone here is quite upset. These kids know they live in a tough city, but when it hits this close to home . . . What can I do to help?"

"We realize it's the middle of a school day," Kylie said, "but we'd like to talk to Tripp Alden."

"Tripp?" Anderson said. "Oh, he's not here today. Under the circumstances, I'd have been surprised if he had come in. I know he was very fond of Peter."

Tripp had never showed up. Point for Gittleman.

"He has a friend," I said. "Someone he's shooting a film with."

"Lonnie Martinez," Anderson said. "Just a second." He ran his finger down a computer printout and stopped midpage. "I thought I'd seen his name on the absentee sheet. He's not here today either."

Another point for Gittleman.

"We know how to reach the Aldens," Kylie said, "but it would help if we could talk to Lonnie's parents. Do you know how we can get in touch with them?"

"I have every student's contact numbers right here," he said, sitting down in front of his computer. "Here we go: Alonso Martinez. Everyone calls him

Lonnie. He lives with his grandmother, Juanita Martinez. He's a scholarship student—great kid. Very popular."

"What else can you tell us about him?" I asked.

"What you said before about Tripp and Lonnie shooting a film together—they're quite good at it. Mr. Madison, who chairs our film studies department, says both boys have a bright future in the industry. In fact, he can probably tell you more about them than I can. We have a mentoring program here at Barnaby, and because of their passion for film, putting Lonnie and Tripp with Ryan Madison was a perfect match. I'm sure he was in touch with both boys over the holiday break—the deadline for a lot of college applications was December thirty-first."

"How soon can we talk to Mr. Madison?" I asked.

"Immediately. I'll send for a runner to escort you to his class." He jotted a phone number on a piece of paper. "This is my personal cell," he said. "Whatever I can do to help."

We thanked him, gave him our numbers, and waited for the runner.

"You making any sense of this?" I asked Kylie.

"I totally figured it out," she said. "Tripp sent a text to say his car was at Riverside Park, but the car turned out to be on 136th Street. Alden told us Tripp was in school, but Tripp isn't here. Gittleman said some guy in a red wig and a phony red beard cuffed Tripp and hauled him off in a van, but Alden swears he heard from Tripp last night, and all's right with the world."

"That about sums it up," I said. "So what did you figure out?"

She cocked her head to one side and grinned. "Elementary, my dear Jordan. Clearly, somebody is lying their ass off."

Chapter 11

IN THE POST-COLUMBINE landscape, classroom doors have to be tough enough to deter an intruder. But because the maniac with a gun is often a student, school officials always have to be able to look inside. The doors at Barnaby Prep were all solid oak with thick two-by-two glass inserts at eye level.

Our runner, Jeffrey, was a tall, gangly kid with age-appropriate acne and braces. He walked us up to the third floor, stopped in front of room 314, and pointed through the glass. "That's him," he said, laughing. "That's Mr. Madison."

We peered inside. A man wearing black jeans and a navy turtleneck was standing on top of the teacher's desk, his arms raised high. He had a Barbie doll in one hand and pounded his chest with the other. Every kid in the room watched with rapt attention.

"Film class," Jeffrey said. "They're studying *King Kong*."

Kylie threw him a look. "Really, kid? I was going to go with *Bambi*."

Madison jumped up and down on the desk, swatting at imaginary airplanes. Suddenly he jerked backward in pain, mortally wounded. He slunk down, gently set Barbie on the desk, and slumped slowly to the floor.

"It was beauty killed the beast," Jeffrey the ever-helpful tour guide said. "I took the class last year."

The kids applauded. Madison stood up, ran his fingers through his hair, then looked our way. I beckoned with one finger. He smiled, said something to his students, and came out.

"I don't think we've met," he said. "Ryan Madison. Are you prospective parents?"

"NYPD. We'd like to talk," I said, "but we can wait till your class is over."

"Hell, no," he said. "This is a perfect chance to sneak a smoke. You're not the tobacco police, are you?" He laughed. "Let's go up to the roof. It's cold as hell up there, but it's legal."

Jeffrey took off, and we followed Madison up three more flights of stairs. He was in his midthirties, full of energy, and loaded with attitude.

"Sorry about the cigs," he said, lighting up. "I watched too much film noir as a kid. How can I help you?"

"We're looking for Tripp Alden," I said.

"He's not here today."

"We know. The headmaster thought you might be able to help us find him."

"Oh, of course. This is about Peter Chevalier's murder, isn't it?"

"Yes, sir. We'd like to talk to Tripp as soon as possible."

"I'm not sure if he even knows about it," he said, turning his head and blowing smoke into the freezing January air. "Wait a minute—that's stupid. He must know about it by now. Hell, everybody in school does. But he didn't seem to know about Peter's death last night. At least he didn't say anything."

"You spoke to him last night?" Kylie said.

"Texted."

"What time?"

Madison dug into his jeans pocket and pulled out his cell. "It was 12:07."

"Tripp Alden sent you a text after midnight," I said. It was half statement, half question. "What did he say?"

He read the text to us: "Lonnie and I are headed

upstate for a few more interviews. Sorry to blow off class tomorrow and Friday. Back Saturday. Can we book the editing room over the weekend?"

Madison showed us the text, then put the phone back in his pocket. "Today's our first day after the Christmas break," he said. "Can you believe they started us back up on a *Thursday*? Tripp and Lonnie aren't the only kids cutting school today and tomorrow. So I wrote back, 'Don't sweat it,' and I booked the editing suite for them. Haven't heard from him since."

"What interviews was he referring to?" Kylie asked.

"He's making a film about his grandfather. The old man has family in Rochester. Tripp and Lonnie have gone up there a few times to interview some of his cousins."

"Do you know any of their names?"

Madison had one of those boyish grins that I'm sure endeared him to his students. He tried it out on Kylie. "I'm going to go out on a limb and say some of them are probably named Alden, but I have no idea."

She did not grin back.

"Sorry if that sounded snarky, Detective," he said, going from boyish to sheepish. "My job is to give these kids guidance on mise-en-scène, but I'm not involved in production."

"How would they get upstate?" I asked.

"Tripp has a car—a Prius."

"Thank you," I said, giving him my card. "If you hear from either one of them, have them call this number."

"Hey, why wait? I'll text Tripp. I'll bet he and Lonnie would love to hang with you guys." He stubbed out his cigarette. "I'm freezing. Let's get inside."

We reentered the building and walked back down to the third floor.

"Why do you think Tripp and Lonnie would want to hang out with us?" I asked.

"Are you kidding? Those two are crime film junkies. They've staged a bank robbery, a carjacking—all that cool stuff you guys do in real life."

Kylie blurted out the obvious next question before I could. "Did they ever stage a kidnapping?"

"Not that I know of," Madison said, "but that's a cool idea. They're pretty good at staging these crime scenes. The irony is that they do it all guerrilla-style. No permits, so technically, they're breaking the law every time they shoot. Are we good for now? I've got to get back. Now that I've got their attention with the monkeyshines, I want to get into the good stuff, like the film's blatant undertones of racism during a period of increasing racial and social tension in America.

You're welcome to sit in. Don't worry: I won't blow your cover."

"Thanks," I said, "but I think we'll pass." My cell phone rang. I looked at the caller ID. "That's our boss. Now I'm sure we'll pass."

Madison went back inside the classroom, and I took the call from Cates. "Yes, Captain," I said.

"I just heard from Mayor Sykes," she said.

Red had been held in very high esteem by the previous administration, and we were all hoping that the new mayor would be just as supportive. "That's a good sign," I said. "I think she's going to be your new best friend."

"*Our* new best friend," Cates said. "She wants a rundown on the murder of Alden's driver. She'll be here in fifteen minutes. You be here in fourteen."

Chapter 12

"HE WAS CUTE," Kylie said as she sped downtown on Central Park West.

Kylie is a world-class ballbuster, and I knew she was going to retaliate for my crack about feisty women hogging all the glory. This was her first attempt.

"He was okay," I said.

"Okay? Zach, he was hot. I'd go out with him."

"I don't know," I said. "He seems a little young for you. I think you and Jeffrey should at least wait till his skin clears up and his braces come off."

"I'm talking about Madison, and you know it," she said. "I'd take the class just to look at those gorgeous blue eyes."

"Oh, you mean the teacher—Madison? He was freaking adorable," I said. "Definitely the second cutest guy up there on the roof."

She laughed, and I felt like maybe I'd won that round. But just to be on the safe side, I swiveled my body and edged closer to the passenger side door so she couldn't punch me again.

We whipped across the 65th Street transverse to the east side and pulled up in front of the One Nine on East 67th five minutes ahead of our deadline.

We were walking up the steps of the precinct when the front door flew open, and Cheryl came racing out.

"Zach," she said.

"Hey . . . I thought you were taking the train up to the hospital this morning."

"I made the mistake of coming in to wrap up some work, and I was bombarded with calls from people who spent the holiday making big plans for the new year and needed to pick my brain on all of them immediately."

"Aren't you the shrink who taught me that 'No' is a complete sentence?" I asked.

"I did say no to most of them," Cheryl said, "but Captain Cates needed me for something that couldn't wait. I called Fred and asked how Mildred was doing, and he said she might only have a few days. Cates only needed me for a few hours, so I stayed. I finally pried myself loose."

"I'm sorry to hear about your ex-mother-in-law," Kylie said.

"Thanks," Cheryl said. "I can't even think of her as my ex-anything. She's the mother of my ex-husband, and I really have to see her before she dies. The best thing about my marriage to Fred was the quality time I spent with Mildred." She gave me a quick hug. "I'll catch a late train back."

"I'll be pulling a long shift, so how about a late dinner," I said. "We can order in, open a bottle of wine—"

Her cell phone rang, and she grabbed it. "Fred, I'm on my way. I'll be on the 1:47. Pick me up at the Mount Kisco station."

I could see she was ready to hang up, but apparently Fred kept talking. Cheryl listened patiently, punctuating the one-sided conversation with the occasional "Mmm hmm," which is what shrinks say when they've heard it all before.

Finally, she jumped in. "Fred, if you keep talking, I'll miss my train. Good-bye."

"So, about tonight," I said as soon as she hung up. "About what time do you think you'll be—"

"Zach!" she said. "How can you expect me to plan a dinner date now? Fred is a total wreck. He's already called half a dozen times."

"Maybe next time he calls you can remind him that he's no longer married to you," I snapped.

I regretted it as soon as I said it. In a heartbeat, the calm, compassionate therapist reverted to hot-blooded, quick-tempered Latina.

"Do you hear yourself?" she said, clenching her jaw to keep the anger from exploding into a scream. "His mother is dying. How insensitive can you be?"

"I didn't mean it to sound so callous," I said, backpedaling. "It's just that Fred is engaged. Why is he calling you instead of his fiancée?"

"Not that it's any of your business, but his fiancée left him."

I hadn't expected that. "I . . . I thought she was pregnant."

"She is," Cheryl said. "But Fred found out that he isn't the father, which is why he's been calling me and not her."

"I'm sorry," I said. "I didn't know."

"Not knowing is acceptable. Not thinking isn't."

She stormed down the precinct steps just as a black Escalade pulled up. The driver jumped out and opened the back door, and Muriel Sykes, the city's new mayor, stepped out.

Kylie and I had a history with Sykes. Evelyn Parker-Steele, the murdered wife of the hotel magnate who upgraded Cheryl and me to a palace in the clouds, had also been Muriel Sykes's campaign manager. At first we had butted heads with Sykes, but once we solved the crime, we became her go-to cops.

"Detectives," she called out as soon as she spotted us. "Hell of a way to start my second day on the job, but I'm happy to see you two on the case."

I could see Cheryl halfway up the block trying to flag down a cab on Lexington Avenue. One stopped, and she got in.

Oh good, I thought. *Don't want her to miss the train that's taking her back to Fred.* My brain began to race, and my mind conjured up thoughts of their tearful reunion. Cheryl was a natural-born caregiver, and I knew she'd be there for Fred in his hour of despair, consoling him, comforting him, offering him a shoulder to cry on . . .

"Zach!"

I snapped out of my self-inflicted misery montage. It was Kylie.

"What?" I said.

"Can we get back to work? The mayor is on her way upstairs."

"Sorry. I was just thinking . . ."

"No, Zach. Cheryl's right. You weren't thinking.

The only thing on your mind was your bruised male ego. You want my advice?"

"I can't wait. Lay it on me, Dr. Phyllis."

"Don't get tangled up in whatever soap opera you're creating in your head. You've already botched things up with Cheryl as it is."

"Yeah, I guess I really shot myself in the foot."

"Oh, you're right about shooting yourself," she said, grinning. "But you've got the wrong body part, Casanova. It definitely wasn't your foot."

Chapter 13

KYLIE AND I took the stairs two at a time and made it to the third floor just as the mayor was getting out of the elevator. We followed her into Captain Cates's office.

Sykes wasted no time. "Where are you on the murder of Hunter Alden's driver?"

"Alden would like us to believe that Peter Chevalier was a womanizer who was probably murdered by a jealous husband," I said. "But something else is going on. Alden's son didn't show up at school today, and he's not at home grieving."

Most politicians have very little understanding of the inner workings of the criminal justice system, but Sykes was a former U.S. attorney. She had prosecuted criminal cases for the federal government for sixteen years. "And you suspect it's not just another rich kid playing hooky?" she said.

"We have a witness who says she saw Tripp and a friend of his taken into custody by an undercover cop yesterday, hours before Peter was killed," Kylie said. "But we know for sure the precinct never sent a cop. It sounded to us more like both kids were abducted."

"How reliable is your witness?"

"To us or to a jury?" I said. "Her name is Fannie Gittleman. She's at least eighty years old. She's a bit off the wall, but definitely not delusional. We're convinced she got it right. Those kids were taken."

"What does Hunter Alden say?"

"He swears that Tripp is fine. Says he got a text from him last night—after he was supposedly kidnapped. Of course, if Tripp is being held for ransom, the kidnappers would have told Alden to keep the cops out, which is why he'd be lying to us."

"So then we went to the kid's school," I continued. "One of the teachers showed us a text he got from Tripp—also late last night. He bailed out of classes for a couple of days. Said he was going up to Rochester for this film project he's shooting for his father."

"The kidnapper could have sent that text so the school wouldn't report the boy missing," Sykes said. "Let's get back to the murder of the driver. Are you anywhere on that?"

"No, but if Tripp Alden was abducted, that might

explain why Chevalier was killed and beheaded. One of the scenarios we've run is that his head was sent to Alden as a warning—pay the ransom or your son is next."

"Detectives, it all makes sense, but you're walking a fine line trying to solve a crime that nobody has yet reported."

"Mrs. Gittleman reported it," Kylie said.

"Before you confront Hunter Alden with an eighty-year-old eyewitness, why don't you talk to the parents of the other victim? See if they're willing to work with us."

"The other kid lives with his grandmother. From what I hear she's lucky to have rent money, let alone ransom money."

"All we need is for her to file a missing persons report. Then I don't care how poor she is—she gets all the resources of NYPD Red," Sykes said. "One more thing. Hunter Alden can be overbearing, but don't let him push you. He's not your boss—even if he tries to act like it. Oh, who the hell am I kidding? Hunter is a lot more than overbearing. What I should have said was, he's a major pain in the ass. If you think his son is a crime victim, and he doesn't cooperate, talk to me. I'll connect you with someone much easier to deal with."

"We may well take you up on that," I said. "Who are you talking about?"

"His father, Hutch Alden."

Cates finally spoke. "Madam Mayor, thank you. Having you back us up means a lot."

"Don't thank me," Sykes said. "The Aldens might have a lot of political clout, but this isn't politics. This department gets my support before they do."

Chapter 14

SILAS BLACKSTONE PARKED the Audi and stared up at the cluster of identical redbrick buildings. They looked harmless on the outside, but he knew better. He'd grown up in public housing in the Mott Haven section of the Bronx. Violence was everywhere. If the gangs and the drug dealers didn't get you, a random bullet could. The first thing you teach a kid living in the projects: Never stand in front of a window.

The fact that Lonnie Martinez went to a rich white kids' school meant nothing. This was a whole other world. Blackstone checked his gun. "Better safe than sorry," he said, tucking it back into his holster.

He got out of the car, locked it, and then looked up and down Paladino Avenue. Calling it an avenue was a joke. It was nothing more than a service road running along the Harlem River Drive. Just as well.

No kids walking around with nothing better to do than key every car on the block.

The tiny vestibule of 64 Paladino smelled faintly of disinfectant. Eau de Pine-Sol, his father used to call it. He found the name Juanita Martinez on the panel of doorbells and pressed the button.

The intercom crackled. "Who is it?" a woman's voice said.

"I have a package for Lonnie Martinez. It's from Mr. Alden."

She buzzed him in.

He took the elevator to the sixth floor. He knocked on the door to apartment 6H, and an attractive woman opened it halfway and leaned against the doorjamb.

"Where's Lonnie?" he said.

"Lonnie no here. I take package."

"Package? No. I said I have a message from Mr. Alden."

"Alden?" she repeated. "Tripp Alden—he no here."

Blackstone took another look. Her English sucked, but the rest of her was drop-dead amazing. Five foot two, with a tight little body, thick dark hair, and skin the color of warm honey. She was wearing a blue uniform with the Costco logo on the shirt. The name tag said Juanita, which was the grandmother's name, but he had been expecting some fat old broad with her hair in a bun. This chick had it going on.

"Are you Lonnie's grandmother?" he said.

Her eyes lit up when she heard the name. She flashed a smile. "*Sí, sí. Soy Lonnie abuela.* Gronmodder."

"You speak English?"

She shrugged. "*Un poco.* No much."

"Mr. Alden wants to hire Lonnie to help Tripp with another movie."

She gave him a smile and a vacant stare.

He shook his head. "Let me leave a note for Lonnie," he said, writing in midair with an imaginary pencil. "You got paper and a pencil? *Papel? Lápiz?*"

"*Sí, sí,*" she said. "*Papel y lápiz.* I get for you."

She turned to go inside to find something for him to write with, and the door swung open.

"Son of a bitch," he said. He followed her into the apartment and grabbed the newspaper off the kitchen table.

"The *New York Post*?" he said. "You don't read *El Diario*?"

"*No comprendo,*" she said.

"Is that how you're going to play this?" Blackstone said. "You *no comprende* my English? You work at Costco, you read the *Post*—I'm pretty sure you *habla inglés* like a pro."

She smirked. *"Quién sabe, señor?"*

Blackstone knew it was a lost cause, and with his ninety-thousand-dollar wheels parked in this dicey neighborhood, he wasn't going to stick around.

"Fine. Play it your way," he said. "Your grandson is not in trouble—not yet—and if you want to keep it that way, you'll drop the act and tell him to call me at this number." He handed the hot little grandmother his card.

She took it. *"Gracias,"* she said as he walked out the door.

He didn't look back. *"De* fucking *nada,* bitch," he mumbled to himself.

Chapter 15

"WELL, WELL, WELL," Kylie said. We were driving down Paladino Avenue, and she slowed the car to a crawl. "Guess who's here." She pointed to a black Audi A8 L that didn't fit the profile of the neighborhood. The vanity plates said SDB.

"Gosh," I said. "I wonder what that stands for."

"Short Dickless Bastard," Kylie said.

"The good news is," I said, "if Blackstone is here, then he and Alden are as clueless as we are about where Tripp is."

We parked out of sight. Ten minutes later, SDB came out of Lonnie Martinez's building, then circled the Audi, inspecting it for damage.

"What's he going to do if he finds a dent?" Kylie said. "Call a cop?"

He drove off, and we walked up a neatly shoveled

path to number 64. We got lucky. Somebody was coming out, which let us go directly upstairs without having to ring the bell. Kylie knocked, and Juanita Martinez opened the door.

"NYPD," Kylie said.

"You real cops or bullshit cops?" she said.

Kylie flashed her shield. "Homicide detectives. We're as real as it gets."

"Good, because I had my share of bullshit from the last one."

"Short guy? Big ego?"

"Blackstone." She let us in. The place was compact, neat, and whatever was simmering in the big stew pot on the stovetop smelled fantastic.

"What was Blackstone doing here?" I asked.

"Looking for my grandson Lonnie. Even if I knew, I wouldn't tell that *pinche cabrón*."

"Would you tell us?" I said.

"Why do homicide cops want to know where Lonnie is?"

"We want to talk to his friend Tripp Alden, and we thought Lonnie might know where he is."

"I don't know where either of them are."

"When did you last see Lonnie?" I asked.

"Yesterday for breakfast. Then he went out with Tripp—they're shooting a movie. Later on he sent me a text. Said he was going to spend the night at Tripp's house. This morning I find out about the murder." She held up today's *Post*. "That's why you're here, right?"

"Did you know the victim, Peter Chevalier?" Kylie asked.

"He was Tripp's driver. Of course I knew him. You think I'm going to let my kid ride around in a car without meeting the guy behind the wheel?"

"And?"

"He passed the test. I trusted him with my grandson. But now I'm nervous. I haven't seen Lonnie since yesterday. Should I be worried?"

"We have no reason to think anything is wrong," Kylie lied. "We'd just like to talk to both boys."

"I'll give you Lonnie's cell number. If you find him, tell him to call me."

She wrote down the number on a scrap of paper and held it out to Kylie. "You think you can catch the bastard who killed Peter?"

"I don't think so," Kylie said. "I *know* we'll catch him."

The tears came without warning. Juanita pressed her hand to her eyes, trying to hold them back, but a mournful wail came from deep down inside, and her body convulsed with the pain of loss.

Kylie rested a hand on her shoulder. "You and Peter were close, weren't you?"

She shook her head. "We dated. He was such a wonderful man. He gave so much of himself to others. How could such a beautiful life be cut so short?"

"We see it all the time," Kylie said. "It's senseless, but I promise you we will find the person who killed him."

Juanita lowered her head. "It was my fault," she said, still sobbing.

"How so?" Kylie asked casually. But I knew her antenna had gone up just like mine had as soon as we heard the words *my fault*.

"There's a couple on East Seventy-Third Street," Juanita said. "Very nice people. I clean their apartment every Wednesday. This year they had a New Year's Eve party, and they asked me to help out. I got there at five o'clock to set up, then I was serving, and I didn't finish cleaning everything up until two in the morning. They paid me well, but I was so busy, I forgot to throw the water out the window."

Kylie looked confused. "What water?"

"It's a Puerto Rican custom," I said. "Cheryl told me about it. You pour a bucket of water out of a window at the stroke of midnight at the beginning of each year for good luck."

"Not luck," Juanita said. "It washes away the evil spirits."

"Ms. Martinez," Kylie said, "I've been around a lot of evil people, and I can tell you this: the only thing that can come from dumping a pail of water out the window and onto East Seventy-Third Street is a dry cleaning bill or a big fat lawsuit."

She laughed, took a dish towel from the counter, and wiped her eyes. "Lonnie doesn't know about me and Peter. It was private."

"And that's the way it will stay," Kylie said. "You have my word on it."

"Thank you. I knew you'd understand. Secrets of the heart. We all have them, don't we, Detective?"

"Yes we do, Ms. Martinez. Yes we do. We are so sorry for your loss."

She gave Juanita her card, and we took the elevator down to the lobby.

"I'm glad you were there," I said as we got into the car. "I couldn't have handled it nearly as well."

"It's called empathy, Zach. Men aren't very good at it."

"Hey, I may not be in the Sisterhood of the Traveling Pants, but I'm as empathetic as they come."

"Yeah, I was deeply moved by the way you told

Cheryl to say good-bye to her dying friend and get her ass back to New York as fast as she can."

Before I could even buckle up, she gunned the engine and tore down Paladino Avenue.

"For somebody who's so damn smug about her ability to get in touch with her inner woman," I said, "you drive like you've got a hell of a lot of testosterone coursing through your veins."

"Testosterone?" she said. "Me?"

"Yeah, you."

"Hmm . . . I never really thought about it."

Her right fist shot out like lightning, and she gave me another solid punch to the shoulder.

She smiled. "But you may have a point."

Chapter 16

SILAS BLACKSTONE TURNED into the driveway on East 81st Street and looked at his watch: 3:45 p.m. By now the Hunter Alden Happy Hour would be in full swing.

He took a deep breath, exhaled slowly, and mentally braced himself—a bit of emotional Kevlar for the inevitable verbal pummeling. Blackstone knew what he was: an indentured servant working for a heartless prick. But that prick accounted for 90 percent of his income. Quitting was not an option.

He tapped the intercom button on the front gate, smiled at the security camera, and waited until he was buzzed through. He took the stairs, then waited again until Janelle took her sweet time opening the door.

"Mr. Blackstone," she said without any of her usual

charm. She didn't like him, what he did, or how he did it, and she did little to hide her feelings.

"Mrs. Alden," he said as amiably as he could. "How are you doing today?"

"We had a death in the family. How do you think I'm doing?"

"Oh yeah. Terrible thing. Peter was a good guy. We'll all miss him." He capped the hollow sentiment with an equally disingenuous shake of his head. He waited for her to invite him in.

She didn't. "My husband is downstairs," she said, turning away and leaving him standing in the open doorway.

In the real world, *My husband is downstairs* might mean *He's in the rec room* or *He's working out in the gym next to the boiler.* But Hunter Alden didn't live in the real world. He was in the 1 percent of the 1 percent. His downstairs was a cedar and stone grotto that housed a swimming pool, a sauna, and a hot tub—a lush tropical paradise that cost millions to build, and millions more to maintain a perfect temperature-humidity balance during the grim New York winter.

Hunter was soaking in the tub, a glass of red wine in his right hand, two cell phones sitting on a towel within easy reach of his left.

His eyes were lethal weapons, and they were

locked and loaded with loathing and disgust. They drilled into Blackstone. "What do you have on the Puerto Rican kid?" he said.

"Lonnie may not be the friend Tripp thinks he is. He's gone. In the wind."

"Of course he's gone. He got taken when they took Tripp."

"Or maybe it was just staged to look that way. His grandmother didn't seem to be too worried that he's missing. She played dumb, but I'm sure she knows plenty."

"Then put somebody on her around the clock."

"Waste of time, boss. Lonnie's not stupid. He's not going home to Grandma. I have a better idea. Let me scrub Tripp's computer."

"His computer? Really? You think he put it in his calendar? 'Shoot movie. Get kidnapped.'"

"Look. Eight times out of ten," Silas said, inventing a statistic, "when somebody takes a kid, it's someone he knows. If Tripp was in touch with this guy by email or through chat rooms, I'll find him."

"And then what?"

"Tripp comes home safe and sound. We turn this guy over to the cops—"

"Have you not been paying attention? The last thing I want is this guy talking to the cops, or a DA, or a judge. I don't want him talking to anyone. Ever. I want him dead."

Blackstone didn't blink. He'd heard it before. No euphemisms. Not "I have a business problem." Not "I want him eliminated." Just a flat-out "I want him dead."

"I'll call Wheeler and get a price."

"I don't have time to dick around. Tell him I'll pay him double what I paid him the last time."

"Will do. Anything else?"

Alden polished off what was left in his glass and lifted it above his head. Blackstone reflexively took it and walked to the bar. The wine bottle was nearly depleted. He poured what was left into Hunter's glass and handed it back to him.

He downed it in one swallow. "The computer is in Tripp's room," he said. "If Janelle asks you why you're taking it, tell her Tripp called, and you're running it up to his school for him."

"She doesn't know he's missing?"

"Why would I tell her? What is she going to do besides annoy the shit out of me? She knows Peter is dead. Apart from that, she doesn't know anything about anything, and it better stay that way. So keep your mouth shut."

"I always do," Silas said. "You want me to open another bottle of wine?"

Hunter lifted himself out of the hot tub. "I'll get my own wine. You just call Wheeler and tell him I'm making room in my freezer for another head."

Chapter 17

TRIPP ALDEN WAS huddled in a corner on the floor, his six-hundred-dollar goose down parka zipped and wrapped tightly around him. "I'm sorry," he said.

Six feet away, Lonnie Martinez, wearing a Barnaby Prep hoodie and a polyester fleece jacket, sat with his knees pulled up to his chest. "You said that already."

"I know, but I can't stop thinking about it. You're only here because of me. It's my fault."

Lonnie shook his head. "Is it your fault that some nut job snatched you off the street?"

"Hey, I've known my whole life that this could happen to me. My father's rich. Ever since I was a little kid he'd pound into me, 'Watch who you talk to, watch where you go.' So what do I do? I go up to Harlem, and I wind up in the back of a van. When I get home he's going to tear me a new one."

"Tripp, I know you think your dad is a dick, but what are you supposed to do? Live in a bubble? Dude, if some wacko with a stun gun wants to grab you, he's going to grab you. It doesn't matter if you're in Harlem or on Park Avenue."

"Tell that to my old man."

"The only thing I want to tell your father is, 'Thank you very much, Mr. Alden, sir, for coughing up the ransom money to get me and Tripp out.'"

"He's not going to cough up anything so fast," Tripp said.

Lonnie scooted his butt across the floor so he was toe to toe with Tripp. "What are you saying? He's going to let us rot here?"

"Relax: we'll get out. But not because my father is all heart. He's got ransom insurance."

Lonnie lifted both shoulders in a shrug. "Never heard of it."

"You know how people have car insurance?" Tripp said. "If you're in an accident, the insurance company pays to have the car repaired. I have ransom insurance. Somebody takes me, the insurance company pays off the kidnapper."

Lonnie stood up. "Then why the hell are we still locked up, starving, and freezing to death? Where's the insurance guy with the check? He can settle up with the asshole who took us and get us out of here."

Tripp laughed. "It's a little more complicated than that. Plus I know my father. However much money this guy asks for, he'll negotiate."

"Why? I thought you said the insurance company pays."

"Up to a point. After that it comes out of my father's pocket."

Lonnie leaned against the wall and stared down at Tripp. "Then I'm dead."

"What are you talking about?"

"I'm talking about your father. If he starts negotiating with this guy, then I'm dead meat. That crazy-ass dude will kill me."

"Kill you? Why would he kill you? We're not worth anything to him dead."

"*You're* not worth anything dead. You're this guy's hole card. Me? I'm not worth shit. Use your brain, Tripp. Your father has more money in his sock drawer than my entire family has had since . . . since forever. My grandmother makes twelve fifty an hour as a food demonstrator. What's she going to do? Pay a kidnapper off with samples of Greek yogurt and Bavarian sausage?"

"Chill out. My father will pay for both of us."

"Oh yeah. I bet he can't wait to fill up a duffel bag

with a couple of million to save my sorry Puerto Rican ass."

"My father is *not* going to let you die."

"Tripp, think about it. This guy who put us in here, he knows how much money he wants. The number doesn't matter. Let's just say it's X dollars. He tells your father how much."

"Okay."

"But then your father starts haggling with him. He says 'How about half of X?' So now the kidnapper gets all pissed off."

"My father pisses everybody off when he negotiates. It's how he wears people down."

"But the kidnapper isn't like a regular business guy. He knows your father can afford X, or ten X, or a hundred X. So he figures, 'Okay, I'm going to send this asshole a message.'"

"Like what?"

"Like in *The Godfather* when the Hollywood producer wakes up and finds a horse's head in his bed. That's the kind of message kidnappers send. That's the way they get what they want."

"So what are you saying? This guy is going to kill me to get my father to pay the full amount?"

"No, Tripp. He's not going to kill *you*. He's going to kill *me*. Don't you get it? I'm the horse's head!"

Tripp wanted to argue, but he couldn't. It all made too much sense. He folded his arms and hugged the parka to his chest. "Oh," he said, looking up at his best friend. "Then I guess I know what that makes me."

Chapter 18

WE PULLED UP to the Alden town house for the second time in a few hours. This time it came as no surprise that Blackstone's Audi was parked out front.

Kylie flashed her badge at the security camera, and we were buzzed through the gate. A familiar face opened the door. I'd seen pictures of Janelle Alden, but they didn't do her justice. Up close she was heart-stopping. Green eyes, blond hair, pink sweater, blue jeans—all my favorite colors on one incredible-looking woman.

"Mrs. Alden," I said. "NYPD."

She let us in. "Thank you for coming," she said, a soft, sweet smile on her face like she'd invited us over for cocktails. "Do you have any—what's the right word—leads?"

"We're working on it," I said. "We spoke to your

husband earlier, and we're here to do a follow-up. Is he home?"

"Hunter is at the pool," she said as casually as most people might say "He's in the kitchen." To her, having a private indoor pool on the Upper East Side of Manhattan must have seemed perfectly normal.

We took the elevator downstairs, and she led us through a jungle of lush, exotic trees.

Silas Blackstone saw us first. "Detectives," he said. "We meet again. How goes the homicide investigation?"

I ignored the question and looked down at Hunter Alden, who was soaking in a hot tub, a glass of wine in his hand. The flushed skin, drooping eyelids, and sagging cheeks let me know this was far from his first drink of the day.

"Any news on Peter?" he asked.

"Not yet," I said. "Have you heard from your son?"

"Not since last night," he said, putting a little spin of exasperation on it to make sure we knew that we were wasting his time.

"He wasn't in school today."

Alden shook his head. "Kids," he said as if a single word could explain away the disappearance of a person of interest in a murder case.

"Tripp texted one of his teachers last night. He

said he was on his way to Rochester to interview some people for that film he's shooting."

Hunter nodded. "That makes sense. My father has family up there."

"We found his Prius on 136th Street this morning and impounded it," Kylie said. "We were wondering how he'd get upstate without a car."

"Yeah, that's a real stumper, Detective," Alden said. "But I'm going to take a wild guess and say train, bus, plane out of La Guardia. The kid is resourceful. He'll figure it out. What I *can't* figure out is why you're not looking for Peter's killer. Why are you so focused on Tripp? Do you think he's got some magical lead that will solve this case for you?"

"Sir," Kylie said, "we told you this morning that—"

"And I told you this morning that Peter Chevalier was a skirt chaser. There are a dozen jealous husbands and boyfriends who'd be happy to cut his head *and* his balls off. There's your lead. As for my son, I promised you that when I heard from him, I would have him call you. The fact that you're back a few hours later badgering me with the same request borders on harassment. Do you understand that, or would it help if I called your superiors and had them explain it to you?"

Before Kylie or I could answer, one of the cell

phones sitting on the towel rang. Not the one with the leather case embossed with the initials HHA, but the piece of crap AT&T flip phone you can pick up at Best Buy for twenty bucks.

Silas jumped. Hunter stared at it but didn't move.

"You want me to answer it?" Janelle Alden said after the third ring.

"Let it go," Hunter said, "but I would very much appreciate it if you showed these two officers to the front door."

Another ring, but Hunter didn't budge. He stared at us over the rim of his wineglass, defiantly ignoring the phone.

"Thank you for your time, Mr. Alden," I said, slowly, deliberately. Kylie and I weren't going anywhere.

"We realize this has been a stressful day for you," she said.

The phone rang two more times. And then it stopped.

"We'll be in touch," I said, waiting for the burner phone to ring again. It didn't.

We took the elevator upstairs with Janelle. "You'll have to forgive my husband," she said. "He's very upset about Peter's death."

"We completely understand," I said, my response

as full of crap as her explanation of Alden's behavior. "Do you know where your son is?"

"No, but he's eighteen. I can't always . . ." She shrugged off the rest of the answer.

"Did he contact you last night?"

"No." She shook her head. "No," she repeated.

"It's important that we talk to him," I said. "Here's my card. If he calls you, please have him call me."

"Absolutely," she said, flashing me a beauty-pageant-winning smile.

So far our investigation hadn't turned up much, but there was one thing I knew for sure. Of all the people who had lied to me today, Janelle Alden was by far the prettiest.

Chapter 19

THE MAN WHO knew the one secret that could destroy Hunter Alden's life, his legacy, and his entire financial empire sat in his Subaru Outback, heater running, watching the people come and go at the house on East 81st Street.

He had no idea who the short man in the Audi was, but the vanity license plates were a good place to start. He Googled "SDB" and came up with assorted acronyms—a talent agency in Los Angeles, a website for the school district of Beloit, Wisconsin—and then, jackpot: SDB Investigative Services in New York, New York.

A picture of the founder, Silas David Blackstone, was on the home page. The diminutive Mr. B was a private eye.

The two cops who showed up ten minutes later

were much easier to identify. Detectives Zach Jordan and Kylie MacDonald had made the front page twice, for taking down the two most notorious serial killers in recent New York history: first The Chameleon, and then the Hazmat Killer.

Peter Chevalier's murder had also made page one. If it bleeds it leads, and a headless body in the park always helps sell newspapers. But the man in the Subaru didn't care about getting ink. He wasn't killing for glory. He was only in it to make a buck—a hundred million of them, to be exact.

He wished he could see the look on Hunter Alden's face when he heard that number. Calling the burner phone while the cops were in the house hadn't been part of his original plan. It was pure inspiration. A little improv. Alden wouldn't dare answer with Jordan and MacDonald breathing down his neck. They left within minutes of the call, obviously booted out by a control freak desperately trying to control something.

The two cops were smart enough to know that Tripp had been kidnapped, but without a formal complaint from the Aldens, they were bound by the rules of NYPD to stay out of it.

Silas Blackstone, on the other hand, was a hired gun who made up his own rules as he went along. SDB would be trouble.

The man in the Subaru was prepared for trouble. Overprepared. He had studied *The Art of War,* the definitive Chinese treatise on military strategy written twenty-five hundred years ago by the brilliant general and philosopher Sun Tzu. He had then spent three months and thousands of dollars planning every detail of the operation with military precision. And when he was finally ready, he had stepped back and asked himself, "What haven't I thought of?"

He didn't know what he didn't know, but if the goal was to be ready for any situation, he needed an arsenal. Not just weapons, but the same sophisticated equipment that was used by anyone orchestrating a clandestine operation.

He had found everything he needed on the Internet. There were hundreds of online retailers selling surveillance devices and other tools of the espionage trade to jealous wives, paranoid employers, Peeping Toms, or, in his case, a kidnapper with a hundred million dollars at stake.

For his money, the best one on the Web was Cheaters Spy Shop. There was a backpack on the floor of the car filled with covert paraphernalia he'd bought from the company, much of which he had ordered "just in case." He pulled it up on the passenger seat, rummaged through it, and found what he was looking for: a micro GPS tracker. Weatherproof, magnetic, and, most important, wireless.

He got out of the Subaru, walked toward Blackstone's car, bent down as if to tie his shoe, and within seconds the tracker was held fast to the underbelly of the Audi.

He returned to his car, and thirty minutes later, Blackstone emerged from the town house carrying a laptop under his arm. He got into the Audi and drove it to 89th and York. The man in the Subaru tracked his journey every inch of the way without even moving from his parking spot on East 81st.

The GPS worked perfectly. He smiled as he realized that, like the legendary General Sun Tzu, the vehicle tracker was another glorious gift from the land of dragons and emperors.

Chapter 20

KYLIE COULD BARELY wait till we got back in the car.

"Holy shit," she said as soon as the doors were closed. "Do you realize who just called Alden while we were standing there?"

"Well, gosh, Detective," I said in my best country bumpkin voice, "I know you graduated first in our class at the academy, and I only came in sixth, but since Mr. Alden didn't pick up the phone, I'm going to take a wild stab at it and say it was one of them telemarketers."

She actually laughed. "All right, all right, I know you know. I just mean wasn't that amazing? We were standing right there, and the damn throwaway phone goes off. Did you see the look in Alden's eyes? He didn't know whether to piss his pants or butter his toast. Blackstone too."

"But not Janelle," I said. "She was ready to answer the call. Do you think that means she doesn't know Tripp is missing?"

"Or it could mean that she thinks like a mother hen—she knows he's been kidnapped, and she's taking the ransom call no matter who the hell is in the room."

Gracie Mansion was only two minutes from Alden's house. We checked in with security, asked to speak with the mayor, and in less than five minutes we were escorted to her office.

It was the same office Mayor Spellman had occupied until midnight on December thirty-first, but it had been completely redecorated in less than two days. The walls, the carpeting, and the upholstery had gone from serious blues and brooding browns to more hopeful, playful shades of peach, mint green, and pale yellow. The ponderous mahogany command post of a desk had been replaced with a sleek, efficient chrome and glass table. Most important, the anxiety-plagued, glass-is-half-empty, sky-is-falling man who had hidden behind the desk was now a confident, upbeat woman in a cheery turquoise Hillary pantsuit.

"Wow," my never-too-shy-to-offer-up-her-opinion partner said. "Madam Mayor, you've transformed this place."

"Thanks. It's a work in progress," the mayor said, shrugging off the dramatic makeover. "What's happening on the Peter Chevalier investigation?"

"I wish we had half as much progress to report," Kylie said. She recapped Alden's drink-addled poolside tantrum.

Sykes said nothing until Kylie got to the part where Alden didn't pick up the burner phone.

"He just let it ring?" Sykes said. "How could he not answer a phone call from the person who abducted his son?"

"He must be playing by this guy's rules. I guess that's what you do when your kid's life is on the line."

"It's not what I'd do," Sykes said. She had four kids and, judging by the family photo on the wall, a busload of grandkids. "That arrogant son of a bitch is stonewalling the very people who can help him."

"He specifically told us he doesn't want our help," I said. "At least not as far as Tripp is concerned."

"He might get his way if this were just about NYPD suspecting his son was kidnapped," Sykes said. "But this is a homicide investigation. The police have to work under the assumption that whoever has Tripp in their custody also killed Peter—or at least has information that will help you find the killer. Hunter Alden is obstructing justice. Let me see if I can help."

She picked up the phone. "Wait in my outer office," she said. "It's never pretty to watch a politician sucking up to a billionaire."

"Did you see that?" Kylie said as soon as we closed the door behind us. "It's about time the city of New York finally elected a female mayor."

"Hey, I'm all for girl power," I said, "but it looks to me like all she's doing is calling in a chit."

"Mayor Spellman would have called in a committee—all men. You don't get it, do you Zach?"

"Enlighten me."

She immediately launched into a manifesto about why women should run the world. "Bottom line," she said, three minutes into her impassioned speech, "women are like heat-seeking missiles. We see what has to be done, and we slam into action. We know how to take charge."

"Some women are especially good at that," I said. "If I recall, you've earned at least three commendations for slamming into action. Oh, no, wait—those were disciplinary reports that were filed because you forgot to tell the person in charge that you were taking charge."

"Those weren't disciplinary reports," Kylie said. "That was pure bureaucratic bullshit—"

The mayor opened the door and cut her off

midsentence. "Bureaucratic bullshit is highly under-appreciated," she said. "In some circles it's considered an art form. I myself just had to tell my wealthiest supporter that his son was drunk, belligerent, and refused to cooperate with the police in the very first homicide investigation of my fledgling administration."

We went inside and shut the door. "How'd he take it?" Kylie said.

"To his credit, Hutch is genuinely upset about Peter's death and said he'd do whatever he can to help us find the killer. I told him the two lead detectives would be right over to ask him some questions."

"Did you tell him we're looking for his grandson?" I asked.

"No. That's police work, not politics. Besides, I think you should be there and get a firsthand look at his reaction when you tell him."

I was beginning to think Kylie was right. Sykes was highly enlightened, extremely effective, and delightfully human. Maybe women should be in charge for a couple of hundred years and we'll see if they screw things up any worse than men have.

"Thank you, Madam Mayor," I said. "This is a big help."

"Anytime," she said. "And I mean that. But do me one favor—don't be too tough on him. This place is starting to grow on me. I may want to renew my lease down the road, and I definitely will need Hutch Alden on my side."

Chapter 21

FIVE MINUTES AFTER the cops left, Hunter Alden finished his second bottle of wine and announced to Janelle that he was taking a nap.

He woke up two hours later, showered, went to his study, and popped a Lavazza Espresso Classico into his Keurig. The sleep and the coffee helped, and as he sat at his desk, sipping his third cup, he started to feel his brain coming back online.

He tried to put the pieces of the puzzle together.

Fact: Anybody could have taken Tripp.

Rich families were always a target. That's why he had kidnap and ransom insurance. For less than twenty thousand dollars a year, the K & R covered Tripp for up to ten million. If this was just a kidnapping, he told himself, he'd have called in NYPD and paid the kidnappers out of his insurance company's pocket.

Fact: Whoever took Tripp knew about Project Gutenberg.

That was clear from the five-word note that came with Peter's head. This was more than a kidnapping. This was blackmail.

He knew there were other investors involved in Gutenberg, but he had no idea who they were, and they in turn wouldn't know him. Joost, the lawyer, couldn't be behind it either. He was a functionary, not a kidnapper. That left the nameless blond man who had orchestrated the entire operation. Hunter had no idea who he was, where he came from, or where in the world he could be now. But for the moment he was the only logical choice.

The door to his study opened. It was Janelle. "Were you able to sleep?" she said.

"A couple of hours."

She sat down in the leather chair on the other side of his desk. "Can I get you some dinner?" she asked.

"The coffee is all I need right now. You want some?"

"No. Well, maybe just a taste of yours," she said.

He passed her the cup. He knew she wasn't

interested in how the coffee tasted. Only in how it smelled.

She inhaled deeply and took a small sip. "Mmm," she said. "It's excellent."

Translation: It's alcohol-free.

"Can I ask what went on downstairs at the pool before?" Janelle said.

"Nothing you need to worry about. It's under control."

"Then where's Tripp?"

"You heard the cops," Hunter said. "He went up to Rochester to get some more footage of the family."

"Oh, you mean Uncle Gavin and Aunt Lucy."

Hunter nodded. "Exactly."

"I just called Gavin," Janelle said. "He and Lucy are in Atlantic City. They've been there since New Year's Eve, and they're not going home till Saturday. So let me ask you again: Where's Tripp? He hasn't called and he hasn't answered his phone."

"For God's sake, Janelle. Last night you were telling me he's a big boy—stop chasing him."

"Last night Peter Chevalier wasn't murdered. Last night the cops weren't here looking for Tripp. Last night you were micromanaging—now you're hiding something."

"I'm not hiding anything."

"Then whose cell phone is that?" she asked, pointing to the burner on his desk.

"Mine," Hunter said.

"But you don't answer it when the cops are in the room? What if it rings now? Will you pick up with me in the room?"

Hunter's voice kicked up a notch. "It won't ring with you in the room, because you're leaving. Now."

"Leaving? You think I'm one of your flunkies, like Silas Blackstone? By the way, he left the house with Tripp's computer—told me he's dropping it off at school for Tripp. You two really ought to get your story straight. Is Tripp in school? Is he in Rochester? Or are those two cops right—he's missing?"

Hunter didn't answer. For Janelle, the silence was answer enough.

"He is missing, isn't he?" she said. "That's why the police were here. They want to help. Why won't you let them? Hunter . . . he's our son."

Hunter pounded a fist on the desk and bolted to his feet. "No, Janelle. *My* son, not yours. *My* problem to solve, not yours. *My* decision to make, not yours."

She stood up, reached across the desk, and slapped him across the face. "Fuck you, he's not my son," she said. "He's missing. I don't care if you need my help or not. Tripp does."

"Stay out of it, Janelle," Hunter said, lowering his voice to a menacing whisper. "I'm warning you. Stay out of it, or I'll—"

"Or you'll what? Bully me like you bully everyone else? Shit on me like you shit on Marjorie? I'm not everyone else, Hunter, and I'm certainly not Marjorie. I don't know what's going on, but I'm going to damn well find out."

She walked out of the room and slammed the door.

Hunter picked up his cup and walked to the bar. He added a shot of Scotch to the espresso, sat back down, and stared at the burner phone.

His cheek stung, and he massaged it with one hand.

"Bitch," he muttered.

He knew her well. She was definitely going to be trouble.

Chapter 22

"THE FDR OR FIFTH?" Kylie asked as we got to the top of the driveway at Gracie.

"I'm busy," I said. "Surprise me."

She turned left and headed south on East End Avenue. "Busy with what?"

"I'm checking out Hutch Alden." I had pulled up Safari on my iPhone and typed his name in the Google search bar. "According to *Forbes*, he's the forty-second richest person in America and number seven in the state of New York."

"That's a big help, Zach. Why don't you try asking the Magic 8 Ball if he knows where his grandson is?"

My phone rang, and Cheryl's picture flashed on my screen.

I answered, still haunted by the high-school-sophomore, but-I-thought-you-were-going-to-the-prom-with-me tantrum I had thrown that afternoon. "Hey, how's it going?" I said with every ounce of sensitivity my bruised male ego could drum up. "How's Mildred?"

"It's almost over," she said, and I could hear the resignation in her voice. Cheryl doesn't create drama. "Almost over" meant exactly that.

"I'm sorry. But I'm glad you got up there in time," I said.

"Thanks. I think she recognized me when I got here, but an hour later she slipped into a coma. I'm just sitting here at her bedside, holding her hand, talking to her, hoping she can hear me. I can't leave her. I'm spending the night."

I, on the other hand, have been known to create drama. Especially in my own head. I'd have liked myself a lot more if my natural instinct was to be compassionate and supportive, but I wasn't thinking about Cheryl being there for Mildred. I was thinking about the fact that Mildred was going to die, and then Cheryl would be spending the night in Westchester being there for her needy ex-husband.

I reined in the craziness. I'd already spent enough time today with my foot in my mouth. "She's lucky to have you," I said. "I'll see you tomorrow."

"Thanks. Good night." She hung up. I sat there, not happy about the situation, but relieved that I hadn't made it any worse.

We had crossed 79th Street, and Kylie turned left onto Fifth Avenue. "I only heard one side of the conversation," she said, "but it sounded like you handled it very well."

"And I have you to thank, Dr. MacDonald. With all that good advice you gave me on the precinct steps this afternoon, I couldn't possibly have screwed it up."

"I'm glad I could help. It's just too bad you're dining alone tonight."

"It's the manly man thing to do," I said. "Any time the asshole who dumped your girlfriend needs her back at his side so he can have a shoulder to cry on, a real man ships her out and tells her to spend the night with him."

"Zachary Jordan, you are the poster boy for benevolence and understanding. And as good fortune would have it, my current husband is in drug rehab, so I have some room on my dance card. Can I interest you in an evening of wings, beer, and cop talk?"

"Yes, yes, and no."

"So that would be a yes on the wings, another yes on the beer, but you're not in the mood to ruin dinner by discussing the shit we've had to wade through all day," she said. "Sounds reasonable. It's a date."

I'd like to think of myself as a mature, enlightened man. The fact that Cheryl was willing to stay and help a jerk like Fred was a testament to what a sympathetic and caring soul she was. You'd hope I might feel good about that. But there was another part of me that was insanely jealous and downright pissed. What I really wanted to do was call Cheryl back and say, "Hey, it's fine with me if you're up in Westchester holding your ex-husband's hand. While you're doing that, I'll be in New York, pounding down beers with my ex-girlfriend. Have a nice night."

Of course, I'd never do it. I may not be all that mature, but I'm definitely not stupid.

Chapter 23

AS SOON AS we pulled up to 808 Fifth Avenue, the doorman hustled out and opened the driver's side door.

"We're here to see Mr. Alden," Kylie said.

"Police?" he said.

"Are we that obvious?" Kylie said.

"No, no. Mr. Alden told me to keep an eye out for you." He escorted us to the elevator.

"Alden is in the triplex," the elevator operator said. "Thirty-one, -two, and -three. They told me to take you to thirty-two. Someone will be there to meet you."

The elevator door opened onto some kind of palatial foyer, but I didn't have time to take it in. A man in a dark gray suit was waiting for us.

"This way," he said. "Leave your coats on. It's freezing out there."

He ushered us briskly through opulence and grandeur that few people ever get to see even fleetingly, led us up a flight of marble stairs to the thirty-third floor, and opened a glass door to a vast terrace that could only be described in architectural terms as fucking awesome.

It was colder out here than it was thirty-three floors below, and I pulled my collar up and put on my gloves.

"He's waiting for you over there," our escort said. He quickly hopped back inside the warm and cozy little mansion in the sky and closed the door behind him.

"Over there" was a corner of the terrace where a man in a gray parka with a fur-lined hood was standing behind the biggest telescope I'd ever seen outside of a planetarium.

"Officers," he said. "You got a minute? Take a look at this before we start."

He stood me behind the monster telescope.

"Quadrantids," he said as I leaned into the eyepiece. "The January meteor shower. It's nature's version of the Fourth of July."

"I don't see any fireworks," I said.

"They go by intermittently. You may have to wait an hour or so, but this is the best night of the year to see them. Meanwhile, you're looking at Arcturus—fourth brightest star in the sky. Most people in New York can't see it, but this is a decommissioned telescope I bought from Butler University. Pretty spectacular, isn't it? Let your partner have a look."

"Mr. Alden," Kylie said, "I'd be happy to gaze at the stars with you all night, but right now we're on a much less heavenly mission."

"Sorry. I can get caught up in these things and lose all track of time," Alden said, walking toward the terrace door. "I don't know how I can help you solve Peter's murder, but I'll do what I can."

The manservant opened the door for us and took our coats, and Alden led us to a crackling fireplace. A maid materialized and set down three steaming cups of hot cocoa.

"Muriel Sykes called," Alden said. "Told me my son was being uncooperative. I don't understand. Peter was family. We'll do whatever we can to help."

"Thank you, sir," I said. "For starters, what can you tell us about his personal life?"

"He has a brother in Haiti. A doctor."

"How about his friends in New York? He worked for your family a long time. Surely you must know something about his habits, who he hung out with when he was off the clock—those are the kind of details that would help."

Alden smiled. "Did you ever hear the story of the man who walks past the mental hospital?" he said. "He can hear all the patients inside shouting, 'Thirteen! Thirteen! Thirteen!,' but the fence is too high for him to see what is going on. Then he spots a knothole in one of the planks. He looks through it, and bam—a stick pokes him in the eye, and he hears the inmates all shouting, 'Fourteen! Fourteen! Fourteen!'"

He took a sip of his cocoa. "I mind my own business, Detectives."

I was doing my best to abide by the mayor's don't-strong-arm-the-rich-guy rule, but I could see that Kylie had zero tolerance for stargazing and folksy anecdotes. "Mr. Alden," she said, "we have reason to believe that your grandson Tripp was abducted yesterday."

She had his undivided attention. His face went from down-home Norman Rockwell grandpa on the cover of the *Saturday Evening Post* to steely-eyed tycoon on the cover of *Forbes*.

It took less than five minutes to give him the whole backstory. He sat quietly till we mentioned Blackstone.

"That little turd—he's more con man than private eye."

"Whatever he is," Kylie said, "your son hired him to find the kidnappers. It's a serious mistake. Kidnappers always tell their victims' families not to call the police. And if they set fire to your house, they'd tell you not to call the fire department. The fact is, a kidnapped child has a better chance of survival if the distraught parents bring in trained police professionals as soon as possible."

"Without a ransom call, none of this is conclusive," Alden said. "Right now, all you have is some old lady's testimony and a gut feeling."

"And my gut tells me there are two young lives at stake, and your son is standing in the way of saving them," Kylie said. "Sir, we need someone to talk some sense into him."

He shook his head. "Only two people could ever reason with Hunter. His mother, who passed in 1997, and his wife Marjorie, who died in the North Tower on 9/11."

"What about you?" Kylie asked.

"Me? Young lady, my son is a grown man, and there is nothing I can say or do to influence his actions or his behavior." He stood up. "My grandson, on the other hand, is eighteen, and I'll be damned if I'm going to bed until I know where and how he is. I'll call you in the morning."

Chapter 24

KYLIE AND I were headed south on Fifth when I figured it out. I'm a better than average detective, but I'd completely missed the first clue. That morning, on the steps of Hunter Alden's town house, Blackstone had asked Kylie about Spence. She had responded with, "He's on the mend, thank you."

On the mend? Who says crap like that? The Kylie I know cuts off personal questions from assholes like Blackstone with a quick verbal one-two punch. Verb. Pronoun. Bam—end of discussion.

The second clue was more obvious. As soon as Cheryl called to say she was spending the night in Westchester, Kylie asked me out for a night of wings and beer. Not pizza. Not Chinese. *Wings and beer.*

And then the clincher. She turned left onto 20th Street, and all the pieces came together. Spence wasn't on the mend; he was in bad shape, which meant Kylie's marriage was in worse shape. And we weren't just going for wings and beer; we were going back to one of the happiest chapters in Kylie's life—a time when she was a young recruit following her dream and madly in love with a man who wanted to be with her forever. Me.

Wing Nuts was around the corner from the academy, and it was the go-to watering hole for recruits who wanted to eat and drink all night on the cheap. It's where Kylie and I had dinner the first night we made love. And for the next twenty-seven days, it was our favorite pre- and post-coital haunt.

We walked in, and it looked, smelled, and felt just the way I'd left it. Same menu, same decor, same bartender, same everything. The only thing missing was my after-sex glow.

We ordered a bunch of wings and a pitcher of Brooklyn Blast and found a table as far from the crowd as we could.

Kylie poured two beers. "So what's going on with you and Cheryl?"

"Nothing's *going on*. Everything's great. We spent New Year's together, and all of a sudden Fred shows up out of left field. One minute I think he's going to get married and have a baby; the next minute I find out he's none of the above, and he wants to lean on Cheryl. You were right. My male ego got in the way. But I'm over it. She'll be back tomorrow; everything's cool."

Kylie gave me one of her signature head tilts, complete with dubious smile and a slow eye roll. She didn't buy my fairy tale with the tidy little happy ending.

A white-haired waitress showed up with two trays of wings. "Well, would you look at who's back," she said.

"Hey, Gladys," Kylie said.

"Don't ask me to remember your names, honey," she said, "but you're the three-alarm, and your boyfriend is the mild." She set the wings down and left.

"Brings back memories," Kylie said, biting into a wing.

"Beer will do that for you," I said.

She kicked me under the table. "Come on, Zach. Whatever else happened over the past eleven years, you have to admit we had some good times back in the day."

Whatever else happened? Spence Harrington managed to kick his cocaine habit just as I was getting into my Kylie MacDonald habit. She took him back, married him, and for ten years they were one of the beautiful couples you see in the Style section of the *Times*. New York royalty. And then Camelot exploded. A killer that Kylie and I were chasing decided to get back at her by targeting Spence. He survived the attack, but he was no match for the Percocet he took for the pain. He was in and out of one rehab in three days. Last month he flew to Oregon for another shot at recovery.

"Yeah, we had fun," I said, getting back to her stroll down memory lane. "And look at us now—two hot shit detectives just hanging out in a joint filled with wannabe cops."

"Yeah, that's us," she said. "One kick-ass hot shit team."

She smiled. The beer was doing its job. This was as good a time as any to see if my trouble-in-paradise theory was right. "So how's Spence doing?"

The smile vanished. "I spoke to his counselor last week. He said Spence just won't *give himself* to the program. Then Spence called me New Year's Eve. He says he's *fine*, but he can't imagine another ninety days away from home. So me, I immediately go into recovering-drug-addict's-wife autopilot, and I told him to take it one day at a time. He goes, 'Oh Christ, Kylie, not you too.' He said 'Happy New Year' and slammed the phone down."

I responded with a noncommittal nod. "So what are you going to do now?"

"I know exactly what I'm going to do," she said, waving at Gladys. "I'm going to order us another pitcher of beer."

We chowed down on wings, and halfway through the second pitcher she was leaning across the table, one hand resting on my arm, and starting every other sentence with "Do you remember when?"

Boy, did I remember. I remembered the first day I looked up and saw the green-eyed, golden-haired beauty walk into my life. I remembered the first kiss, and the tender lovemaking, and the joy of realizing I'd met the woman I wanted to be with forever. And then I remembered the last night we sat in this seedy old wings joint, and Kylie told me she was going back to Spence. "He's recovered," she said. "I have to give him one more chance."

And now it sounded like Spence was as un-recovered as possible.

We talked for two hours. Somewhere along the way, I realized that the crowd had thinned out, and that our third pitcher of beer was dangerously low. Kylie topped off both our glasses, and we asked Gladys for two coffees, one Mississippi mud pie, and two forks.

We dug into the pie like two kids on a sugar binge. Forks dueling, vying for the best chunks of chocolate, and Kylie doing what she always does: play hard to win.

She doesn't like to lose at anything. Especially relationships. Her parents set the bar low. Their marriage failed. Then her father struck out two more times, her mother once. Kylie's goal was to get married and make it stick.

But it's not easy for an ambitious cop to stay married to a drug addict.

We'd played this Mississippi mud wrestling game before, and as usual, Kylie grabbed the last piece. That's when I had my three-pitchers-of-beer epiphany. *This morning I woke up in a penthouse suite with Cheryl and thought,* I've never been happier. *Tonight I'm in a Third Avenue dive, getting hammered on Brooklyn Blast with Kylie, thinking,* I've never been happier.

We were both legally too drunk to drive, and while Kylie loves to break the rules, that's the one we never even bend. Luckily there's no rule dictating how long two cop partners can hug when they're saying good night, because we'd have gone way over the limit.

I put her in the first cab, and she gave me one final hug. "Thanks, Zach," she said. "I really needed this."

I was about to say something like "I'm really sorry about you and Spence," but I kept my mouth shut. Who the hell was I kidding?

Chapter 25

THE ROOM WAS dark, dank, dungeon-like. Tripp Alden stood spread eagle, his wrists and ankles shackled to iron-forged rings set in the stone wall.

In front of him loomed the tall blond man, dressed only in skintight black leather pants, his golden mane pulled back into a tight ponytail, his bare chest oiled and glistening in the orange glow cast by a pair of torches on the wall.

"Your father cares more about money than he does about you," he said, unsheathing a curved sword from the steel scabbard that hung at his side. He positioned the blade an inch from the boy's neck.

Tripp was sobbing. "Please. He'll pay whatever you want. I know he will. Just call him back. Please."

A phone rang.

"That's him," Tripp screamed. "He's calling you back."

"Too late," the tall blond man said. He grasped the hilt with both hands and drew the sword back, ready to deliver a single deadly strike.

The phone rang again, louder this time, and Hunter Alden snapped awake, slamming his knee on the underside of his desk. He yelped in pain and fumbled for his iPhone. Hutch's face appeared on the screen.

"Dad? What's going on?"

"The police were just at my apartment. They think Tripp was kidnapped."

Hunter forced a laugh. "Dad, Tripp is fine. Go back to staring at the moon, or the planets, or whatever else is up there in the stratosphere."

"The only thing I'm staring at is your front gate," Hutch said. "I didn't ring because I don't want Janelle to know I'm here. Open up. I'm freezing."

An op-ed piece in the *Times* once said that Hutch and Hunter Alden were men of biblical proportions. One was Solomon, a man of wisdom, wealth, and power; the other was the serpent who slithered through the Garden of Eden.

The snake buzzed his father through the gate, shoved the burner phone into his pocket and made his way to the foyer, his mind churning, trying to hash out a plan for dealing with Solomon.

"Dad," he said, opening the front door. "I was just going to call you."

Hutch Alden stood there, hatless, gloveless, his parka unzipped. "Where's Tripp?" he demanded, his breath a white puff of smoke in the cold air.

"Don't worry about him," Hunter said. "Come on in. I'll pour you a drink."

"What's going on?" Hutch said as he followed Hunter to the office.

"What's going on is the cops are driving me crazy. They're supposed to be looking for Peter's killer, but they keep coming around asking for Tripp."

"They said he was abducted. There's a witness."

"They came to me with the same bullshit. The truth is the kid was out filming one of his crazy movies, some old lady saw it, and she thought it was for real. It's not. End of story."

"Then where is Tripp?"

"Tripp?" Hunter said, pouring from a three-thousand-dollar bottle of Richard Hennessy cognac. "Getting drunk, or shacked up with some girl, or whatever it is eighteen-year-old kids do when someone they love gets murdered."

Hutch cupped the crystal snifter and slowly

swirled the amber liquid around the bowl. "Be that as it may, what does it hurt for him to talk to the cops? Maybe he knows something that will help."

"Dad, I talked to him. He never connected with Peter. The cops should be interviewing Peter's drinking buddies, not some kid who knows nothing. And the worst part of it is they keep coming back here. It's upsetting Janelle. I'm at the end of my rope. But they won't quit. I don't know what to do."

Hutch snapped at the bait. "You should have called me. I know exactly what to do."

Hunter held up both hands. "I know, I know. I was going to call, but I hated to ask you to use up a chit with the new mayor on her first day."

"I don't have to call the mayor," Hutch said, raising the glass to his nose and breathing in the aroma. "I'll find out who those two detectives report to, and I'll talk to their boss."

Hunter shrugged. "I don't want to put you to any trouble . . ."

"Are you kidding? I have enough juice to call the head of Homeland Security or the goddamn president of the United States. How much trouble is it for me to ask some precinct captain to call off his dogs and give Tripp a break for a few days? I'll take care of it first thing in the morning."

He took a small sip of the cognac and let it run over his palate. "This is exceptional, but I'm not going to stick around and enjoy it," he said, setting the snifter down. "You look like hell. Get some sleep."

"Will do," Hunter said, leading his father toward the foyer.

The burner phone in Hunter's pocket rang.

"Don't answer it," Hutch said, stopping at the front door. "Whatever it is, they can call back in the morning."

"Great advice, except it *is* morning in Japan, and I told this developer in Tokyo to call me now."

The phone rang again, and Hunter opened the front door.

"Give me a minute. This damn thing is stuck," Hutch said, struggling with the zipper on his parka.

The phone rang again. And again. And again.

On the sixth ring the old man was still in the doorway, trying to zip up.

Hunter couldn't wait. He dug into his pocket and yelled into the phone, "Hold on." He turned to his father. "Dad, I have to take this call."

Hutch gave up on the zipper and pulled the parka around him for the twenty-foot walk to the curb. Hunter shut the door and pulled the phone to his ear. "Hello, this is Hunter Alden."

The voice on the other end said only two words, but they were all Hunter needed to hear to realize that his worst fears were about to be realized.

"Hello, Leviticus."

Chapter 26

HUNTER STEELED HIMSELF. He had known this call was coming, and he had two ways to deal with it. The first was to come on like a freight train. His reputation for bullying, browbeating, and psychologically eviscerating his opponents was notorious. *Victoriam terrore*. Victory by intimidation.

There was a second way. It went against every fiber of his being, but it was the only way to play it when the other guy had all the cards. *Be nice.*

"Who is this?" Hunter asked politely.

"Why don't we keep it Old Testament, Leviticus? Call me Cain."

"And I'd prefer if you called me Hunter."

"You're a hard man to reach, Hunter." His pitch was flat, his inflection robotic. He was using a voice modifier, and a cheap one at that.

"I'm sorry I couldn't take your call earlier, Mr. Cain, but the police were here, and while I have no experience in these matters, I felt it wise not to negotiate ransom money in their presence."

"Good call. Bringing the cops in on this would not be in either of our best interests."

"Perhaps you should have thought of that before you killed my driver. Decapitations have a way of attracting law enforcement."

"I'm sorry for that. It couldn't be avoided."

"And what about kidnapping my son? Could that have been avoided?"

"I'm not sure I follow. I'm holding Tripp for ransom. Logic would dictate that the process begins with an abduction."

"I beg to differ," Hunter said. "You're blackmailing me, Mr. Cain. You have—or at least you think you have—information that I don't want to become public knowledge, and you want me to buy your silence. That's extortion, plain and simple. So let me repeat the question: Why did you take Tripp when all you had to do is negotiate?"

"Oh, I see where you're going," Cain said. "Easy answer. I did that to help you."

"Now I'm not sure that *I* follow," Hunter said.

"Simple logic. Paying off a blackmailer has a way

of—as you put it—attracting law enforcement. And once their interest is piqued, they tend to start digging into what it is you're willing to pay to hide. But if you're paying off a ransom demand, nobody bats an eye. It lets the whole world see you as the loving father, the sympathetic victim, instead of the monster we both know you are."

Hunter took a deep breath. He'd made his decision. *Don't intimidate; manipulate.*

"I appreciate your concern for my public image, but I could have easily paid you in cash if you had asked. Nobody would know about the transaction, and life would go on."

"I doubt if you have that much cash on hand to meet my price."

This was it. Let's get down to business, Mr. Cain. "And how much are we talking about?"

"Ten percent."

Hunter had been ready for a dollar amount, but this was a punch in the gut. "Ten percent of what?" he asked, but he was afraid that he already knew the answer.

"Of the money you made from that little Bible study group of yours. Let me do the math for you. Project Gutenberg netted you a one-billion-dollar profit. My 10 percent comes to a hundred million."

Hunter sat down on the foyer steps, barely able to breathe. He'd heard the unhearable. Cain knew the unknowable. Not just the vague notion of Project Gutenberg, but numbers. Real numbers.

Hunter changed the subject. "Let me speak to my son."

"He can't come to the phone, but I can assure you he is alive and well."

"Prove it. Bring him here tonight, and I will pay you five million dollars. No questions asked."

"That sounds like a fair price for your son. But if you want to protect your reputation"—Cain paused—"and your freedom, I'm going to need another ninety-five mil. I have an account in the Caymans, so the logistics are simple."

"On your end, maybe, but not on mine. Do you know what it takes to pull together that kind of money?"

"No, I don't, but I'm sure you do."

"The first step is to know what I'm paying for. How do I know my son is still alive? Let me speak to him."

"That's not going to happen. You people have codes, secret words. I'll get you proof that he's alive, but I don't trust you to talk to him on the phone."

"As for this fantasy of me netting a billion dollars from this so-called Project Gutenberg, how do I know you have any evidence whatsoever to back up that ridiculous claim?"

"You *don't* know," Cain said. "You're a risk taker, Hunter. You look at the upside, and you look at the downside. So here are your options. If, after all I've revealed already, you think I can't hurt you, then don't pay me. But I think you sense the truth. I know enough to bury you. And once the details of Project Gutenberg get out, you'll make Bernie Madoff look like a choirboy. Sleep on it, Leviticus. I wouldn't want you to make any rash decisions."

Cain hung up.

"Oh, I've already made my decision, Mr. Cain," Hunter said. He put the burner phone back in his pocket and headed for the secure landline in his office.

By now Blackstone should have gotten a price from Wheeler.

Part Two

THE SINS OF THE SON

CHAPTER 27

WHEN HE WAS twelve years old, Silas Blackstone's father taught him the secret to success.

"Most people are only good at a couple of things, and they suck at everything else," Kurt Blackstone said one night as he nursed his third beer. "If you want to get ahead in life, focus on the stuff you're good at and get even better."

Young Silas smirked.

Kurt caught it and knew what it meant. "Yeah, I know I'm just a lousy trackwalker for the MTA, but that's because when I was a kid nobody ever taught me nothing. But if you want to make a nice living, get really good at one thing, and you've got the world by the balls."

Silas knew what he was *not* good at: playing sports, making friends, and talking to girls. It's why he spent so much time holed up in his room hunched over a computer.

Thirty years later he was still hunched over a computer, only this time he was looking for digital bread crumbs on Tripp Alden's MacBook Air. He was rummaging through Tripp's search history when the phone rang.

Hunter didn't bother saying hello. Just "Did you talk to Wheeler?"

"Yeah, boss. I offered him double, like you said, but he didn't jump at it. He said all the previous jobs have been regular citizens. But now you're asking him to go up against a professional—someone who will fight back."

"Why the hell does he think I'm willing to pay him twice as much?"

"I know," Silas said, "but as soon as I told him you'd pay double, he knew it was dangerous. He's on the fence. He says he needs time to think about it."

"I don't have time. Tell him I'll pay him triple to get off the fence."

Hunter hung up, and Silas sat back in his chair. Working for Alden, he had learned the value of secrets, and he'd successfully kept one secret from his boss.

The truth about Wheeler.

Eight years ago, a seventy-five-year-old council-woman in Vermont stood between Alden Investments and a nine-figure land deal. When Hunter couldn't get her vote, he called Silas into his office and explained the problem.

"How can I help?" Silas asked.

"Find a pro and pay him to kill the stubborn old bitch."

Silas knew Hunter was serious. Hunter was always serious when it came to money. "Kill the bitch" meant exactly that.

"I know a guy," Silas said. "Wheeler."

Hunter held up a hand. "Stop. I can't be con-nected to this. I don't want details. All I want is results."

Two weeks later, the councilwoman's car skidded off an icy mountain road. The coroner ruled her death an accident. The following day, Hunter transferred a quarter of a million dollars to Wheeler's offshore account.

Since then, Wheeler had been called in six more times. Hunter never met the man, but he considered him a valuable asset to his business. What he didn't know was that there was no Wheeler.

If Silas had offered to kill the old lady himself,

Hunter would have laughed. So Silas invented Wheeler, and the more money Hunter made, the more indispensable Wheeler's services became.

"So Mr. Wheeler," Silas said out loud. "He's offering triple. What do you think?"

"I think we can do better, Mr. Blackstone," Silas said, his voice more menacing this time.

"Quadruple?"

"That has a nice ring to it. If Alden agrees, consider me off the fence."

Silas went to the fridge, popped the top on a beer, and called Hunter back. "I spoke to Wheeler," he said. "He'll do it for an even million."

Hunter didn't hesitate. "I'll pay, but it's got to be done by Monday. I spoke to the asshole who took Tripp. He calls himself Cain, and he's smart. He wants a shitload of money. I can stall him, but not for long. How close are you to finding him?"

"I've been digging into Tripp's computer all night. The bad news is it's all password-protected. The good news is I taught him everything he knows about computer security. He's using my methods, which means I can hack his files."

"Call me as soon as you find something, and tell Wheeler to stand by."

Hunter hung up, and Silas sipped his beer. "Looks

like you've got the job, Mr. Wheeler," he said. "What have you got to say for yourself?"

"I'd say your father was right, Mr. Blackstone," the imaginary Mr. Wheeler replied. "If you want to make a nice living, get really good at one thing, and you've got the world by the balls."

Silas raised his beer. "I'll drink to that."

Chapter 28

CAIN SMILED, PLEASED with the way he'd gone one-on-one with Hunter Alden. *Not bad for an amateur.*

The alarm on his phone beeped. He looked at the message on the screen.

FEEDING TIME AT THE ZOO.

Even though he'd written it himself, it tickled him. Kidnapping was a serious business, but a little whimsy never hurt.

He went to the kitchen and opened a jar of peanut butter. The boys hadn't eaten in twelve hours. By now Tripp would be miserable, but the little Puerto Rican would tough it out. Snatching the two kids hadn't been easy, Cain thought, rubbing his arm where Lonnie had slashed him with the box cutter, but the toughest part had been finding a place to hide them once he had them.

The answer had come to him the day before Christmas. He was watching *Eyewitness News* on channel 7 when Art McFarland, the education reporter, came on with a story about high levels of PCBs found in lighting fixtures in eight hundred of the city's schools.

"It will take three years to replace those fixtures," McFarland stated.

Cain had just about tuned out the story when McFarland dropped the bombshell. "The EPA says almost all the schools are safe enough for classes to continue, but some of them are so contaminated that they had to be shut down immediately."

He turned up the volume as McFarland wrapped up. "All city schools are currently closed for the holidays, but twenty-two of them will not reopen in January. A list of the affected schools is posted on the station's website."

Cain had racked his brain trying to come up with a safe place to stash Tripp, and suddenly, on Christmas Eve, the city of New York had presented him with twenty-two possibilities.

He booted up the TV station's website. The schools about to be closed were scattered throughout the city, and he carefully mapped out a game plan in his head. He'd visit each one, and then rate them on location, access to public transportation, and how likely they were to attract eyeballs.

And then one school jumped out at him: PS 114—his alma mater. It had been a wretched place to go through middle school, and the day he graduated, he vowed that he'd never go back.

He was about to cross it off the list when it hit him. Everything that had made 114 unbearable back then might make it perfect for locking up Tripp. Plus it was the school closest to where he lived. He had to at least give it a look.

He waited till midnight before he walked the seven blocks from his apartment on Avenue D in Alphabet City to the rambling old building on Delancey Street, sitting in the shadows of the Williamsburg Bridge. The neighborhood was deserted—no restaurants, no bars, and, except for the school, there was almost no reason for anyone to go there.

It was as desolate a spot as you could find in this thriving city. Even the people who lived in the low-income high-rise on Grand Street knew better than to venture out onto this near-dark stretch of Manhattan, where there was nothing but a fleet of sanitation trucks parked under the bridge. They were sure there would be a mugger behind every truck.

But there was no one. Cain swept the area, one

hand on the Glock pistol in his jacket pocket. There were no guards, no surveillance cameras. The smartest way in was through the basement. He went down the stairs and took a look at the basement door. The flimsy padlock that held it shut would have to be replaced with a heavier-duty lock if he expected to keep people out. But the place was perfect.

After all these years, this shithole is good for something, he thought.

He went home and poured himself a drink.

"Thank you, Santa," he said. "It's just what I wanted for Christmas. A toxic middle school on the Lower East Side."

Chapter 29

THE JANITORIAL SERVICES room in the basement of PS 114 was a burial ground for broken furniture, moldy books, and a fetid lost-and-found pile that had been accumulating since the Truman administration. Nobody went there, especially the janitor.

Then, in 1983, Augie Hoffman took over as head custodian and transformed a vast hellhole into a perfectly organized maintenance command center: maple workbench, neat rows of tools, precisely labeled storage bins, an immaculate kitchenette, and a sleeper sofa for those winter nights when the school's temperamental heating system required round-the-clock attention.

On the south wall were three floor-to-ceiling ten-by-eight-foot wire cages for gym equipment, school supplies, and anything else that might walk out the door if it wasn't locked up.

Tripp and Lonnie were in the center cage along with a case of bottled water, an empty spackle can, and a roll of toilet paper. They were asleep when they heard an upstairs door slam shut.

Cain came down the stairs and entered the make-shift prison. He was in black from his watch cap to his boots, his eyes barely visible beneath a ski mask. He went directly to the janitors' workbench, opened the top drawer, and retrieved the stun gun.

He pointed the fifteen-million-volt Vipertek at his captives, and they backed up to the rear of the wire impound.

"Did you talk to my father?" Tripp asked.

"He wants to make sure you're still alive," Cain said, his voice filtered through a voice changer.

"Doesn't sound like my father. You sure you dialed the right number?"

Lonnie laughed. Cain didn't.

"He wants a proof-of-life call," Cain said, dropping to one knee and shoving a dozen peanut butter and jelly sandwiches under the sweep space.

"You want me to call him now?"

"Not him. For all I know you people have code words."

"Can I call my grandfather?"

"No. I want someone outside the family. Make it casual. Tell them to call your father and say you're fine."

"And to pay the ransom," Tripp added.

"Are you dicking with me, or are you stupid? You say 'Pay the ransom,' and they're not going to call your father. They're going to call the cops."

"Sorry, I didn't mean—"

"It's real simple, kid. Call a friend. Someone you trust. Tell them to tell your old man you're happy and healthy. That's it. Short and sweet."

"Okay. Give me a phone."

"You give orders just like your father, don't you? I'll do it in the morning. He can stew till then."

Cain took a long look around the room. Nothing out of place. He shook the cage door. Locked tight. "Don't eat it all at once," he said, backing away from the cage. "Room service is closed for the night."

He put the stun gun back in the top drawer of the workbench and slammed the storeroom door on his way out. The boys listened as he walked down the corridor and trudged up the stairs. The outer door opened and closed, and he disappeared back into the world.

Lonnie grabbed two sandwiches and tossed one to Tripp. "Who you gonna call?"

"He said a friend. Someone I trust."

"That would be me," Lonnie said, "but I've asked the front desk to hold all my calls."

"There's only one other person besides you that I trust," Tripp said. "I'll call Peter."

Chapter 30

HANGOVERS ARE LIKE snowflakes: no two are alike. Of course, that's just my theory. Truth be told, I haven't had nearly enough hangovers in my life to qualify as an authority on the subject, but even in my limited experience, I find that they each come with their own special brand of physical and mental misery.

Waking up at 5:00 a.m. on the third day of the new year, I found myself with a throbbing head, a rumbling belly, and an overwhelming veil of guilt. Actually, it was more like a guilt, shame, and remorse cocktail. I'd been cheating on my girlfriend, and I felt like shit. Okay, maybe I hadn't cheated on her, but I still felt like shit.

I turned to one of the world's oldest hangover cures: yoga. I pulled out the mat and spent the next half hour stretching my body, cleansing my spirit, and hopefully exorcising the devil's horny ass from my soul.

That, plus a hot shower and two cups of fresh-brewed French roast, left me feeling better. Technically, I hadn't done anything wrong. Kylie was my friend, my partner, and she had needed a strong shoulder to lean on. I was there for her. If I crossed a line, it was only in my fantasies. I'm a man, and men don't always think with their shoulders.

I had just about given myself complete absolution when the phone rang. As soon as I saw Cheryl's picture fill the screen, I froze. The universe was not ready to cut me some slack. There was no time to recite the sinner's prayer.

"Hey . . . how'd it go last night?" I said, my voice appropriately somber, like I'd been holding my own deathwatch for Mildred out of solidarity.

"She's hanging on. I've decided to run into the city, grab some clothes, stop at the precinct to pick up some work, then go back to Westchester and wait for the end."

"Anything I can do?"

"No, I just wanted to connect."

There was an uncomfortable pause, and I knew she wasn't groping for the words to apologize for her behavior on the precinct steps yesterday. She was waiting for me.

"I'm sorry about yesterday. I guess I was a little insensitive," I said.

"No you weren't," she said sweetly.

I couldn't believe she was letting me off the hook. "Really?"

"No, Zach. *I* was a little insensitive. You—and I say this not as your girlfriend, but as a board-certified behavior analyst—you were completely emotionally oblivious."

She was *not* letting me off the hook. In fact, she impaled me with it. But at least she said it with a smile.

"Thank you, Dr. Robinson. I guess I'm lucky to be dating a shrink so I don't underestimate my shortcomings."

"That's me: full-service girlfriend."

"Just don't put it on my departmental evaluation."

"Don't worry—I have a separate file of all your flaws just for home consumption."

"Well, whichever one of them flared up yesterday, I'm sorry, and I'm ready to move on."

"Me too. So, what did you do after I left you high and dry last night?"

"Me?" I said.

"Yes, you. What did you do last night?"

My half-baked brain scrambled for a plausible half-truth. "Well, Kylie and I worked pretty late. Then we grabbed a bite to eat."

"Where'd you go?"

"Some cop bar with halfway decent food," I said. *Nameless sounded harmless. If it had been memorable, I'd have remembered the name.*

"Sounds like fun."

"Not as much fun as two nights in the La-Di-Da Suite at the Steele Towers with you. But you know me—I make the most of what's available. Speaking of available, as soon as you are, there's a new Greek place opening up near my—" My phone beeped. It was Captain Cates. "Sorry, the boss is on the other line. I've got to run."

"I'll see you later," she said.

I took Cates's call.

"Jordan, how fast can you get here?" Cates said.

"Very. I'm just getting ready to leave."

"Make it quick. I'm expecting a visitor in fifteen minutes, and I want you and MacDonald here to help me deal with the politics."

"We'll be there. Kylie and I are starting to build a good relationship with the mayor."

"It's not the mayor," Cates said. "Her I can handle on my own."

"Who is it?"

"It's the man who can get things done around this city faster than the mayor or any one of us. Hutch Alden."

I squeezed my eyes shut. My head was throbbing again.

Chapter 31

IF I HAD ANY doubt who owned the Cadillac limo parked outside the precinct, the license plate spelled it out in orange and black: ALDEN 1.

Kylie was waiting for me on the front steps.

"How'd you get here so fast?" I said.

"I woke up early, picked up the car, and was at the diner when Cates called. Hutch Alden showed up a few minutes ago. He's waiting for us."

"What's his mood?"

"Very chummy," she said. "But guys like Alden never show their cards. He was in full-blown, salt-of-the-earth, man-of-the-people, billionaire mode—just like last night."

"Only last night it was 'Let's watch a meteor shower together,'" I said. "This morning it may be a shit storm. Let's go up to Cates's office and find out."

Alden greeted us warmly. Cates took the lead.

"Mr. Alden was just telling me that the mayor set up a meeting between him and you," she said as if she'd just heard about it for the first time. "And he was generous enough to come to the station to do a follow-up."

"The mayor is busy," Hutch said. "I appreciate her personal concern for our family, but why drag her back into this? I'm sure we can resolve it right here on the departmental level."

The threat was clear. "I'm sure we can," Cates said, playing the game.

"My grandson is fine," Alden said. "As soon as you left, I went to see Hunter, and wouldn't you know it— Tripp called while I was there. I told him you'd like to talk to him, but he's so upset by Peter's death that he needs a few days to himself."

"That's understandable," Cates said, "but in solving any homicide, time is our enemy. Maybe you can set up a phone call between him and the detectives."

"If I thought he could help in any way, I'd be glad to accommodate you," Hutch said. "But I questioned him at length, and he knows nothing. He didn't even know about the murder till it hit the news. I think the best way to handle this is for NYPD to pursue the leads you have, and let Tripp come to peace with his loss. Once he's gone through the grieving process, I'll see to it that he makes himself available for any questions. Can you do that for me?"

Unspoken: If you say "No," I'll call my buddy Muriel Sykes.

Cates graciously agreed. Hutch thanked us and left.

"He's gone over to the dark side," Kylie said. "He's totally in sync with Hunter. No cops. Let the family take care of it."

"I know he's stonewalling, but unless you suspect Tripp of being the killer, let it go," Cates said. "Now fill me in on what you've got so far on Peter Chevalier."

"Hunter would like us to believe a jealous husband did it," I said. "Peter was a lifelong bachelor who loved the ladies, but he played by the rules. He definitely wasn't the home wrecker or the womanizer Alden made him out to be."

"It doesn't surprise me," Cates said. "Hunter Alden wouldn't be the first uptight rich white guy to exaggerate the exploits of a sexually active black man. It sounds to me like Peter was killed because of the man he worked for, not for the man he was."

"We're on the same page," Kylie said. "Tripp Alden was kidnapped, and instead of sending one of his fingers or an ear to his father, the killer sent Peter Chevalier's head. It makes a much louder statement."

"If you're right," Cates said, "Alden is either too smart or too nervous to move it, which means the head is probably on ice somewhere in his house. But there's not a judge in this city crazy enough to sign a search warrant. Based on your conversations with Alden, do you think he'll pay the ransom?"

"Yes," Kylie said. "And the minute he does, the killer is going to disappear off the face of the earth. Screw Hutch Alden. We should be talking to that kid."

Cates set her right elbow on the desk and rested her mouth and chin on the knuckles of her right hand. She was thinking—something she was very good at.

Thirty seconds into her Rodin's *Thinker* pose, she looked up. "I know you don't want to hear this," she said, looking straight at Kylie, "but I want to remind everyone in this room—myself included—that police departments work for the taxpayers. I'd bet a month's salary that someone took Tripp Alden and is negotiating a payoff with his family. But the family flat-out denies it. And now, a man with a lot of juice in this town told us as politely as he could to back off. So until we have proof that's a lot more substantive than an eighty-year-old woman who thinks she saw an undercover cop arrest Tripp Alden, this unit will stand down. Your job is not to solve an unreported kidnapping. Your job is to catch a murderer. Any questions?"

"Just one," Kylie said. "How do you propose we do that if we have to wait for our main person of interest to go through his 'grieving process'?"

"You might start by talking to Peter's family."

"The Aldens *are* his family."

"Peter has a brother in Haiti. He flew to New York last night and is stopping by my office later this morning."

"Yes, ma'am," Kylie said. "He'll probably need reassurance that NYPD is doing everything it can to find his brother's murderer. Would you like me to lie to him, or do you want to handle it?"

She turned and stormed out of the office. Cates looked to me and shook her head.

"Don't be too mad at her, Captain," I said. "She's frustrated."

"That's not my 'I'm pissed at her' look," Cates said. "It's my 'Boy, do I feel sorry for you' look. Have a nice day."

Chapter 32

BY THE TIME I left Cates's office, Kylie was at her desk unleashing her fury on her computer keyboard.

"What are you writing?" I said.

She didn't look up.

"A letter of resignation? A tell-all book on the injustices you've had to endure as a member of New York's Finest? I've heard poetry is an excellent way to express your innermost—"

She gave me the finger. In return, I gave her some time. She stopped typing after a few minutes, then made a violent assault on some of the paperwork we'd amassed on the case. She turned pages with a vengeance, threw a ballpoint pen across the room for failing to write on the first stroke, and stormed to a file cabinet, where she yanked open and slammed shut half a dozen metal drawers.

I loved it.

I don't care what time of day it was, or what she was wearing: Kylie MacDonald was a smoldering-hot woman. And when she was angry, the heat factor went up exponentially.

I thought back to the previous night and the not-so-subtle way she had put her hand on my arm, the two forks interlocking over Mississippi mud pie, and the long good-night hug that didn't last long enough. Then I thought back to the days when we were together, and I'd sometimes go out of my way to piss her off because the make-up sex was so fantastic.

If I was keeping a diary, the entry would have said, "Got exceedingly horny. Could not focus on murder investigation."

After twenty minutes, I decided we'd both indulged ourselves long enough. "If it makes a difference, I'm on your side," I said.

"Then why didn't you back me up, Zach?"

"Because Cates is not the enemy. Because she can get as tormented about the system as any of us. And because when you're a cop you get shit thrown at you from all sides. The only difference with Red is that most of the time the shit gets thrown down from on high. Cates is playing by the rules because she's smart enough to know that she doesn't have enough street cred to go head-to-head with a new mayor who has less than seventy-two hours on the job."

She blinked. Smiled, actually. The ice was broken.

"So now what?" she said.

"I don't know. You were working like a madwoman. It looked like you were onto something."

"I was looking for a loophole, trying to figure out if we could charge Tripp Alden with something. Then we could go after him."

Before I could say "Stop wasting your time," my phone rang. It was Bob McGrath, the front desk sergeant.

I'd prearranged for McGrath to call me when Cheryl arrived. "But don't broadcast it," I'd told him. "I don't want the whole squad to hear you yelling, 'Hey, Jordan, your main squeeze is here.'"

"Don't worry about it," McGrath had promised. "I'm the most discreet six-foot-two, two-hundred-and-fifty-five-pound cop in the department."

I picked up the phone. "Hey McGrath, what's the word?"

"Elvis has entered the building," he said in a gruff whisper. "How's that, Detective? Subtle enough for you?"

I laughed, thanked him, and turned to Kylie. "I'll be back in five minutes," I said.

"Where are you going?"

A simple question, but not for a man who finds himself torn between two women. The official male rules of dating clearly state, "Never let one know how strong your feelings are for the other."

"Cheryl's office," I said, trying to sound like I was heading there on official business.

Kylie didn't buy it for a second.

She winked. "Have fun."

Chapter 33

I WAS TOO conflicted to have fun. In fact, I was a perfect candidate for a session with the department shrink, but that, of course, was out of the question. The best that Dr. Robinson could do right now was welcome me with a good old-fashioned, PG-rated, safe-for-work hug.

I took the stairs two at a time, came bounding through her office door, and kicked it shut behind me.

"Zach," she said, completely taken by surprise. "How did you know I was here?"

"I didn't," I said. "I stop by every five minutes just to bask in your aura."

She wrapped her arms around me. "My aura sucks right now. But it's good to see you."

I pressed her close, and she tilted her head up to mine. Just as our lips touched, the door opened.

I'd never met the man standing in the doorway, had never even seen a picture of him, but I immediately knew who he was.

He was tall, with a runner's body and Paul Newman-blue eyes. His hair was light brown and shaggy, giving him a rumpled surfer look that went well with the carefully groomed stubble on his face.

"Fred," Cheryl said, dropping her arms from around my neck like she'd just been caught behind the barn with the strapping young stable boy.

"You must be Zach," Fred said, flashing me a toothpaste-commercial smile. He reached out, and we shook hands.

I'm a good judge of character. It's one of the prerequisites of the job. One look at Fred, and my first thought was, *Nice guy.* If I wound up sitting next to him on an airplane, we'd probably chat it up. But this was different. Fred and I weren't sharing an armrest on a flight to LA. We were sharing my girlfriend.

"I've heard so much about you from Cheryl," he said.

"So much for doctor–patient confidentiality," I said, trying to keep it light.

Fred laughed. "No, really. She tells me you and your partner are two of the smartest detectives in the city."

"Thank you," I said, looking at Cheryl. "Of course, even the smartest cops can do dumb things from time to time. Am I right, doc?"

She nodded. I got the feeling it was not a happy nod. The conversation we'd had a few hours before was still bouncing around in my head. I hadn't just been insensitive. I was emotionally oblivious. I had to step up my game.

"Sorry to hear about your mom," I said with all the compassion I could muster. "How are you holding up?"

"My mother raised me on her own," Fred said. "We've always been close, and I can't bear the thought of . . ." He stopped, unable to finish the sentence.

He held up a hand and turned his head away from us. It took him a solid ten seconds to regain his composure. "Anyway," he said, forcing energy back into his voice, "your question was, how am I holding up? The answer is, I'm holding up a hell of a lot better than I would have if I were dealing with this on my own. I couldn't have gone through it without Cheryl. She's an angel."

"Don't I know it," I said, putting my arm around Cheryl. "We're lucky to have her."

I stood there, my chest puffed up, a contented smile on my face, as if I were waiting for Fred to pull out a camera and snap a picture of the happy couple.

Fred didn't need a camera. He got the picture. He gave Cheryl an uncomfortable smile. "Why don't I leave you two alone," he said. "I'll wait for you outside. Nice to meet you, Zach."

Then, faster than you can say "Three's a crowd," he was gone.

Cheryl squirmed out from under my arm. "What the hell was that about?" she said.

"What was *what* about?" I said, walking to the door and shutting it again. "And don't tell me I was insensitive. I told him I was sorry about his mother."

"And as soon as he said how grateful he was for me to be there for him, you grabbed on to me, and you were ready to square off like a bull elephant during the mating ritual."

"Hey, you blindsided me. I didn't expect to run into your ex-husband. I thought you were taking the train in by yourself."

"I didn't want to be at the mercy of Metro-North, so Fred drove me in. That's still no reason for you to act like . . . like . . . like a caveman."

"Sorry," I mumbled. "Me jealous. Me not know what else to do."

She laughed. "You're hopeless."

"Not hopeless," I said, moving toward her. "Just a

little damaged." I put my hands around her waist and pulled her body against mine. "All I need is a good therapist."

There was a knock at the door, and without waiting for an answer, Kylie charged in. "Barnaby Prep," she said.

For the second time in a few minutes, Cheryl and I pulled apart in a hurry. "What's going on?" I said.

"That teacher, Ryan Madison, just called me. He just heard from Tripp. He wants us to meet him in the headmaster's office. Now."

I followed Kylie to the door, turned, and took one last look at Cheryl. "Rain check on the hug?" I said.

She nodded, a happier nod this time. "If you're lucky," she said.

Chapter 34

"SO IT LOOKS like you and Cheryl are once again the happiest couple at the One Nine," Kylie said as she peeled out and barreled up 67th Street.

"Circumstantial evidence," I said. "It's not as rosy as it might appear. I was in the middle of begging forgiveness when you busted in on us."

"What dumb thing did you do now?"

"I ran into her ex, and I may have behaved like a bit of an asshole."

"And when you say 'a bit' of an asshole, you mean . . ."

"Flaming."

"For God's sake, Zach. The poor guy's mother is dying."

"We all have our character defects. You, for example, drive like we're in a stolen car."

"At least I get us where we need to go," she said, not easing up on the gas pedal. "You're the one who's going to crash and burn unless you do some immediate damage control on your relationship. And I know just the person who can help you. His name is Scott Coffman. I'll give you his card."

"Are you serious? I'm already dating a therapist. You think another shrink is going to help? Thanks, but I don't need Dr. Coffman to fix my relationship with Cheryl."

She laughed. "You're an idiot. Scott's not a therapist."

"Then what is he?"

"He's my go-to sales guy at Tiffany's."

"I can't afford Tiffany's. But jewelry is a great idea. I think I'll talk to Wally."

"Who's that?"

"He's my go-to sales guy at the dollar store."

We kept up the verbal sparring all the way to Barnaby Prep, and by the time we got to Headmaster G. Martin Anderson's office, I had a smile on my face.

Ryan Madison, on the other hand, did not. He was no longer the happy-go-lucky, let's-sneak-a-smoke-on-the-roof guy we'd met yesterday. The unflappable Mr. Madison was definitely flapped.

"Ryan here is quite unnerved, and justifiably so," Mr. Anderson said, putting it all in headmaster-speak. "As am I. We have liability issues. Barnaby can't be involved in any of this."

"Any of what?" I asked. The four of us were in Anderson's office and Madison had yet to tell us what was going on.

"Tripp Alden left me a voice mail," Madison said. "I'll play it for you."

He set his phone to speaker and played back the message.

"Hey, Mr. Madison. I need a big favor. Please call my folks and tell them I'm fine. I can't come home, and I really can't talk to my dad. Just tell them I'm okay. Thanks."

"And did you call his parents?" I asked.

"No, I did *not* call his parents," Madison said, springing from his chair. "What kind of a schmuck do you think I am?"

"Calm down, sir," Kylie said. "We're all on the same side here."

"No we're not," Madison said. "You're investigating a murder. I'm on the side that wants nothing to do with it. I think the world of Tripp Alden, but what if he murdered his driver? You think I want to get in the middle of *that*?"

"We have no reason to suspect that Tripp killed Peter Chevalier," I said.

"That's your script, Detective. In my script, anything is possible. This whole thing is turning into a bad movie, and I don't want any part of it."

We were in a no-smoking building, and it was clear that Madison's neurons were screaming for a cig.

"That's fine," I said. "We can take it from here. What time did the call come in?"

He looked at his phone. "This morning at 8:11. I was upstairs in my room."

"And where was your phone when he called?" Kylie asked.

"It was on my—" Madison stopped, realizing what Kylie had just done.

"Go ahead, sir," she said. "Where was your phone when the call came in?"

"It was on my desk. And yes, Detective, I heard it ring, I saw it was Tripp calling, and I purposely let it go to voice mail. I don't want to be involved in their drama. Is that a crime?"

"Not at all," she said. "Considering the circumstances, not taking his call is totally understandable. Can I have your phone? I'll record the voice mail onto mine, and my partner and I will relay Tripp's message to the Aldens."

He handed Kylie his phone and pulled out a pack of cigarettes. "I'm going outside to burn one. I'll be back in a few minutes."

"I hope you understand our dilemma," Anderson said as soon as Madison left. "Our job is to develop these young men, not get caught up in their personal lives. We don't know if Tripp's reluctance to call home is connected to Mr. Chevalier's death. That's your bailiwick. Barnaby Prep has to stay above the fray. We cannot be the interlocutor between Tripp and his parents."

"We understand completely," I said, "and we'd be happy to pass Tripp's message along to the family."

The truth was that Hunter Alden was definitely hiding something, and we'd have been happy for any excuse to take another shot at him.

Chapter 35

TWENTY MINUTES LATER, we were back at the Alden house. Janelle answered the door. Like Ryan Madison, she had lost some of the spark she had the day before. She was still beautiful, but today I could see the stress lines in her face, and her green eyes were tinged with red.

"Oh," she said, which is what civilized people say instead of "You again? What the hell do you want now?"

"We have a message for you from your son," I said.

It was like the cop equivalent of open sesame. She swung the door wide, escorted us to her husband's office, and knocked.

One word from the other side: "What?"

"Hunter, the police are back. They have a message for us from Tripp."

Alden opened the door and let us in. Janelle took a seat. We stood.

"Tripp called you?" Alden said.

"Not directly, but we have a message from him for you and your wife," I said.

"Let's hear it," he said, settling into a leather chair behind the desk.

"It's a family matter," I said, pointing to Silas Blackstone, who was standing in a far corner of the room.

"Ignore him," Alden said. "What's the message?"

"It was delivered to one of Tripp's teachers less than an hour ago," Kylie said. "The school asked us to pass it on to you."

Kylie played the voice mail.

Janelle held her breath until she heard "Please call my folks and tell them I'm fine." A wave of relief washed over her, but it was immediately followed by a wince when Tripp said, "I can't come home, and I really can't talk to my dad."

Hunter was stone-faced throughout. "Just like I told you," he said as soon as the voice mail ended. "He's fine. He's okay. You heard every word he said."

"We're more interested in what he didn't say," I said.

"And I'm interested in getting back to work. Thank

you for coming. Janelle, see these two out. Again."

Janelle stood up. "No." She turned to me. "What do you mean you're interested in what he didn't say on the message?"

"We've been told that your son is grieving over Peter's death, yet he doesn't even mention it. Not 'When is the funeral?' or 'Did they catch the killer yet?' Your husband has assured us that Tripp has been calling here regularly, and yet Tripp says, 'I can't come home, and I really can't talk to my dad.'"

"That's enough!" Hunter said, coming out from behind the desk. "Get out."

I remembered the words of our new mayor: "Hunter Alden can be overbearing, but don't let him push you. He's not your boss—even if he tries to act like it." I was hoping she'd remember them, too.

"I'm . . . not . . . done," I said, laying it out like a poor man's version of Dirty Harry.

"Neither am I," Janelle said. "Go on, Detective."

"Mrs. Alden, Tripp's message came in this morning. Not to your home phone or your cell phone, but to his teacher—a third party whose phone wouldn't be set up to trace the call. Tripp has been missing since the murder, and quite frankly this voice mail sounds like a proof-of-life call."

"He's been kidnapped, hasn't he?" Janelle said.

"We don't know, but if he has, whoever abducted him would have instructed the family not to call in the police. That would be a mistake, very possibly one that could cost your son his life."

Janelle didn't say anything. Hunter put a hand on her shoulder. "I hope you're happy, Detectives. You've successfully scared the shit out of my wife. Your work here is done. Unless you have anything to charge us with, leave."

There's no law against being supremely arrogant, so there was nothing we could charge him with.

We left.

Chapter 36

SILAS BLACKSTONE ESCORTED the two cops out and watched as they drove off. Heading back to the office, he could hear the screaming.

He snickered. Janelle was going nuclear.

"Why didn't you tell me?" she shouted.

Hunter kept his cool. His response was so low that Blackstone couldn't make it out. But Janelle's reaction ripped through the thick mahogany door.

"*Spare* me? How? By telling me to stay out of it because I'm not Tripp's mother?"

Blackstone shook his head. *Careful, sweetie. The dead wife is off-limits. You keep this up, and I wouldn't be surprised if Hunter calls in Wheeler to get rid of you next.*

"How much money are they asking for?" Janelle demanded.

This was one answer Blackstone didn't want to miss. He eased closer to the door.

Hunter deflected the question. "A lot."

"It doesn't matter," she said. "We have kidnap and ransom insurance."

Silence.

It was no longer a problem of Hunter's voice not being audible. Blackstone was close enough to hear their body movements. It couldn't have been clearer if he'd bugged the room. Hunter just hadn't said a word.

"Is there a problem with the K & R?" Janelle asked.

"Yeah. The R. The insurance company will pay up to ten million, but this guy is asking for ten times that."

"Are you serious?" Janelle said. "A hundred million dollars?"

Blackstone couldn't believe it either. They both must have heard wrong.

"Great math skills, Janelle. Ten times ten is a hundred. Now subtract the ten the insurance company will pay from the hundred this lunatic wants and see how much has to come out of my pocket."

"I don't care what it costs," Janelle said. "Pay it."

"For a dirt-poor cracker from Alabama you're pretty fast and loose with my ninety million, aren't you?"

"You have more than you'll ever need. You only have one son."

"And before I spend a dime, I had to make sure that one son was alive. Last night I told the guy I wanted a proof-of-life call."

"Now you've got it."

"And so do the cops. I can't believe that asshole teacher dragged them in. Who the hell is he, anyway?"

"Seriously? *You don't know who Ryan Madison is?* Tripp talks about him all the time. He's been a mentor to your son for two years."

"Well, Mr. Mentor is a pussy for calling the cops. And how did he know to send for those two particular detectives? I'll tell you how. They talked to him yesterday when they went to Barnaby, and they told him if he heard from Tripp to call them. So he did."

"Can you blame him for that? The police are in the middle of a murder investigation—"

"I don't care! I've been writing checks to that school since Tripp was in kindergarten. At least a hundred grand a year above and beyond the tuition. You'd think that would buy a little discretion, but no, that candy-ass teacher couldn't wait to dial 911. Well, guess what? I'm going to make sure he doesn't do it again. Blackstone!"

Silas flinched at the sound of his name. He quickly

backed out to the foyer. "Coming," he yelled from the other room. He waited five seconds and entered the office.

Hunter was at the wall safe.

"What can I do for you, boss?"

"Get your car ready. You're my new driver."

"What are you talking about?"

"My car is in the impound lot, and my driver is dead. You're my new driver." He pulled four stacks of cash from the safe and shoved them into a leather envelope.

"You wait here and make yourself useful," he said to Janelle. "Those cops have held on to the Maybach long enough. Call their boss. Hell, I don't care if you have to call the mayor. I want it back."

"And where are you going?"

"Barnaby Prep," Hunter said as he strode out the door. "Parent–teacher conference."

Chapter 37

PATRICE CHEVALIER WAS tall, dark, and probably handsome, but his brother's brutal murder had left his face shrouded with grief, pain, and anger.

Cates made the introductions, Kylie and I extended our condolences, and the four of us sat down in Cates's office to talk about a subject that three of us would have liked to put off.

Cates eased us into it. "Dr. Chevalier and I have been talking, and from what he tells me, his brother was quite the philanthropist."

"That's not how Peter would put it," Chevalier said. "He would simply say he was just a guy helping out his kid brother."

"What did he do to help?" I said.

"He paid to send me to college in France, then four

years of Tulane medical school. I'm a pediatrician in one of Haiti's most impoverished regions, and after Hurricane Gilbert, Peter helped me build a children's clinic."

"That, Dr. Chevalier," Cates said, "is my definition of a philanthropist."

"Thank you, Captain. Now, how close are you to finding Peter's murderer and recovering his remains? The Peter Chevalier Children's Clinic stands as a tribute to my brother's generosity, and thousands of Haitians—many of whom owe him their lives— mourn his death and are waiting for me to bring him home." He paused. "All of him."

"It's impossible to tell you how close, but please know that Detectives Jordan and MacDonald are the most accomplished team under my command, and I promise you that bringing Peter's killer to justice is our highest priority."

It was not what he wanted to hear, but the man was practical. "How can I help?" he asked.

"Did you talk to your brother often?" I asked.

A hint of a smile. "Incessantly. He would often have nothing to do except sit in a parked car waiting for Mr. Alden. So he'd call me. I had to constantly remind him that chauffeurs have more time on their hands than doctors."

"So if Peter had any enemies, he might have told you—"

Chevalier held up a hand. "If you had met him, you wouldn't even suggest that."

"Maybe not enemies," I said, "but a romantic affair that—"

The hand again. "Peter was in a loving relationship with a single woman. But you know that already, Detective. You spoke with Juanita. Now I have a question for you. Have you spoken to Tripp Alden since my brother's death?"

"No, sir. We've been looking for him."

"As have I. And Juanita is worried sick because she hasn't heard from her grandson Lonnie."

"If I may ask," Kylie said, "why are you looking for Tripp?"

"Quite likely the same reason you are. Peter was working for the Aldens when he was killed. If anyone can help you in your investigation, it's the family. But you won't get anything out of Hunter Alden. So last night I went to see Janelle, but she either couldn't or wouldn't tell me where to find Tripp."

"How close was Tripp to Peter?" Kylie said.

"They adored one another. When Tripp was ten years old, he was bored spending the summer in Southampton and asked if he could visit the village where my brother and I grew up. He and Peter flew to Haiti and stayed two weeks. The next summer, he spent a month. And he came back every year until he was fifteen. He is not affected by his wealth. He was right at home in our village—and at this point he speaks fluent Creole. Between you and me, I'd say Peter was more of a father figure to the boy than Alden was. The fact that Tripp hasn't reached out to me after Peter's death has me very concerned."

"It has us concerned too," Cates said. "We will find him and get some answers from him."

"When?" Chevalier snapped loudly. "And don't tell me that you have the most accomplished team under your command looking for him, because I know otherwise. Hutch Alden was here this morning using his boundless political powers to keep you from doing just that, wasn't he?"

Cates didn't say a word.

"Thank you for not denying it. My apologies for raising my voice."

"I can only imagine the stress you've been under these past forty-eight hours," Cates said. "No apologies necessary, Dr. Chevalier."

"Please. Call me Patrice," he said, mellowing his tone. "Last night, when I visited Janelle, I asked if I could go through Peter's personal effects. With her permission, I took his computer and his cell phone."

"We already have his phone," I said.

"You have his business phone. This is his personal cell, and since the police hadn't seized it, I assumed it was not part of your investigation. Once I had his contacts, I was able to reach out to our people."

"Our people?" Cates said.

"There is a strong Haitian community in this city, many of whom work in quiet obscurity for the privileged few your unit was created to serve. My brother was part of that community. They were the glue that kept Peter connected to his Haitian culture."

"And one of those people works for Hutch Alden," Cates said.

Chevalier nodded. "Yes. But I shouldn't have to go underground to get the information I deserve in connection to my brother's murder. In the future, I'd like you and your detectives to be much more forthcoming."

"Understood," Cates said.

"And please tell me that you won't let the politics of wealth and power stand in the way of finding Peter's killer."

Cates rose from her chair and extended her arm. "You have my word on it, Patrice."

He stood and shook her hand. He smiled—all the way this time. His eyes brightened, and his lips parted to reveal perfect white teeth. There was no more "probably" about it. Patrice Chevalier was a handsome man.

"Thank you, Captain," he said.

She smiled back. "Call me Delia."

On the surface, it might have looked like there was a spark between them, a connection that might have led to dinner, and then who knows what. But I knew better. Delia Cates did not allow sparks to fly between her and the family of a homicide victim. The good doctor had caught her in the act of trying to bullshit him, so she turned up the charm, hoping to regain some of his trust. It was a variation on good cop/bad cop with Cates playing both roles.

She only had one agenda. Find the killer and the two missing teenagers.

Chevalier's agenda was the same as hers. Only he had one more priority—one he had shared with us from the get-go.

To bring his brother home. All of him.

Chapter 38

AUGIE HOFFMAN BRACED himself for the frigid blast that would hit him as soon as he made the turn onto the wide expanse of Grand Street. He rounded the corner, and the wind whipped up from the East River and bit into his face. He didn't care. Tomorrow at this time he'd be out of New York. Another two days and he'd be in Florida. Forever.

After thirty-two years, this was the last time he had to make the eleven-minute trek to PS 114. He'd told himself he was going to clean out his desk, but the truth was he needed to say one final good-bye to the old place.

He reflected on the craziness of the last few weeks. He had flown to West Palm Beach to spend the holidays with his brother Joe. Joe's wife, Debbie, had invited Nadine over for dinner, and by the end of the evening, Augie was love-struck. Two days later, he got the email telling him that PS 114 would be closed until further notice. "I don't have a job to go back to," he told Nadine.

"Then don't go back," she said. She didn't have to say it twice. He put in for early retirement, flew to New York, and packed. Tonight, she was flying up, the movers would come in the morning, and he and Nadine would drive back to West Palm to spend the rest of their lives together.

Thank you, God, he thought when he got to the school. *I knew there was a reason why you had all those toxic chemicals dripping out of those light fixtures.*

Since the school was closed, snow had been allowed to pile up everywhere, but there was a clear path from the street to the basement door. *Kids,* Augie thought. Judging by the boot prints, there had been three of them.

He took out his key ring and reached for the padlock. "Son of a bitch," he said. Whoever had been down there had changed the lock.

Damn bureaucrats, Augie thought. *They screw you up, even on your last day.*

He took a closer look at the new padlock. "What the hell?" he said. It was a top-of-the-line, core-hardened steel Abus Granit.

The damn lock must have cost a hundred and fifty bucks, which was a hundred and forty-five more than the school usually spent. It was like seeing filet mignon on the school lunch menu instead of fish sticks. It didn't make sense, and in Augie Hoffman's orderly world, things that didn't make sense kept him awake at night.

Who would change the lock? And why?

He probably should look into it. He had a key to the front door, but that meant trekking all the way around the building in the deep snow.

Hell, no, he told himself. *I don't work here anymore. It's not my problem.*

Sure it is, the little voice inside his head reminded him.

He turned and tromped through the snow toward the front of the building.

Old habits die hard.

Chapter 39

"WHERE IS HE?" Lonnie said, standing at the cage door, his fingers laced around the ten-gauge welded wire mesh.

"He's not coming," Tripp said.

"I swear I heard him upstairs fiddling with the lock a few minutes ago."

"Why would he come back so fast?" Tripp said. "We still have food. Plus, he was here this morning when I made the phone call to Mr. Madison." Tripp lowered himself to the floor of the cage.

"You think Madison called your old man by now?"

"Yeah. I do. I trust him. Don't you?"

Lonnie shrugged. "Not as much as I trust Peter. I don't understand why he wouldn't let you call Peter."

"He said Peter is too much like family. He thinks

we have some kind of secret telephone code, and I'd be able to give Peter a clue to where—"

An upstairs door slammed, and Lonnie jumped up. "I told you he's back. He came in another way."

They listened to the echo of heavy footsteps clomping down a corridor.

"I'll tell you one thing, dude," Lonnie whispered. "If he tries anything, I'm not going down without a fight."

The door to the storeroom opened, and the overhead lights went on. A man in an orange parka entered the room, saw the two teens in the cage, and stopped. He had no idea what to make of them.

"What the heck's going on here, boys?"

"Some crazy motherfucker grabbed us off the street and locked us up," Lonnie yelled. "Let us out, man. Let us out."

"Hang on, hang on," Augie said, hustling over to a lockbox on the wall. He fiddled with his keys while Lonnie bounced up and down on his heels, rattling the wire cage and yelling, "Come on, come on, hurry, hurry, hurry."

Augie unlocked the box and grabbed a key off the rack. "I'm coming, I'm coming."

He unlocked the cage and the door swung open. Lonnie was out first. Tripp was right behind him.

"Thanks, man," Lonnie said.

"How long have you been here?" Augie asked. "Who took you?"

"Three days, and I don't know," Lonnie said. "You got a cell? We need to call 911."

Augie unzipped a side pocket on his parka and reached for his phone. "This is insane," he said. "You've been locked in here for three—" He let out a piercing scream and fell to the floor, writhing in pain.

Lonnie spun around. There, standing over Augie, was his best friend, Tripp, the stun gun in his hand.

"Drag him into the cage," Tripp said calmly.

"Are you out of your fucking mind?" Lonnie yelled.

Tripp held the stun gun steady and pointed it at Lonnie's chest. "I don't want to shoot you too, but I will. I swear. Just drag him into the cage."

"Tripp, I think maybe you went stir-crazy. This guy is on our side. He—"

Tripp waved the gun. "I mean it. Get back in the cage and drag him in there with you, or I swear to God I will fry your ass."

"Go to hell. I've been in there three days. I'm not going back."

"Just get back in there for ten more minutes," Tripp said. "Trust me."

"Trust you? You go home, and I stay locked up?"

"Ten more minutes, Lonnie. I swear I'll call the cops as soon as I get out of here. And I am not going home."

"Where are you going?"

"Anyplace but home."

"Is this about your father, Tripp? You think he's going to punish you for getting kidnapped? What could he do? Take away your Platinum card? Make you fly coach?"

"You have no idea what my father is capable of."

Augie started to move. He tried to sit up.

"Please," Tripp said, "drag him into the cage and give me his cell phone, or I'll zap the both of you."

Cursing, Lonnie grabbed Augie's legs, pulled him along the floor and into the cage, and handed the cell phone to Tripp.

"Mission accomplished," he said. "Now what?"

"I have to lock you in there with him for ten minutes. But first we have to talk. I owe you an explanation."

"You think?"

"Walk me into the hall," Tripp said. "I don't want this guy to hear what I have to say."

With the gun to his back, Lonnie walked out

the door and into the corridor. "This better be good, Tripp," he said. "Or one of these days when you least expect it, I'm going to beat your rich monkey ass."

Chapter 40

THE LEATHER ENVELOPE filled with cash under his arm, Hunter arrived at Barnaby and went directly to the headmaster's office.

"Mr. Alden," Anderson said, a Big Benefactor smile on his lips, a guarded look in his eyes. "We were all so saddened to hear of Peter's—"

"I need to speak to one of my son's teachers," Hunter said. "His name is Madison."

"I'll see if he's available," Anderson said. "The three of us can meet right here in my—"

"Not the three of us. Just me and Madison. Why don't you see if he's *available?*"

"Follow me," Anderson said. He knew better than to say anything else.

They took the stairs to the third floor, and Anderson led Hunter to a large open room. There were a dozen computer workstations, each manned by a teenage boy, his eyes glued to a wide-screen monitor, his ears covered with headphones. None of them looked up.

Hunter shook his head in disgust. *Twelve fathers spending a fortune so their sons can piss their lives away making movies nobody will ever watch.*

"Mr. Madison," Anderson said, crossing the room to where the teacher was leaning over one student's screen.

They had a brief exchange, and Madison walked over to Hunter and extended a hand. "Ryan Madison," he said. "We can have some privacy in my office."

Madison's office was small and cramped. The walls were plastered with movie posters, and the shelves and most of the available floor space were cluttered with camera equipment. Madison took a seat behind his desk.

"From what I understand, my son contacted you twice since the murder," Hunter said, lowering himself into a wicker-backed side chair. "Once by text, once by voice mail."

Madison nodded.

"So it looks to me like you're Tripp's go-to guy," Hunter said. "Knowing the way his brain works, I figure he's going to contact you again."

"If he does—"

"Let me finish," Hunter said. "I understand that those first two times you did what you had to do. Call the cops. Keep the school out of it. I get it. The school pays you. They *incentivize* you to play by their rules."

"Mr. Alden, with all due respect, I didn't call the police because I'm on the payroll at Barnaby Prep. I called because it was the right thing to do."

"And who told you it was the right thing? The cops? All they want to do is hassle my son. You should have called me. But you didn't, because you had no incentive. So I'd like to change the rules."

Hunter reached into the leather envelope, pulled out a stack of bills, and put it on Madison's desk. "That's five thousand dollars," he said. He pulled out a second stack and set it on top of the first. "Ten." He reached in again.

"Stop!" Madison said. "Mr. Alden, I don't accept bribes."

Hunter smiled. "I'm not bribing you. I'm incentivizing you to do the right thing."

He pulled two more stacks of money from the envelope. "Let me start off our new relationship with twenty thousand dollars' worth of incentive."

He slid the money across the desk and watched as the teacher's eyes rested on the four banded packets.

Hunter knew the look. For a working stiff like Madison, twenty thousand tax-free dollars was like winning the lottery.

Madison's phone rang.

"Sorry," he said. "It's my landline. School business." He picked it up. "Film studies."

The voice on the other end exploded in his ear. "Mr. Madison, it's Tripp. I need help. I'm sorry I called the school phone, but your cell number is on my speed dial, and I don't know it by heart, so—"

"Mr. Berger," Madison said.

"No, no, it's Tripp."

"Mr. Berger," Madison repeated. "I can't talk now. I'm in conference with a parent." He turned to Hunter. "Sorry, Mr. Alden. I'll be right with you."

"Oh shit. My father's with you?"

"Yes. May I put you on hold for a minute?" Madison didn't wait for an answer. He pushed the hold button.

He turned to Hunter. "Mr. Alden, I grew up poor. I was jealous of kids like Tripp until I started working at a rich kids' school, and I realized that money doesn't build character. I have four years to work with them, and hopefully help mold their—"

"Are you lecturing me? You think I give a shit about character?" Hunter said. "Just tell me what it will take to get you to wipe that holier-than-thou

215

smirk off your face. Everybody has a price, Madison."

"That's what the last father said when he put five times that amount on my desk. His pothead kid never did a lick of work, so I gave him an F. Daddy wanted to buy an A. I'm not for sale, Mr. Alden. Now if you don't mind, I have a classroom to get back to."

"Thank you for your time," Hunter said, shoving the money back into the envelope. "If you come to your senses, give me a call."

He left the office, closing the door behind him.

Madison picked up the phone. "Tripp, what's going on? Where are you?"

"I'm okay. I'm at a subway station on the corner of East Broadway and Rutgers Street. I need to talk."

"Tripp, I can't just up and leave my classes. I can meet you after work."

"How about that place where we ate dinner after we shot the carjacking scene? You remember it?"

"I do. I'll shoot for five o'clock."

"I'll be there," Tripp said. "Did you say anything to my father?"

"Yes. I told him I'm a teacher, and I had no desire to get caught up in your family drama." Madison exhaled heavily. "But apparently that's unavoidable."

Chapter 41

HUNTER GOT IN the back of Blackstone's Audi and slammed the door.

"Get me home," he said. "You got anything to drink back here?"

Silas rolled his eyes. *Sure. I'll send the sommelier to your table with a wine list.* "Sorry, boss," he said, pulling out. "You want me to stop along the way?"

"No. I want you to call your people and have them do a complete workup on this private school cream puff Ryan Madison."

"What am I looking for?"

"The usual," Hunter said. "Drugs, hookers, cheating on his taxes—anything and everything."

"You were only there fifteen minutes. What did he do?"

"Son of a bitch won't cooperate. Right now he's our

only connection to Tripp, so I tell him, 'The next time you hear from him, call me, not the cops.' One hand washes the other, I say. 'I'll pay for your trouble.' I put the cash down on his goddamn desk."

"And?"

"And the candy-ass Boy Scout says he doesn't take bribes. Fine. Let's just see what kind of a Boy Scout he really is. I want every one of this guy's dirty little secrets. Documents, pictures—everything and anything you can dig up on him."

"What if he's clean?" Silas said, turning onto the 85th Street transverse.

"Nobody is clean. Nobody."

"I get it, but I mean he's a teacher. Teachers get parking tickets. They don't rip off the IRS. They don't run drugs. What if there's nothing?"

"Then invent something," Hunter barked. "By tomorrow this time, I want to own that bastard."

"Okay, okay. I'll get right on it."

"Not you. I said have your people do it. Your job is to sit on Madison. Drop me off at home, then go back and watch his every move."

"Am I looking for anything in particular?" Silas said.

"God, do I have to spell it out for you? This guy is a hotline to the goddamn police. He's done it twice, and he'll do it again. I want you to stay with him. See what he does. See where he goes. And if he goes to the cops, I want to know about it."

"Will do," Silas said, wondering how Peter Chevalier had managed to haul this arrogant prick around for twenty-three years. He stayed silent for the rest of the ride to East 81st Street.

"Don't dick around. Call your people," Alden said, getting out of the Audi and slamming the door.

"Calling my people," Silas muttered. He looked at his watch. It was almost 11:00 p.m. in Mumbai. He pulled up the contacts screen on his phone and tapped a name.

Vivek answered on the first ring. "SDB Investigative Services. Vivek speaking."

"I hope you didn't plan on getting any sleep tonight, Vivek," Silas said. "I've got Hunter Alden up my ass. He wants a level-three workup on a Ryan Madison."

"And what does Mr. Alden think the nefarious Mr. Madison has done?"

"That's the problem. Madison isn't one of our usual power brokers of dubious character. He's a teacher at the Barnaby school in New York. It's possible that the most despicable thing he's done is piss off Alden by turning down a bribe. We may have to get creative."

"In that case, I hope Mr. Madison is a model citizen. It's always more fun for me to fabricate skeletons to put in people's closets than it is to dig up the real ones. What kind of school is this Barnaby?"

"All boys."

"Oh please, Silas," Vivek said, chuckling. "You are making it too easy."

Chapter 42

KYLIE AND I walked around the corner to Gerri's Diner and plopped down in a booth. Gerri Gomperts herself, the proprietor and unofficial den mother of the One Nine, came over to wait on us. "I apologize," she said.

"For what?" Kylie asked.

"For not having a liquor license. You two look like you could use something stronger than a milk shake. What'll you have?"

We ordered. "And from the looks on your faces," Gerri said, "I'm guessing you'd like a side order of leave-us-alone-so-we-can-work."

As soon as Gerri went off to get our lunch, Kylie said, "Patrice Chevalier gave me a whole new perspective on our victim. Isn't it funny how Hunter Alden completely failed to mention that Peter helped build a children's clinic?"

"That's because humanitarians don't get their heads cut off," I said. "Guys who mess with other guys' wives do. Alden wants us to believe Peter deserved what he got. That way we might stop *badgering* him about his missing son."

She grinned. "He doesn't know us very well, does he?"

Her cell phone rang, and she answered it.

"Oh hey, Janet. Tomorrow? Really? Tomorrow's Saturday. No, I don't want to put it off. It's just that I'm swamped at work. Hold on." She turned to me. "It's Janet Longobardi. Can you spare me tomorrow for an hour at three o'clock?"

"It won't be easy," I said, "but I think I can muddle through sixty minutes without having you around to tell me how to do my job."

She was too far away to punch me. She got back on the phone. "Okay. I'll do it. Email me his address and phone number. Thanks. Bye."

"You never take time off work," I said. "What's going on?"

"You know how my friend Janet is. She's a fixer. If someone has a problem, she's got to jump in and help."

"What's she helping you with?"

"I needed a lawyer, and of course not only did she find me the best one in the entire city, she took the liberty of scheduling an appointment with him. She made it for Saturday thinking I'm one of those normal people who have lives on weekends. Don't worry. I'm sure it won't even take me the whole hour."

"Since when do you have legal problems?"

"Not legal," she said. "Matrimonial."

"Whoa. Last night you were telling me how Spence was on rocky ground at rehab, and now you're seeing a divorce lawyer?"

"Zach, I'm not *seeing* a divorce lawyer. I'm just exploring my options. And it's not a sudden decision. I've been thinking about it for a while."

I wondered if she'd been thinking about it last night when we were playfully interlocking forks over the Mississippi mud pie, or when she was giving me a marathon good-night hug on Third Avenue.

"Do you want to talk about it?" I said.

"No."

Damn. I did.

I was trying to think of how to convince her that talking it out would help when my phone rang.

"It's Cates," I said, and I grabbed the phone. "Jordan here."

Cates knew Kylie and I were at lunch, and she wasn't the type to interrupt with something trivial. "Start rolling," she said.

I got up from the table and headed for the door, the phone pressed to my ear. Kylie was right behind me. As we passed the counter, I caught Gerri's eye, and she waved us on. We weren't the first cops to bolt before our order made it out of the kitchen. We ran down Lexington and around the corner to 67th Street. By the time we got to our car, Cates had given me the big picture.

"Where to?" Kylie said, getting behind the wheel of the Ford.

"Go to 329 Delancey, under the Williamsburg Bridge. Nine one one just got a call—two captives were locked in the basement of PS 114."

"Tripp and Lonnie?" Kylie asked.

"Lonnie, yes. The other was a school maintenance worker."

"What about Tripp Alden?"

"According to the first responders, Tripp knocked the maintenance guy out with a stun gun and took off. The kid's in the wind."

"So much for our grief-stricken little rich boy," Kylie said, running the red light on Lex.

"Stop talking and drive faster," I said.

Chapter 43

"NOBODY'S HERE," KYLIE said when we got to PS 114. And by nobody she meant only five cop cars, a fire truck, and an EMS unit, which is not exactly a massive turnout for a school 911.

"There were no kids inside, and dispatch put it on the air as a B and E, so nobody's connected the dots yet," I said. "Let's get in there before they do."

We started with the maintenance worker. Augie Hoffman was the witness every cop hopes for. Organized, clearheaded, and in complete command of the details. But he was dumbfounded.

"It doesn't make any sense," he said.

Then he told us what had gone down. *Good Samaritan rescues kidnap victim. Victim zaps Samaritan with stun gun.* He was right. It didn't make any sense.

Augie turned down a free ride to the hospital in

the EMS bus. "I'm fine, but my new girlfriend will kill me if I don't pick her up at the airport on time. I have to check her flight, but the kid took my phone. You got one I can borrow?"

"If he has your cell, we can track him," Kylie said. "What's your number?"

He gave it to us along with his girlfriend's number so we could reach him.

Lonnie Martinez was next. His account of the abduction matched Mrs. Gittleman's. The only difference was that she referred to the man with the red beard as an undercover cop. Lonnie called him the kidnapper. After all the denial we'd heard from Alden, it was nice to finally hear one of the victims using the K-word.

"Did he say anything about ransom?" I asked.

"Like how much? No, but he said Tripp's father wouldn't pay unless Tripp made a call to prove he was alive."

"Did he tell Tripp who to call?"

"No. Just who *not* to call. No family. He pulls out Tripp's cell and says 'Pick one of your contacts.' Tripp says 'Peter, my driver.' The guy says no way."

I looked at Kylie, then back at Lonnie. "Did he say why?"

"He said 'Peter's like family—he's too close. Pick

someone else.' So Tripp called one of our teachers, Mr. Madison."

I believed him. Partly because it synced up with what I already knew, but mostly because after listening to Augie, I knew this wasn't the part that Lonnie Martinez was going to lie to us about.

"One last question," I said. "When the police arrived, you and Mr. Hoffman were in the cage, and Tripp was gone. How'd that happen?"

"It was crazy," Lonnie said. "Just when Hoffman was cutting us loose, the guy comes back. He sees us, and then bam, bam, he drops me and Hoffman, but Tripp runs for it."

"Where do you think he ran to?" Kylie asked.

He gave us his best clueless look.

"I didn't realize he shot you too," I said. "You need to get to a hospital."

"I'm fine. What I need is to get to a pizza joint. I'm starved."

"We can't let you go until we take a look at the wound," I said. "Can you show me where it hit you?"

He pulled up his shirt and showed us a bruise on his shoulder.

"Nasty," I said. "Let me see the wound from the day you were abducted."

"Oh . . . that one healed," he said. "I was wearing

a coat so it wasn't too bad. All I have is the one from today."

"Sit tight for a few more minutes," I said. "We're going to call your grandmother, then one of the officers will drive you home."

Kylie and I walked out into the hall.

"Nicely done, partner," she said. "That mark on his shoulder was brown instead of bright red. And there was no swelling. It's not a fresh wound."

"So now we've got the rich guy *and* the poor kid lying to us," I said.

"Forget all the bullshit he was shoveling," she said. "I'm still reeling from the truth. Did you catch what he said?"

"Did *I* catch it? I looked over at you to make sure *you* caught it. Tripp wanted to call Peter. All this time you and I are trying to question Tripp about the murder, and now we find out that the kid doesn't even know Peter is dead."

Chapter 44

FOUR HOURS AND twenty minutes into Silas Blackstone's stakeout at Barnaby Prep, Ryan Madison stepped out of the front door, unzipped his jacket pocket, and pulled out a set of keys. Car keys.

"Hallelujah," Silas muttered. "The man's got wheels."

He had hated the thought of abandoning the Audi on the street and following his target into the subway, and now he didn't have to. Madison walked a block, pulled his low-rent teacher car out of a postage stamp lot attached to the school, and headed north on Central Park West.

Silas kept five car lengths behind him. Fifteen minutes later they had driven across Manhattan and onto the RFK Bridge toward Queens.

We're not in Kansas anymore, Silas thought. *Where*

the hell are you going? Not home. Vivek had confirmed that Madison lived in lower Manhattan.

It was just after 5:00 p.m. when Madison got off the Grand Central Parkway at Hillside Avenue. A mile later he turned onto Musket Street and pulled into the parking lot of the Silver Moon Diner.

Silas was starting to wonder if he'd made a mistake. He had decided that Hunter was being a jerk, and that tailing Madison would be a waste of time, but nobody drives this far for diner food. Something was going on.

Madison parked the car and went into the Silver Moon. The building had wraparound windows, and Silas watched as Madison scanned the room, saw what he was looking for, and joined someone at a booth that looked out onto the parking lot.

Silas pulled a pair of binoculars from the glove compartment so he could get a better look at Madison's mystery dinner date.

"Son of a bitch," he said as soon as the image of the disheveled, sleep-deprived teenager filled the lens. Tripp.

Silas grabbed his cell phone. His finger was on Hunter's speed dial when he stopped. Too soon. First find out what's going on.

Sitting in the diner window munching on a burger,

Tripp Alden sure as hell didn't look kidnapped. But he had been—Silas was positive. Even if the old lady had lied to the cops. Even if Hunter had lied to Janelle about the hundred million. Peter's head in a box with the burner phone—that was the clincher.

The only thing Silas could figure was that Tripp had gotten away. The kidnapper was a bumbling amateur. The back doors of his van were held together with a bungee cord. He let the Puerto Rican kid slash him with a—. *The other kid.* Where the hell was *he?*

Nothing made sense. Including the baby-faced teacher driving out to a diner in Queens. One thing Silas knew for sure. There was a million bucks in it for him if he killed Cain, but Alden wouldn't pay him an extra dime if all he did was bring his son home.

There was only one way that Silas had a shot at a big payday. He had to talk to Tripp. Alone.

Almost on cue, Madison stood up. Tripp didn't budge. He sat there, mopping up a puddle of ketchup with a handful of fries. Madison left the diner, walked five steps from the entrance, and lit up a cigarette.

He took three quick drags, put it out, pulled his collar up, and walked into the parking lot. Not toward his car, but straight for the Audi.

He made me, Silas thought. *And now he's going to hassle me.*

Madison tapped on the driver's side window, and Silas rolled it down. "Can I help you?" he asked.

In the last few seconds of his life, Silas Blackstone realized that he had completely misjudged Ryan Madison. The teacher was standing there, a nine-millimeter Glock in Silas's face, a six-inch suppressor on the business end.

All of Blackstone's instincts kicked in. *Don't do anything stupid. Try to calm him down.* "Mr. Mad—" was all he managed to get out before the bullet drilled a tiny circle in his forehead and hurtled blood, brain, and the back of his skull all over the passenger seat of the Audi.

Madison tucked the gun back under his jacket, lowered himself to the ground, removed the GPS tracker from under Silas's car, and put it in his pocket.

He looked around the parking lot. Twenty cars. No people. He took one final look at the bloody heap in the front seat of the Audi. "This was not part of my plan, Mr. Blackstone," he said. "You have nobody to blame but yourself."

He turned and headed back to the Silver Moon to get Tripp. It was time to get this kidnapping back on track.

Chapter 45

AS SOON AS Madison stepped out of the diner for a smoke, Tripp dug into his pocket and pulled out Augie's phone. After the calls to 911 and Barnaby, he'd kept it off. By now the cops would have the number, and they could ping him.

But he had to talk to someone. Madison was starting to scare him. As soon as Tripp told him what had happened, the teacher had leaned across the table, his eyes on fire. "What the hell were you thinking?" he growled.

Tripp tried to explain, but Madison could focus on only one thing. "So by some miracle you managed to lock them both up, you got away, and then you decided that the smartest thing you could do was to call the cops?"

"Mr. Madison, I couldn't just leave them there. I

knew you weren't going to go back. They'd starve to death."

"Very noble, Tripp. And unbelievably stupid. Now the cops will know you're in on it."

"No, they won't. The guy was too out of it to know what happened, and Lonnie won't rat me out. He's going to say you stun-gunned them, and I got away."

Madison exploded. "*Me?* You told him I was there?"

"Not you by name. Trust me: I just spent three days in a cage with him. Lonnie has no idea it's you. We're good."

"No, Tripp, we're not good, but I'll just have to deal with it." He looked out the window at the parking lot. "You stay here. I'm going out for a smoke."

Tripp knew he didn't have much time. He had to risk it. He turned on Augie's phone and dialed the one number he had known by heart since he was a kid.

The voice on the other end said hello, and Tripp said, "Peter. It's Tripp. I need you."

"Tripp? This isn't Peter. It's Patrice."

"Patrice, what are you doing in New York? And where's Peter?"

"Oh, Lord," Patrice said. "You don't know."

"What?"

A pause, then: "Tripp, there's no easy way to tell you. Peter is dead."

Tripp tried to speak, but he couldn't. He choked back the tears.

"I'm so sorry," Patrice said. "I know how much you loved him."

"What did he die of?"

"He was murdered. Wednesday night when he drove to Riverside Park to pick you up, someone attacked him, and . . ." Patrice held back the details. "Someone attacked him and killed him."

"Wednesday night?" Tripp said. "I wasn't in the—" Even in his state of shock he could put the pieces together. Madison.

"Tripp, you and I should sit down and talk," Patrice said. "Where are you?"

"It doesn't matter. I'm getting out of here."

"Stay where you are. I'll come and get you. I'll take you home."

"No."

"I understand if you don't want to go home. At least let me take you to the police. They need your help finding Peter's killer."

"I can't talk to the police. Not yet."

"Okay. Maybe I can help you. Why are you calling Peter?"

"He was holding something for me. I need to get it back, but if he's . . . if he's dead, I don't know what to do. He was the only one I could trust."

"I've known you all of your life," Patrice said. "If you can trust my brother, you can trust me. What was Peter holding for you?"

"A flash drive."

"I've just gone over all his things. I have his computer. But there was no flash drive."

"It doesn't look like a regular flash. It's shaped like a—"

Madison ripped the phone from Tripp's hand. "Are you out of your fucking mind?" he said, disconnecting the call. "You're supposed to be a kidnap victim. Who are you calling?"

"Lonnie. I called Lonnie. I wanted to make sure he's okay. Don't worry. He knows I'm not kidnapped."

And I know you're lying. I took Lonnie's phone away from him three days ago. Madison didn't know who Tripp had called, but he wasn't going to stick around and find out. He dropped a twenty on the table. "Come on. We have to go."

They left the diner and walked out into the cold night air. "Can I at least get the phone back?" Tripp said.

"Jesus, kid, use your head," he said. "You carry

this thing in your pocket, and it's like calling the cops to come find you. And I think you've called the cops enough for one day."

He flung Augie Hoffman's phone into the weeds on the far side of the parking lot. He shoved Tripp toward the Subaru. "Now move it. Get in the car."

"I'm going. What's the big hurry?"

Madison stole a quick look at the Audi with the open window. "No hurry. It's dinnertime. I just want to get out of here before it gets crowded."

Chapter 46

THE FACT THAT Kylie was planning to talk with a divorce lawyer was none of my business. And yet it was all I could think about. I wanted to know more, but that wasn't going to happen as long as we were sitting in the office.

I looked at my watch. "It's twenty after five," I said. "I'm starved. What do you say we walk over to Gerri's Diner and see if she's got our lunch order ready?"

"Good idea," she said. "I haven't eaten anything since those chicken wings last night."

I got up from my desk, and my phone rang.

"This is Patrice Chevalier," the caller said. "I just got a call from Tripp Alden."

I sat down and grabbed a pen. "Where is he?"

"He didn't say where he was, but from the

background noise it sounded like some kind of bar or restaurant."

"How did Tripp know you were in New York?"

"He didn't. He was calling Peter. When I told him my brother had been murdered, he sounded genuinely shocked. It was all he could do not to cry."

"Did you ask him why he was calling Peter?"

It was a simple question. Patrice took too long to answer. "I . . . I was going to ask, but while we were talking someone snatched the phone away from him."

"Someone?"

"All I heard was a man's voice, and he was angry. Then we got cut off. I'm very concerned, Detective Jordan. I think Tripp is in over his head. I offered to help, but—"

"Can you check the caller ID on your cell? We can track the number."

"Yes, I've done that. It's a nine one seven number." He gave it to me.

"Thank you, Dr. Chevalier. This is a big help."

"Big enough for me to be kept in the loop from now on?"

"Yes, sir," I said. "As much as possible."

I hung up and handed the phone number to Kylie. "Tripp just used this phone to call Peter."

"*Peter?*" Kylie repeated.

"According to Patrice, Tripp had no idea Peter was dead. Patrice had to break the news to him. Have Matt Smith run this number."

"I don't need Matt," she said. "I recognize it. It's the phone Tripp took from Augie Hoffman. He used it to call 911. I have Matt pinging it, but so far nothing. The kid is smart enough to keep it off."

Her phone rang. "Speak of the devil," she said. She took the call. "Hey, Matt, Zach and I were just talking about you."

She turned to me. "He's got a location on Augie's cell. Yeah, Matt, give me the address."

"Drop everything." I looked up. It was Cates.

"Give us a minute, Captain," I said. "It looks like we've got a trace on Tripp Alden."

"And I've got a body with a bullet in it. He's in the parking lot of the Silver Moon Diner, 235-20 Hillside in Queens."

Kylie had been listening to Matt with the phone pressed to one ear while trying to focus on Cates with the other. "Oh shit," she said. "Matt, thanks. I've got to go." She hung up.

"What's your problem, MacDonald?" Cates said.

"Matt just tracked the cell phone Tripp Alden has been carrying. It's in Queens. Hillside Avenue and Musket Street."

"That's where your body is," Cates said.

"Then Tripp is dead," I said.

"I don't think so," Cates said. "Dispatch said the victim is a white male, about forty-five years old, sitting behind the wheel of a late model Audi, license plate SDB. Looks like your old PI buddy Silas Blackstone was getting close to whoever killed Peter Chevalier."

"Sounds like Silas got a little too close," Kylie said, putting on her coat and heading toward the stairs.

I was right behind her. My lunch plans would have to wait.

Chapter 47

AS IT TURNED out, Kylie and I wound up at a diner after all. But instead of sitting in a cozy booth at Gerri's, we were standing in a freezing parking lot at the Silver Moon. And instead of listening to Kylie bare her soul about her dying marriage, I got to listen to Chuck Dryden doing a postmortem on the late Silas Blackstone.

"Single nine-millimeter shot to the head," he said, stating the obvious.

One shot was all it took. Going in, it made a relatively neat hole in the center of Blackstone's forehead. But there's nothing neat about exit wounds, and after working its way through bone, brain, and tissue, the bullet blew out the back of his skull, and left the inside of the Audi looking like a Crock-Pot had exploded.

"Blackstone knew the person who killed him," Kylie said.

"And how did you determine that, Detective?" Dryden asked.

"If a stranger knocks on your car window, you only crack it open a few inches. This one is rolled all the way down. Plus Blackstone's gun is still holstered, so he not only knew the killer, he probably trusted him."

Chuck looked bemused. "Interesting theory, but I prefer more empirical evidence."

"Then by all means get me some empirical evidence on the shooter," she said. "Until then, I'll just have to rely on unsubstantiated wild guesses."

"Are you also guessing that Tripp did this?" I asked.

"A few hours ago I wouldn't have thought Tripp would pull a stun gun on Augie Hoffman. Now I don't know what he's capable of. Somehow Blackstone figured out where he was, and he was staking him out. There's a pair of binoculars on the seat. Let's see if we can find out what he was looking at."

We started with the woman who discovered the body. Leslie Stern had just pulled into the parking lot when she spotted the open window of Silas's car. She took a peek inside, called 911, told the dispatcher what she'd seen, then ran to the diner to tell everyone else.

By the time the cops arrived, a throng of people had gathered, cell phones in hand, and #DeadGuyInAnAudi was trending on Twitter.

Next we talked to the manager of the diner, who was irate because it was Friday night and his parking lot was packed with looky-loos, but he couldn't convert their curiosity into cash. NYPD had closed him down. There was no sense explaining to him that crime scene investigations trump commerce, so we showed him a picture of Silas Blackstone that we had pulled up from the DMV.

"Never saw him," the sullen manager said.

"How about him?" I asked, showing him a photo of Tripp Alden.

He grumbled a "Yeah," and I pressed him for details.

"He came in about four thirty. Said he was meeting someone and asked for a booth. It was early, so I gave him one by a window."

"We'd like to talk to whoever waited on him."

Her name was Denise, and she had the look of a veteran diner waitress who was always there to top off your coffee before you asked. But clearly Denise was more shaken than her boss. She practically cried when I showed her Tripp's picture. "Oh God, is he the one that got shot?"

"No," Kylie said. "What can you tell us about him?"

"He ordered a cheeseburger, fries, and a Pepsi. Nice kid. Said 'Please' and 'Thank you.' But that's it. Teenage boys don't talk it up when the waitress is old enough to be their mother."

"Was he alone?"

"At first. Then this guy sits down. He was white, maybe thirty-five. I gave him a menu, but he said he's not staying, so I didn't pay much attention to him. At one point he went out. When he came back, I could see he was pissed at the kid for something. He tossed a twenty on the table, and the two of them left."

The uniforms canvassed the crowd, and while the speculation ran from gang shooting to jealous husband, there was none of what Chuck Dryden had called empirical evidence.

He was waiting for us when we got back to the Audi. "This was under the front passenger seat," Dryden said, holding up a laptop. "It belongs to Tripp Alden. I dusted it, but instead of tying it up in the lab, I'll get it over to Matt Smith. I have a feeling he'll find more on the inside than I will on the outside."

A cell phone rang. It was Blackstone's. I answered.

James Patterson

"Damn it, Silas," Hunter Alden bellowed. "Where the hell are you?"

"Mr. Alden, this is Detective Zach Jordan. I have some bad news. Mr. Blackstone has been shot. He died instantly. I'm sorry for your loss." I told him what had happened.

"A diner in Queens? What was he doing there?"

"It looks like he tracked down your son. Tripp had dinner here earlier."

"Do you have him now? I'll pick him up."

"No, sir. A lot has happened since we spoke to you this morning." I filled him in on Tripp's escape from PS 114.

"So this guy had Tripp locked up," Alden said. "The kid gets away, and instead of coming home, he takes off?"

"Yes, sir. We're still looking for him, but he's no longer considered a hostage. It appears he was in collusion with whoever was trying to shake you down, and your son is now a suspect in two homicides. So this time we expect a lot more cooperation. If you hear from him, I need you to contact us immediately, or you'll be aiding and abetting—"

He hung up before I could finish.

Chapter 48

I STOOD THERE with the dead PI's dead phone in my hand. "Son of a bitch cares even less about Blackstone than he did about Peter."

"Some people are better than others at coping with having their valued employees murdered in parking lots," Kylie said. "But let's try to do something more productive than vent about Hunter Alden."

"If you're thinking 'late lunch,' it's not going to happen. The diner's closed."

"No. I'm thinking 'find Augie Hoffman's phone.' I just got a text from Matt. The signal he picked up before is holding. The phone is on, and it's nearby."

We pulled together a dozen uniforms and gave them all latex gloves. "Listen up, everybody," Kylie said. "We're looking for a cell phone. If we're lucky, we'll get a ringtone. If it's on vibrate, it's a lot harder to pick up, but not impossible. Half of you start along the Hillside Avenue perimeter, and the other half position yourselves in those weeds."

The cops spread out, and Kylie and I joined the group lined up in a patch of frost-covered vegetation at the far end of the lot. "Okay," she yelled, holding up her cell, "I'm activating my high-tech phone finder."

She dialed Augie's number. Five seconds passed. Then I heard music. *I hear the train a-comin'. It's rollin' round the bend.* Johnny Cash. "Folsom Prison Blues." I knew I liked Augie Hoffman.

A cop fifteen feet away yelled out, "Got it." He bent down, picked up the phone, and walked it over to me.

Kylie and I got back in the car, and she turned up the heater.

Augie had an ancient flip phone with no password protection. I pulled up the Recent Calls screen. "There's a slew of incoming from Florida," I said, "but the last four are outgoing. The first is to 911 at 2:09 p.m., which matches the time 911 dispatched units to the school. A minute later he dialed 411—information."

"Makes sense," Kylie said. "It's not his phone. He wouldn't have his usual contacts. Who'd he call after information?"

"It's a two-one-two number, so it's Manhattan. He talked for two minutes, then the phone went silent for about three hours. The final call was at 5:17. I recognize the number. It's the one he made to Patrice."

"Hit redial on the two-one-two number," Kylie said.

"No. It's fifteen digits, which means Tripp dialed the ten-digit number first, got a recording, then responded to the voice prompts. You can't duplicate that with auto redial. You have to punch it in the same way he did. Take out your phone, put it on speaker, and dial this number."

I read off ten digits, and she dialed her iPhone. A machine answered.

"Thank you for calling Barnaby Prep. If you know your party's extension, please dial it now. To access the school directory, dial nine."

"Nine is the next number Tripp dialed," I said. "Do it."

She did, and another prompt came on. "Please enter the first four letters of your party's last name."

"Six, two, three, four," I said.

She entered the numbers.

The extension rang, and voice mail answered. "Hello, this is Ryan Madison. I'm not in my office right

249

now, but leave a message, and I'll get back to you as soon as possible. Thank you."

Kylie hung up. "Madison? For a guy who says he doesn't want to get involved . . ."

"He didn't call Tripp," I said. "Tripp called him."

"Why?"

Before I could come up with an intelligent answer, she hit the steering wheel with the palm of her hand. "I'm an idiot," she said. She lowered her head and began hitting the keys on her iPhone.

"What are you doing?" I said.

"If I were standing up, I'd be kicking myself." She tapped away furiously, then she stopped and held the screen up for me to see.

"The waitress," she said.

She bolted from the car, ran back to the diner, and pushed open the front door. I was right behind her.

"Denise," she yelled.

Four waitresses were sitting at a table having coffee, most likely wondering if they'd get back to work that night.

Denise looked up. "Yes?"

Kylie shoved her phone in front of her. "Do you recognize this man?"

Denise took a quick look. "That's him," she said,

giving Kylie back the phone. "That's the one who left the diner with the kid."

"Are you sure?" Kylie said, trying to give the waitress the phone back. "Look again. Take your time."

"Honey, I don't have to take my time. I know faces."

"Please. It's important."

It wasn't important to Denise. Whatever good will we might have established with her was long gone. She stood up and took the phone back reluctantly.

Kylie had gone to the Barnaby Prep website, drilled down to the faculty bios, and pulled up a picture of Ryan Madison. Denise stared at it.

"Okay, one more time," she said, exasperated. "This is the guy I told you about before. He sat down with the kid. He didn't want to order. Then he went outside for a cig—oh my God. He didn't go for a smoke. He killed that man in the parking lot. No wonder you're making such a big—oh my God." She took another look at Madison. "That's definitely him. That's the guy you're looking for."

"You're sure," Kylie said.

"Honey," Denise said, not able to take her eyes off the prep school teacher's smiling face, "I have never been so sure of anything in my life."

Chapter 49

TRIPP WAS CURLED up in the front seat of the Subaru, pretending to sleep.

Peter was dead. Murdered. Wednesday night after they had staged the kidnapping. He wanted to scream at Madison, "Why did you kill him? What happened to 'Nobody gets hurt'? What happened to 'Your father deserves this, so it's a victimless crime'?"

But he couldn't say anything. He'd made enough mistakes. Trusting Madison was the dumbest thing he'd ever done in his life. The best thing to do now was to act normal until he could figure out how to get away.

It took them an hour to get into the city, and then they crept down Park Avenue in Friday night traffic, heading for the Holland Tunnel.

Tripp decided it was time to open his eyes. "Where are we?" he said.

"Somewhere in the middle of the rat race," Madison said. "I can't believe people do this every day."

"I'll turn on 1010 WINS and get a traffic report," Tripp said, reaching for the radio dial.

Madison smacked his hand away. "Don't," he said. "They're just going to tell me that traffic sucks, which I already know. I drive better without the radio."

"Okay, man," Tripp said. "No traffic report." *And no news stations.*

It was another forty-five minutes before Madison drove into the parking lot of the Liberty Harbor Marina in Jersey City.

"Recognize that beast?" he said as he pulled the Subaru alongside a blue 1998 Dodge Caravan.

"Is that the piece of shit you had us in?" Tripp said.

"Don't knock it," Madison said. "I got it on Craigslist. Eight hundred bucks—as is. Plus the guy threw in a bungee cord to keep the back doors from flying open."

"It would have helped if he threw in some shocks. It rides like a tank. Especially when you're lying on the cold floor."

"Oh, you poor spoiled rich kid. Next time I'll kidnap you in a Maybach."

Just the mention of the Maybach conjured up

Peter. The cheeseburger roiled in Tripp's stomach, and he felt like puking.

They walked down to the slip where Madison's aging twenty-two-foot cabin cruiser was docked. "Too many people are looking for you," he said as they boarded, "so until I tell you otherwise, this is your new home sweet home. A few ground rules: no contact with the outside world."

"How could I? You took my cell phone. Can I at least have it back so I can play some games?"

"I took out the SIM card so they can't track it. So no games, no email, no texts, no phone."

"Can I have my wallet back?"

"You don't need it," Madison said. "You're not going shopping. You're not going anywhere."

"So it sounds like now I really am a hostage," Tripp said, faking a smile.

Madison didn't smile back. "Don't be cute. We're in this together. But you're running scared, and I'm trying to keep you from blowing this up in our faces. Here's the deal. There's no TV, no radio—"

"And no heat," Tripp yelled, folding his arms and hugging his parka to his body. "Can't we go to a hotel? It's freezing on this tub, and I'm not exactly dressed for yachting."

"Tough shit, Richie Rich. You try checking into a

hotel, and you'll be on a dozen security cameras before you get to your room. This boat was plan B. You wouldn't be here if you hadn't screwed up plan A, so stop bitching and get to bed. We've got three more lousy days, then the partnership is dissolved, and you can take your ninety million and spread it around like Johnny Fucking Appleseed."

"And what about you?"

"I'll tell you what I won't be doing," Madison said. "I won't be at Barnaby Prep kissing fat rich asses for a lousy forty-eight thousand a year. You got the top bunk. Lights out in five."

Chapter 50

WHEN YOU WORK high-profile cases, getting a search warrant is easy, even on a Friday night, and by eight thirty Kylie and I were heading downtown to see what we could dig up on Ryan Madison.

He lived in a four-story prewar building on the corner of East 4th Street and Avenue D in Alphabet City, about a half mile from where Tripp and Lonnie had been locked up.

The apartment fit the single-guy-living-alone pattern we'd seen before. Cluttered, but habitable. There were the predictable movie posters on the walls, shelves full of film books, and DVDs scattered everywhere. Adding to the ambiance, the entire place smelled like the bottom of an ashtray.

There was nothing in the living room to connect Madison to the crimes, but the bathroom was much more promising. There on the sink was a can of Bactine antiseptic spray, a roll of gauze, and another of adhesive tape. The wastebasket contained half a dozen long strips of bloodied gauze bandages.

"He was either shaving drunk," Kylie said, "or some kid came at him with a box cutter."

We headed straight for the kitchen trash can. Kylie popped the top, and we didn't have to look too hard to find what we were searching for. A gray Yankees hoodie with blue trim. The left sleeve was slashed and thick with dried blood.

"Note to self," I said. "Send lovely thank-you card to Fannie Gittleman at 530 West 136th Street."

We checked the bedroom. There was a pile of clothes on the floor.

"Head to toe all black," I said, "which matches the outfit Lonnie told us the kidnapper wore."

Kylie laughed. "Zach, this is New York. All black isn't exactly damning evidence. It's a fashion statement."

I opened the closet door. "Okay, then, how fashionable is a couple of boxes of surveillance and security equipment from Cheaters Spy Shop? What does *Vogue* say about that?"

"Let's find this creep," Kylie said.

Thirty-five thousand cops have a better chance

than two, so we called the precinct and had them issue a BOLO. Then we called the lab and sent for some techs to tag and bag everything we thought we'd need in court.

The only thing we couldn't figure out was Tripp Alden's role in the murders.

"Is he a victim, an accomplice, or did he mastermind the whole operation?" Kylie said.

"Scratch that last one," I said. "Whatever this kid did wrong, I can't believe he planned or had anything to do with Peter's murder. And based on what we heard at the Silver Moon, he might not even know about Silas getting killed."

"He's guilty of something."

"We're all guilty of something," I said. "But I still can't wrap my head around his motive. There's got to be an easier way to get money from your billionaire father than to stage a kidnapping and ask for ransom."

"At this point, I'm not sure I can wrap my head around anything," Kylie said. "It's ten p.m., and I haven't eaten all day. Detectives shouldn't try detecting when they're running on fumes."

"In that case, can I buy you some lunch?"

"Sure. Someplace quiet."

"It's Friday night in New York. Anyplace worth going to will be jammed with supercool people dressed in black." And then, without thinking about it, I said, "How about my place? That's quiet."

She was as surprised to hear me say it as I was.

"Where have I heard that line before? The first time I ever went up to *your place*, all you had was half a bottle of cheap vodka, leftover pizza, and the new Radiohead album. Real class."

"Hey, give me a little credit here. I've come a long way since the academy. I've got some chilled Stoli, we can order a fresh pizza, and I'm sure I can download whatever hip sounds you kids are into these days."

"You're on," she said. "But same ground rules as last night. We've put in a fifteen-hour day, and the weekend is going to be even more intense. I have to give my brain a rest. No shop talk. Let's just keep it personal."

I shrugged. "Okay with me."

It was better than okay. For the past ten hours I'd been dying to know if Kylie was going to dump Spence and jump back into the dating pool. It doesn't get more personal than that.

Chapter 51

BY 11:00 P.M., KYLIE was sitting barefoot on my sofa, legs tucked under her, slice of pizza in one hand, tilting a bottle of Blue Moon to her lips with the other.

Discussing the case was off the table, so we slid comfortably into rehashing our days at the academy, laughing about the pranks we had played, and carefully avoiding any reference to our emotional baggage.

But for me, it was in the air, and the old feelings crept back quickly. Probably because I'd never totally been able to shake them.

Kylie was on her second beer when I got around to the subject that had been gnawing at me all day.

"I know Spence has put you through the wringer with his drug problem, but divorce—that's pretty drastic."

"Nothing is drastic yet," she said. "I told you, I'm just testing the waters. I want to understand my options."

"You've got to do what you've got to do," I said. It was meant to be supportive. Or, at best, noncommittal. But Kylie responded like it was judgmental.

"Hey," she snapped, "I love Spence, but if he can't kick it, I'm not sticking around. That was the deal I made with him when we got married ten years ago, and it's the same deal today. Do I sound like a coldhearted bitch?"

"No, not at all," I said, making sure she knew whose side I was on. "You sound like a woman who's already given Spence a second chance. He blew it. And now he's blowing his third."

"Exactly. Three strikes. I'm a cop, Zach. I can't be married to a drug addict."

"Whatever you do, I got your back."

I heard a key in the front door, and my stomach dropped. Timing is everything, and mine was disastrous.

The door opened. It was Cheryl. "Well, hello. I thought I heard voices."

"You did. It was us," I said, hoping I didn't look as guilty as I sounded. "I thought you were spending the night in Westchester."

"Mildred passed."

"I'm so sorry," Kylie said.

"Me too." I stood up and gave Cheryl a half-assed hug.

"At this point it was a blessing. Fred is with Mildred's sister and some of his cousins, so I thought I'd come home and go back for the wake on Tuesday. I came to your apartment because I wanted to make up for blowing off dinner last night. But if you guys are working, I'll go to my place."

"No, no—working is the one thing we're definitely not doing," Kylie said. "That's been the pact two nights in a row. Strictly social. Are you hungry?"

"Starving," Cheryl said, reaching for a slice of pizza.

"Can I get you a beer?" I said, heading toward the fridge.

"Please," she said. "And hurry."

I brought her back a beer from the kitchen. She took a long swallow and exhaled slowly. "I can tell you right now that one won't be enough," she said. "It's been a hell of a day."

"Same for us," I said. "Why don't I pop downstairs and make a quick beer run?"

I dashed out of the apartment before they could answer. I didn't even bother with a jacket.

I replayed the scene in my head, trying to picture what Cheryl saw when she opened the door. *Oh look, there's Zach on his sofa, all nice and cozy, sipping beers with his ex-girlfriend, totally confident that his current girlfriend is out of town comforting her dying friend.*

Not a pretty picture. Even so, there was one brief moment when I had a shot at redemption. It was when Cheryl said, "If you guys are working, I'll go to my place."

And then Kylie nailed the coffin shut.

Hell, no, we're not working. We're just having fun. That's been the deal two nights in a row. What? He didn't tell you about the trip down memory lane we took last night? It was magical. Just Kylie and Zach—the same asshole who bitched and moaned about you spending any time with Fred.

I bought two more six-packs at the bodega, but deep down inside I knew that no amount of alcohol was going to salvage my evening.

It was the first thing I'd been right about all night.

Chapter 52

"TIME TO POKE the bear," Madison said, zipping up his jacket.

Tripp was under a blanket staring at the ceiling. "Where are you going?"

"I've learned from your father's mistakes. Handle all your business transactions in private. I'm going out. You're not."

He grabbed a clean burner phone and padlocked the cabin door.

It was a clear, crisp night, and the moon lit the way to the Subaru. There was no sense warming it up. This would be a short call. He lit a cigarette and dialed Hunter Alden's number.

Ten seconds into the conversation, it was clear that Hunter's legendary negotiating skills were impaired by exhaustion, booze, and rage.

He flew into a tirade. "You should have taken the five million I offered last night. Now that I know my shit-for-brains son is in on it, you get nothing."

"News flash, Hunter. Tripp is not just *in on it*. The whole thing was his idea."

"Bullshit. He's already got a half-a-billion-dollar trust fund and a shitload more down the road. Why would a kid like that need another hundred million?"

"To punish you, Hunter. And to make reparations to your victims."

"*Reparations?* Is that his ingenious blackmail scheme? Give me your money, and I won't tell your secrets? But once I get the money, I'll give it away, and it will be on the front page of every newspaper on the planet."

"What can I say? The kid's an idealist."

"Well he can shove his ideals up his ass. I don't have any *victims,* and you're not getting any money. Fuck you and Tripp. You can kill him for all I care."

"I'd be happy to accommodate you," Madison said. "But it will cost you a hundred million dollars."

"What the hell are you talking about?"

"You haven't figured it out yet? I thought surely by now you would have grasped the finer points of my brilliant business model."

"Illuminate me, asshole."

"Tripp knows everything. As soon as you pay the ransom, he'll go straight to Homeland Security, tell them what a bad daddy he has, and put you behind bars for the rest of your life. I didn't kidnap Tripp so I could send him home once you pay the money. I'm only planning to let Tripp go if you *don't* pay me."

Hunter inhaled sharply, audibly.

"Aha . . . that sounds like a gasp of enlightenment. It's quite simple, Hunter. If you fail to see the wisdom of my business proposition, I'll cut my losses, turn your son loose, and within a few hours, men with buzz cuts and badges will appear at your front door. Need I go on?"

Hunter didn't say a word.

"Your silence is heartening. It means you're finally processing the upside of my proposal. Shall I text you the number of my account in the Caymans?"

"These things take time," Hunter said.

"I come from humble beginnings, but I've familiarized myself with a few of the basic rules of international banking. It's now almost midnight on Friday. The Fed reopens for immediate, final, irrevocable wire transfers at nine p.m. on Sunday. That gives you forty-five hours to contemplate your future, my future . . . and of course Tripp's future."

"Spell it out for me," Hunter said. "Exactly what am I buying?"

"Total silence. As soon as the wire transfer clears, Tripp and I will take off on a little sea voyage, and you'll never hear from either of us again. Good night, Leviticus."

He hung up and walked back to the dock. Silver beams of moonlight streaked the Hudson, and looking east, he could see the tip of Manhattan. *The heart of the financial district. The Street. Home of the robber barons.*

He tossed the cell phone into the water and watched it sink without a ripple. Then he extended his arm, stuck up his middle finger, and yelled into the cold, quiet night.

"My name is Ryan Madison, and you can all kiss my hundred-million-dollar ass."

Part Three

PROJECT GUTENBERG

CHAPTER 53

IF YOU HAVE to be anywhere at six o'clock on a cold Saturday morning, Gerri's Diner is one of the better places to be. The food is always good, and at that hour the place is relatively empty, so Gerri has time to come to your table and shamelessly meddle in your life.

Sometimes I steer clear of her unsolicited advice, but after last night's disaster with Cheryl and Kylie I was ripe for her take-no-prisoners brand of grandmotherly wisdom.

She brought two cups of coffee and a basket of muffins and sat down across from me.

"Sorry I ran out on the check yesterday," I said.

"Yeah, I called the cops," she said, pushing the muffins in my direction. "They're looking all over for you."

"What do I owe you?"

"I don't know yet. It depends how long this therapy session lasts. You've got 'needy' and 'confused' written all over you."

I told her what had happened the night before. She didn't say a word until I got to the point where I bolted out the door.

"You *left* the scene of the crime? I hope you brought back a third woman, because you don't have a chance in hell with the two you left in your apartment."

She nailed it, and the look on my face let her know she was right.

"Anyway, I get back with the beer, thinking, 'How do I do damage control?,' and as soon as I walk in the door, Cheryl says she's exhausted from a long day, gives me a half-assed peck on the cheek, and leaves. Then Kylie, who's clueless about what's going on, says she better be going too, and *she* leaves."

"And there you are with all those party supplies and no party."

"I felt like a total asshole."

"You want my take on it?"

I knew I wasn't going to like what she had to say, but I needed to hear it. "Sure. Lay it on me."

"You're right about one thing," she said. "You were a total asshole. Someone Cheryl loves is dying, she's devastated, and all you can think about is your manly ego? She was married to Fred for more than ten years. It's over. And you're upset because she's got compassion? My take on you—" She picked up a spoon and banged it on the tabletop like a gavel. "Guilty of bad behavior.

"Next case: Cheryl was right to chew you out after the way you behaved when she showed up with Fred. But then she walks in on you and Kylie, gets her own nose out of joint, sends you on a fool's errand, then walks out when you come back? Classic passive-aggressive shit. Verdict on Dr. Robinson: guilty." The gavel-spoon came down again.

"And finally, Kylie. Do you really think she was clueless about what was going on between you and Cheryl? Women are not remotely as clueless as men would like to think. As for coming up to your apartment for pizza so she could tell you how her marriage is going south, she knew exactly what she was doing. She wants to play out the old girlfriend–boyfriend scenario, only without the sex . . . for now. But that's like Spence spending the night with a bottle of oxy on the dresser and promising himself he won't even look at it."

"So you think she wants to get back together with me?"

"I'm not saying she's ready to jump into bed with you, but she definitely remembers the times when she did, and it's not an option she's ruled out. And you—you had the same thing on your mind. You weren't just sitting on the sofa drinking beer so you could help save her marriage. Both of you: guilty." She pounded the gavel-spoon two more times.

"Okay, but at least you're saying we're all equally at fault."

"You're not listening. Yes, you're all at fault, but not equally. You started it, Zach. You're the one who got upset with Cheryl because you let your ego take over for your brain. And you're the one who invited Kylie up to your apartment for a six-pack and sympathy, only it wasn't your ego that made that stupid decision. It was your—hey, do I have to spell it out for you? Court is adjourned."

She gave one last hit with her gavel and stood up.

"You need protein," she said. "How do you want your eggs?"

Chapter 54

TRIPP WOKE UP to the smell of fresh coffee. He'd slept in his parka and hugged it to his body. "Worst night's sleep of my life," he said, easing himself out of the top bunk.

"I'll call the front desk and see if I can arrange for an upgrade," Madison said. "Till then, suck it up, princess."

"I'm sorry about yesterday," Tripp said. "That guy walked in out of nowhere and opened the cage. I had no choice."

"There's always a choice," Madison said. "But what's done is done."

"I guess my father is pissed at me now that he knows I'm not really kidnapped."

"I hate to break it to you, kid, but he didn't seem to give a shit about you. Mostly he's crapping in his pants that I know about Project Gutenberg." He poured himself a cup of coffee. "I'm going up top for a smoke. Help yourself to coffee. There are some power bars in the cabinet."

Madison went up to the deck and lit a cigarette.

Tripp poured himself a cup of black coffee and followed him upstairs. "You think he'll pay the hundred million?"

"Oh, he'll come around," Madison said. He took a drag on his cigarette, turned away from Tripp, and blew the smoke in the other direction.

Tripp braced himself. *Now or never.*

As Madison turned back to look at him, Tripp's arm flew up and unleashed a full cup of scalding hot coffee at his face.

Madison screamed, dropped his cigarette and coffee cup, and threw his hands against his seared skin. Tripp dug into the pocket of his parka, produced the stun gun, wedged it under Madison's jaw, and shot fifteen million volts into the teacher's neck.

Madison crumpled to the deck. One hand still clutching his face, he struggled to get to his feet, but Tripp fell on him, jammed the stun gun against his ass, and squeezed the trigger.

All it took was three seconds and Madison was immobilized. Tripp rifled through his pockets. Money.

Car keys. No phone—and no time to go back to the cabin and hunt for one. Shoving his arms under Madison's torso, he dragged him across the deck and, with one adrenaline-charged motion, heaved him over the side into the icy Hudson.

Tripp ran for the starboard side and vaulted onto the dock. It would have been an easy jump if he hadn't caught the toe of his boot on a cleat. He landed hard, and both ankles buckled on impact. The stun gun flew from his hand, skittered into a wooden pile, and bounced into the water.

He staggered to his feet. The parking lot was only a hundred yards away. He started to run, but it was like a dream where he willed himself to go faster, and his body refused. His ankles were on fire, his legs were leaden, and the best he could do was painstakingly limp his way up the icy path toward the Subaru.

He was almost there when he heard the scream. He turned. Madison was out of the river, slowly slogging toward him.

Tripp threw himself against the driver's side door of the Subaru and, with two hands on one key, put it against the lock. It didn't fit. He fumbled for the other key. That didn't work either. Cursing, he tried the first one again. Still nothing.

Madison, waterlogged and weighed down, was

halfway up the hill, screaming Tripp's name, swearing that all was forgiven, promising that everything would be all right.

Tripp tried the second key one more time. He held it as steady as he could, put the tip against the lock, and pushed. It didn't fit. By now Madison was fifty feet away, panting, his pace slower, but closing in.

Tripp had two options: try to outrun him or stay and fight. And then his eyes fell on the useless car keys, and his brain zeroed in on the Pentastar logo.

It wasn't the Subaru key.

Madison was less than twenty feet away when Tripp unlocked the front door of the rusty old Dodge Caravan, shoved the second key in the ignition, turned the engine over, threw the van into reverse, and hit the accelerator.

The van lurched back into the empty lot. Ten feet, twenty, fifty.

He was crying now, overwhelmed by fear and the new reality. Peter was gone. Madison had betrayed him. His father despised him. For the first time in his privileged life, Tripp Alden was on his own.

He shifted the van into drive, and then, pointing toward freedom, careened out of the parking lot and headed north on Marin Boulevard toward the Holland Tunnel, into the city.

Chapter 55

AFTER A MEMORABLE breakfast of eggs, bacon, and a side order of analysis, I walked to the office to face my second challenge of the morning. Matt Smith.

Matt is our resident technical virtuoso—an affable Brit who's easy to like and easy to work with. He's also annoyingly good-looking, which for me makes him harder to like and harder to work with.

A few months ago, I caught him being overly attentive to Cheryl, and I was sure he was hitting on her. But I was wrong. Matt was much more fascinated by Kylie. He never acted on his feelings because he knew she was married. But in my never-ending quest to drive myself crazy, I wondered what he'd do if he found out Kylie was thinking about becoming unmarried.

She was in Matt's office when I got there. "Zach,

Matt's been working on Tripp's computer all night, and he's got something."

"Correction," he said, flashing a self-congratulatory smile. "Half the night. And *two* somethings."

He tapped on the tracking pad, and an email popped up on one of the two thirty-inch monitors on his desk.

> *Mwen te kite flash la nan chanm ou. Èske ou te jwenn li? Tripp*

"It's in Haitian Creole from Tripp to Peter Chevalier," Matt said. "It says 'I left the flash drive in your room. Did you get it?' Here's Peter's response."

> *Te resevwa li. Pa enkyete. Mwen pral kenbe l 'fèmen. Pyè*

"Translation: 'Got it. Don't worry. I'll keep it close. Peter.' There was nothing in the evidence report that indicates they found a flash drive on Peter's body. Did you find one in his room?"

"No, and we released his personal effects to his brother," I said. "None of it was crime scene evidence, but we'll get the computer back if you want it."

"Absolutely. In the meantime, you should talk to

her," Matt said, flashing a picture of a woman on the second screen. "Irene Gerrity, eighty-five years old. According to the file I found in Tripp's computer, she's the first employee ever hired by Alden Investments. She was Hutch's personal secretary until Junior joined the family business. Then she was assigned to him—probably because in the beginning she knew more than he did. She worked for him till she retired seven years ago. Last November, Tripp shot an interview with her."

"He's putting together a movie for Hutch's seventieth birthday," I said.

"Tell me about it. I found the folder with twenty-three different interview subjects, each one more boring than the next."

"How'd you happen to zero in on Irene?"

"It's the only one shot by Peter Chevalier."

"Roll it," Kylie said.

"Trust me," Matt said. "If you had to sit through the entire forty-seven minutes, you'd blow your brains out. I pulled out a few highlights. Here's the first one."

Irene was in a formal living room, sitting on a love seat, wearing a blue dress, minimal makeup, with her silver hair neatly done in a no-nonsense cut. Tripp Alden was adjusting her mic. "You look great, Irene," he said.

"Bullshit. I look like the wreck of the *Hesperus*."

"No, really, you look beautiful," Tripp said, stepping off camera.

"You haven't changed a bit, have you, Hunter? Still blowing smoke."

"It's Tripp, Irene."

"Of course it's Tripp. What did I say?"

"You called me Hunter."

"I did? Peter, did I?"

"Don't worry about it, Miss Irene," the off-camera voice said. It was slightly nasal, with a distinct French lilt. "And for the record, you do look beautiful."

Matt stopped the video. "She called the kid Hunter five more times. He finally gave up on correcting her. But apart from a spot of dementia, Irene's quite the feisty old broad."

"Zach doesn't like 'em feisty," Kylie said.

Matt laughed, but he knew enough to stay out of it. "Next clip," he said.

Irene was now sitting at a piano, singing the last few notes of "Happy Birthday." Applause came from behind the camera, and she responded with the classic lounge singer bow. "Thank you, thank you, thank you."

"Thank *you*," Tripp said. "Not only were you terrific, but this room will be the best-looking one on the video. Your house is incredible."

"Couldn't have afforded it without you, Hunter," Irene said.

"You can thank Hutch for that," Tripp said. "He's always paid people well."

She waved off the remark. "Hutch had nothing to do with it. I'm talking about . . ." Irene leaned forward and whispered toward the camera. "Project Gutenberg. Just you and me, Hunter. We both hit the jackpot on that one."

She waited for an answer. Tripp didn't have one. She put her hands to her mouth. "Oh shit. Cat's out of the bag. Hunter, please don't be mad."

Tripp entered the frame and sat next to her on the piano bench. "It's okay, Irene. Whatever it is, I could never be mad at you."

"I kept all your secrets. Especially Gutenberg. But I had a little secret of my own. I always felt bad about hiding it from you."

"Don't feel bad," Tripp said. "I'm fine. I don't care what it is."

"Screw it. I opened my big mouth. It's time I got it off my chest."

Matt stopped the tape again.

"Hey," Kylie said. "Don't stop now. It's just getting interesting."

"Oh, would you like to see the rest?" Matt said. He

pushed play. The screen filled with white noise.

"What the hell?" Kylie said.

"It's been redacted. Censored. Wiped clean. Whatever it was she confessed, Tripp didn't want anyone else to hear, so he erased the tape."

"But not right away," I said.

"Meaning what?" Kylie said.

"Meaning that Irene thought Tripp was Hunter, and she dropped a bombshell on him," I said. "How does an eighteen-year-old kid handle something like that? Does he quickly destroy the evidence? Or is he more likely to share the footage with the one person he trusts?"

"Son of a bitch," Kylie said. "Before he erased it, Tripp showed it to Ryan Madison, the dedicated teacher who gives young filmmakers guidance on mise-en-scène."

We still had no idea where Madison was, or what he was planning, but we finally knew one of the cards he was holding.

Chapter 56

LONNIE MARTINEZ LEFT his apartment, rang for the elevator, and then backed off when the doors opened. He'd spent enough time trapped inside a small box. He walked down the six flights of stairs.

There was a man sitting on the floor of the vestibule, his head buried between his knees. Lonnie tapped him on the shoulder. "Hey, dude, you can't park your ass here. Find a shelter."

The man looked up. "Lonnie, I need help." It was Tripp.

Lonnie exploded. "You *need?* You've got some balls. I took a couple of million volts trying to save your ass, spent three days locked in a cage, and when I finally get out, you put a stun gun in my face, and shove me back in. Get out, or I'll call the cops. No, wait: your buddy still has my cell phone, so I can't call anybody. But I can still beat the shit out of you."

"The guy who took us isn't my buddy."

"I'm not an idiot, Tripp. I don't know what your deal is, but you and that so-called kidnapper were in it together. It wasn't even a real kidnapping. The whole thing was a scam. Three days, Tripp. Three days of my life. You want to know how crazy my *abuela* was when I finally got home?"

Tripp held up his hands. "I'm sorry. You're right. It was bullshit at first, but last night he changed the rules. He locked me up in his boat, but I got away."

"I don't give a shit. Now get up and—"

"He killed Peter!"

"Who?" Lonnie said.

Tripp struggled to his feet. "I banged up my ankles pretty bad," he said.

Lonnie grabbed Tripp by the shoulders. "Who?" he said, his voice dropping to a menacing whisper. "Who killed—"

The outside door opened and two women walked in. Lonnie nodded and pulled Tripp out the door. "Start walking."

"I'm freezing, and I can't walk," Tripp said. "I've got wheels. I'm parked around the corner."

Lonnie recognized the Dodge Caravan as soon as they turned onto 120th Street. "If you think I'm getting back in there so you can pull that stun gun on me again, you're crazy."

"I don't have it." Tripp spread his arms and legs, and Lonnie patted him down.

"Open the back of the van," Lonnie said.

"Empty," Tripp said once the doors were open. "Get in. It's smarter if we keep moving."

"You try anything and I'll punch your lights out," Lonnie said, climbing into the passenger seat. Tripp put the van in gear and headed east.

"Now tell me who your partner is in all this rich-boy crazy kidnapping shit."

"Mr. Madison."

"*Our* Mr. Madison? From school?"

Tripp nodded. "I had a plan—to get money from my dad."

"And you needed it so bad that you had to kill Peter?"

Tripp pulled the Dodge Caravan to the curb and jammed on the brakes. "I didn't fucking kill Peter. I didn't even know he was dead till last night," he said, tears streaming down his face. "Madison did it, and I'm probably next."

"So," Lonnie said, "do you think Madison killed Blackstone too?"

"What are you talking about?"

"The private eye who works for your dad. Somebody put a bullet through his head last night. He was in his car at the Silver Moon Diner—same place we went to after we finished shooting the carjacking scene."

"Madison and I were at the Silver Moon last night," Tripp said, "and trust me, I didn't kill anybody."

"Are you telling me that some preppy-ass, white-bread teacher from Barnaby did Peter *and* Blackstone?"

"I didn't see him do it, but yeah."

"Why?" Lonnie said. "Blackstone I can almost understand, especially if he tracked you down, but why would Madison kill Peter?"

Tripp shook his head. "I can't tell you."

"You can't *what*? You put me through hell, you come back begging for help, and now you're holding out on me?" Lonnie opened the van door.

Tripp grabbed onto his jacket. "Wait. I'm sorry. Please."

"Hands off me, Alden. I'm not your bitch. I'm the best friend you ever had. So either answer the question or find another ghetto kid to kiss your ass."

Tripp let go of Lonnie's jacket. "Do you remember Irene Gerrity?"

"Never met her. I was sick that day, so Peter shot for me. What about her?"

"Near the end of the shoot she told me something

about my father. Something that could put him in jail for the rest of his life."

"Did you believe her? That old broad was crazy as a shithouse rat."

"She had proof—real evidence—and she gave it to me. I didn't know what to do. Peter said I should talk to Hutch, but I decided to show it to Madison, and he came up with this plan to get my father to pay back the people he hurt."

"I watched the video. She never said anything bad about your father."

"Madison erased it before you got the tape. But Peter heard every word of it, and I think that's what got him killed."

"So why don't you just take this *real evidence* the old lady gave you and turn it over to the cops?"

"I would, but I don't know where it is. I gave it to Peter for safekeeping."

"Shit, man," Lonnie said, still holding the van door open. "Being your cameraman is a dangerous job. I think I should resign while I still can."

"Please, I know I screwed up bad, but you're the only one I can turn to."

Lonnie took a deep breath and let it out. "Damn your ass," he said, pulling the door shut. "What do you need?"

Chapter 57

"I DON'T KNOW when Irene Gerrity started losing her marbles," Matt said, "but she had them all when she was pulling off this Gutenberg deal. I've tapped into all her available bank records, but the money she made never saw the light of day in the U.S. It's got to be squirreled away offshore."

"What about her house?" I said.

"She bought it eight years ago, just before she hung up her hat at Alden Investments, but there's no paper trail on how she paid for it," Matt said.

"I'm sure it's just one of the little skill sets she picked up working for Hunter," I said. "I'll ask her about it. Kylie and I are headed straight up to Fieldston as soon as she gets back from the dentist."

Kylie had left five minutes earlier. "Dental emergency," she had said to Matt as she bolted out the door.

It was, of course, pure fiction, but telling your coworkers you have a loose filling is much more discreet than saying "My marriage is on the skids."

I went back to my desk, which is in the wide-open bull pen that Red occupies on the third floor of the 19th Precinct. I decided to use the time to catch up on a growing pile of paperwork that's part of the glamour of being a cop.

Five minutes later, the elevator doors opened. I looked up, and there, heading my way, was the last person I ever expected to see. He stopped at my desk and grinned. "Happy New Year, Zach."

It was Spence Harrington, Kylie's husband.

I stood up and shook his hand. "Spence . . . Kylie didn't tell me you were coming home."

"That's probably because I didn't tell her. It's kind of a surprise. Where is she?"

That's kind of a surprise, too. "Dentist," I said, sticking to the cover story. "If you're back so soon, I'm guessing Oregon didn't go so well."

"Oregon? Zach, I'm an addict. You can say *rehab*. Actually, they have a damn good program out there, but I had a long talk with my counselor, and he figures it'll take me six months to a year to get through it. Despite what Kylie thinks, that's too long to be three thousand miles away from my wife. So,

I found something in New York, and, like it or not, here I am."

"Well, I'm sure Kylie will be . . ." I groped for the right words to finish the sentence.

Spence did it for me. "She'll be pissed to the gills, but that's her problem. This is my last chance to salvage my marriage, and I decided I'd have a better shot at it if I were closer to home. So, what have you and Kylie been up to?"

Up to? I'm sure he meant work, so I started making small talk about NYPD closing out last year with the fewest homicides in the city's history, and staying away from any reference to the Aldens. As awkward as it was, it beat the alternative of sitting there like an idiot and not talking to him.

After ten minutes, the elevator doors opened, and Kylie stepped out. She took one look at Spence and shook her head in disgust. "What the hell are you doing here?"

"Hey, sweetheart, I'm happy to see you too," he said.

"Let me rephrase the question," Kylie said. "When did you lose your mind?"

"It's not as crazy as you think," Spence said. "I signed up for a program right here in the city. It's called Better Choices."

"And what makes Better Choices any better than the one in Oregon?"

"It's not in Oregon," he said with a boyish smile that fell flat. "Come on, Kylie, don't judge it before you know anything about it. It's in Tribeca. It goes from eight in the morning to five at night, six days a week, and it has one of the best success rates on the East Coast."

"It's a *day* program?" Kylie said. "And where are you spending your nights? Because I can tell you where you won't be spending them."

Spence looked at me. "I told you she'd be pissed."

"Pissed doesn't begin to describe it," Kylie said. "We had a deal, and you are not moving back in at this stage of your recovery."

"I know. I called Shelley. He's letting me use the corporate apartment. For the record, he's not happy I'm back either. He said he can put a roof over my head, but I don't get my job back till I graduate."

"Spence, this is your third rehab in less than two months. What makes you think this one is going to be any different?"

"It won't be," he said. "Unless I have you on my side. I'm just asking you to believe in me one more time. That's it. I'll let you guys get back to work. Nice to see you, Zach."

Spence didn't wait for the elevator. He hightailed it down the stairwell. Kylie stood there in silence, watching him go, her anger and frustration palpable.

I decided this would not be a good time to ask her how it went with the divorce lawyer.

Chapter 58

KYLIE AND I got in the car, and she drove across Central Park without saying a word. I knew she was stewing about Spence, so I decided to give her all the space she needed.

We were headed north on the Henry Hudson Parkway when she finally broke the silence. "It's too bad Cheryl's not around," she said.

I couldn't believe it. Why would she want to open *that* wound? But I couldn't let it go either. "Why would you say that?" I asked.

"Irene Gerrity has serious comprehension and memory issues, and Cheryl could have given us some direction on the best way to handle her."

I let out a long slow breath. I'd been so obsessed with Cheryl, my girlfriend, that I'd forgotten she was also Dr. Robinson, my go-to departmental psychologist.

"I could call Cheryl and ask," I said, "but first I'd need some direction on the best way to handle *her*."

"Trouble in paradise, Detective Jordan?"

"You know damn well there is, Detective MacDonald. You were in paradise chomping on pizza and knocking down brewskis last night when the trouble hit the fan."

She gave me a wide-eyed smile that said "Look at me—I'm innocent." She was anything but. Gerri Gomperts was right. Women are not remotely as clueless as men would like to think. Kylie had no interest in talking about her relationship issues, so she brought up mine.

And I, of course, couldn't resist taking the bait. "As long as we're on the subject of last night," I said, "did Cheryl say anything about me when I went out to get more beer?"

"Not a lot. Just that you owed her a major apology for your childish behavior over Fred."

"Damn. She said that?"

"No, Zach, she didn't. But I'm having much more fun analyzing your relationship problems than I'd be having ruminating about my own."

"Sounds like it all went swimmingly at the *dentist's office*," I said.

"*Swimmingly* is the perfect choice of terms. The

man was a shark. All he cared about was how much Spence earned, how much I'd contributed to his income over the past ten years, how much is our apartment worth, and do we own any cars, boats, life insurance policies, or livestock. It was all about money, money, money."

"Kylie, he's a divorce attorney. What did you expect?"

"I don't know. I guess I was naive enough to think that there would be some compassion to go along with the legal advice."

"Hey, if you want compassion, go to a diner, not a law firm."

"I guess that means you woke up early this morning and poured your heart out to Gerri."

"Don't knock it. Not only did she give me excellent advice, but it came with eggs over easy, bacon, and a toasted blueberry muffin. See if your guy can top that."

She laughed. "My guy gets five hundred an hour. Six hundred if I want breakfast with it. Can we get serious for a minute?"

"We can try."

"I've handled more than my fair share of EDPs over the past ten years," she said. "And my track record is less than stellar."

NYPD responds to a couple of hundred thousand emotionally disturbed persons calls a year. Most are harmless, but some can be homicidal. It's always a challenge dealing with the mentally ill, and the department is constantly evaluating how to improve our training. But the simple fact is that some cops are better at it than others. I wasn't surprised to hear Kylie admit that she fell short.

"Irene is not exactly your typical threat-to-the-neighborhood EDP," I said. "She's a rich old lady who's losing her mental faculties as part of the aging process."

"Even so, I don't think I can remember any of the training we had at the academy on how to interview someone who has dementia. How about you?"

"I remember the basics. Make eye contact, talk slowly, try to engage them in shared experiences, and no waterboarding unless they really have it coming to them."

Kylie laughed. "You take the lead with Irene," she said.

"You sure? I think she'd be more comfortable talking with a woman."

"No, no . . . I caught part of your conversation with Spence," Kylie said. "You seem to be very good at communicating with delusional people who are incapable of living in reality."

We drove the rest of the way in blessed silence.

Chapter 59

ASK YOUR AVERAGE New Yorkers what they know about the Bronx, and they might recall their first Yankees game in The House That Ruth Built, or rave about the cannoli-to-die-for on Arthur Avenue, or dredge up the wave of arson that ravaged the South Bronx in the seventies.

None of them would mention Fieldston.

Less than twenty minutes from the precinct, Fieldston is one of the best-kept secrets in the Bronx: a privately owned community of tree-lined streets, landmark-status homes, and well-heeled white people.

"Miss Irene seems to have done pretty well for a secretary," Kylie said as we turned onto Goodridge Avenue and parked in front of her imposing stucco-and-stone Tudor revival–style house.

We rang the bell and ID'd ourselves to a woman in a nurse's uniform.

"Is this about the stolen pearls?" she asked.

"No, ma'am," I said. "Did you report a robbery?"

"Miss Irene did last week. She hid her pearls so no one would steal them, then she forgot she hid them, so she called 911. Yesterday I was taking the ornaments off the Christmas tree, and guess what I found? A string of pearls. I called the precinct and unreported the crime."

"This is about Peter Chevalier," I said. "Is she aware of what happened?"

"She saw it in the newspaper, and she was very upset at the time. But *aware?* I can't tell you what she's aware of. It changes from minute to minute."

She escorted us into the living room. It was the same one we'd seen in the video, and there on the settee was Irene Gerrity sipping a cocktail.

We introduced ourselves, and she raised her glass. "It's a Perfect Manhattan," she said. "My doctor lets me have two a week."

The nurse, who had stepped off to the side, rolled her eyes, and I got the feeling that math was not Irene's strong suit. Delusional *and* tipsy. I'd just have to wing it.

"Miss Gerrity," I said, "we're here to ask you about Peter Chevalier."

"Beautiful man," she said. "How do you know Peter?"

"I don't, but I understand you saw him recently."

She looked at me. She needed another prompt.

"He was here with . . ." I hated lying to her, but I had to work within the bounds of her reality. "He was here with Hunter Alden. They were shooting a video for Hutch's birthday."

"Oh yes. I remember. We had a few laughs. Told some war stories."

"Hunter told us you're quite a smart investor."

"He's the smart one. That boy kicked ass up and down the Street."

"Looking at this beautiful home, I'd say you kicked a little ass yourself."

She took a sip of her drink. "Are you here about the pearls? I can tell you who stole them."

I didn't know the rules, but I was determined to play the game. I took out a pad. "That would help us a lot," I said. "Did you see who took your pearls?"

"Damn right. I saw him skulking around here a bunch of times. It was Truman."

I rolled with it. "And what's Truman's last name?" I asked, pen poised.

Irene turned to Kylie. "Is he stupid? Truman *is* his last name. Harry S. Truman. He's the goddamn president of the United States. All those Democrats are after my money, and he's the ringleader."

"That's a big help, ma'am," Kylie said. "I'm sure we'll be able to find your pearls. Thanks for your help. We'll be going now."

Kylie gestured at me with her head, and the two of us were starting to leave when she stopped and turned back to Irene. "I do have one last question," Kylie said sweetly.

Irene smiled, determined to help us find the dead president who had made off with her pearls.

Kylie smiled back. "It's about Project Gutenberg—"

Irene snapped. "Get out!" she screamed. "Both of you. Out!"

She tried to stand, but the nurse jumped in and grabbed her. "Get your hands off me, Lorna. Just throw their asses out of here now."

Lorna calmly eased her back onto the settee. "I'll see them out, Miss Irene. Why don't you enjoy your drink? And when I get back we can play a little canasta."

Irene didn't go for the drink. She glared at Kylie, teeth gnashed, one fist clenched. "Fucking asshole bitch," she said.

Sweet little old Irene Gerrity had just shown us her dark side.

Lorna ushered us to the front door. "And don't come back!" she yelled loud enough for an octogenarian to hear in the next room.

Then she leaned forward and dropped her voice to a whisper. "Wait in your car. I'll be out in ten minutes."

Chapter 60

"I'M NOT THE keenest judge of human nature," I said as Kylie and I walked to the car, "but I'm guessing you two feisty females are not going to be BFFs."

"Hey, you were getting nowhere, so I threw a Hail Mary. It didn't work. No apologies."

"None expected, but it would be a nice gesture if you let me drive."

She tossed me the keys, and we got in the car.

Ten minutes later, Lorna, bundled up in a heavy coat and with a scarf over her head, came out of the house, walked toward us, then kept going. When she got half a block away, she turned and gestured for us to catch up. We followed her around a hairpin turn onto Fieldston Road and pulled over.

"I couldn't let her see us talking. She watches me out the window," Lorna explained, getting into the backseat. "I told her we were low on bourbon, and I had to get to the liquor store before it starts to snow."

"Where's the store?" Kylie asked. "We can drive you."

Lorna laughed. "Honey, don't worry. We've got plenty of booze. I keep it hid. Reenie can drink like a sailor with a hollow leg. Sorry she cursed at you."

"Thanks," Kylie said, "but you didn't go to all this trouble to apologize."

"I'm with her twelve hours a day," Lorna said. "So I hear a lot. But I don't want Mr. Alden to fire me for speaking out of turn."

"Hunter Alden pays you to take care of Irene?"

"Hell, no. That man ain't called or come once since the day she retired. Mr. Hutch foots the bill. I wouldn't do nothing if it would upset him."

"Hutch wants us to find Peter's killer as much as we do," Kylie said. "If you help, I promise he won't be upset."

"My husband Findley's been driving for him more than thirty years. Me and Findley, we both knew Peter since we were kids. What do you want to know?"

"Have you heard of Project Gutenberg?"

"Yes. That day when they made the video. Miss Irene said it by accident, then she got upset, because it's a secret. It didn't seem to bother Tripp, but then Irene says she wants to confess everything, and she pours it all out."

"Can you tell us what she said?"

"It was all business talk. So when I got home I told it to Findley to see if he could make sense of it. You can talk to him if you want."

"Give us the gist of what you remember."

"Don't hold me to the words, but the upshot is that Miss Irene was spying on Hunter. He'd invest a pot of money, like a million or something, and she could see what he was doing, so she'd do the same thing, but maybe like five thousand. He makes a lot, she makes a little, everybody's happy—only he don't know she's copying all his moves."

"That doesn't sound illegal," I said.

"That's just what Findley said. But this Gutenberg is not like the others. It's all hush-hush. Hunter doesn't even tell Irene what's going on, so she knows it's big. And by now she's getting used to the easy money, and she wants in."

Lorna was sweating. She took off her head scarf and dabbed her face and neck with it. I killed the heater. I had a bottle of water on the front seat. I handed it to her, and she downed it.

"Thanks. Where was I?"

"Gutenberg," Kylie said. "Irene wants in, but Hunter's keeping her out of the loop."

"Right. But she's cagey. She's already one step ahead of him. All along she's been taping his phone calls and copying his email, and going over them at home every night. So when Hunter starts pumping a shitload of money into the Gutenberg deal, Irene decides this is her one big chance, and she bets the farm."

"And what happened?" Kylie said.

"Sweet Jesus, you seen the damn house, didn't you?" Lorna said, cackling. It took her a few seconds to regain her composure. "So she gets it all off her chest, and Tripp, he's cool. It's not like she stole anything. If Hunter would have lost money, so would she. Finally she says the one thing that's been eating at her all these years: 'It's too bad we had to make all that money in the wake of all that suffering.' Them's her exact words. 'The wake of all that suffering.'"

"What suffering?"

Lorna shrugged. "She didn't say, but does it really matter? Honey, I'm from Haiti. We've had more than our fair share of suffering. It's a story that's old as time—rich people getting richer off poor people's misery. The only difference with Irene's story is that she feels bad for whoever got the shit end of the stick."

"You've been very helpful," I said. "Thank you for stepping forward."

"This meeting is just between us, right?" she said.

"You have my word." I gave her my card. "And if you think of anything else, call me anytime."

Lorna opened the back door.

"One more question," Kylie said. "Did Peter ever say anything to you or your husband about a flash drive he was holding on to for Tripp?"

"No." She pondered for a beat. "You talking about the flash drive I gave Tripp that day they shot the video?"

I motioned for her to shut the door. "What flash drive?"

"I told you Irene was taping Hunter's phone calls and copying his email so she could take them home and study them at night. She put it all on a flash drive. And when she told Tripp the story, he asked if she still had it."

"And she did?"

"Kept it in a music box on her dresser. She sent me upstairs to get it, and I gave it to Tripp, but I don't know anything about him giving it to Peter."

We thanked her again, and she left.

Kylie and I sat there not saying a word. We didn't know exactly what Project Gutenberg was, but it was pretty clear that whatever was on that flash drive could destroy Hunter Alden's life.

I was looking forward to finding it.

Chapter 61

HUNTER ALDEN PULLED up Silas Blackstone's name and contact information on his iPhone. "Idiot," he said, staring at it. "What kind of a PI gets shot sitting in his own car in a parking lot?"

Sixteen hours after Silas's death, Hunter was beginning to realize how much he had relied on the man. Too much. He'd never wanted to meet anyone else from SDB Investigative Services. Silas had been the go-between on everything.

He took one last look at the phone, tapped Delete Contact, and in an instant Silas Blackstone was gone. There was no time to find a replacement. Hunter Alden was on his own. He reached down and removed the .38 from his ankle holster.

His gun-loving friends enjoyed busting his balls. *With a name like Hunter, how come you never hunt?* Just because he had no desire to fly eight thousand miles to slaughter a rhinoceros didn't mean he knew nothing about guns. He knew enough. Still, he kicked himself for never getting Wheeler's phone number.

The intercom buzzed. He tucked the .38 back into the holster and looked at the closed-circuit monitor on his desk to see who was out there. "Son of a bitch!" he said.

Hunter jammed his finger on the button that released the gate, stormed to the front door, and yanked it open. "What the hell do you want?" he said.

Lonnie Martinez looked up at him with complete contempt. "I have a message from Tripp."

Hunter returned the hateful look. "How are you even walking the streets? The cops should have locked you up."

"For what?"

"You were part of it, and you still are," Hunter said. "Have you seen my son since his so-called escape?"

"Yeah. We just grabbed some lunch together. He paid." Lonnie sneered. "With your money."

"Where is he?"

"I don't know where he is now, but I can tell you where he's going to be." He handed Hunter a single sheet of paper.

Hunter scanned it. "What the hell is this?"

"You just read what it is. It's an access pass to Costco."

"What do I need it for?"

"It's the only way you can get into the store. They run it like a club. Members only."

"I'm not interested in joining."

"You don't have to. Tripp joined, and he added you to his account. Congratulations. It's a great store. My grandmother works there."

"Tell Tripp if he wants to meet me, he can come here," Hunter said.

"He said you'd say that, but for some reason he feels safer meeting you in public. Costco is in East Harlem. On 117th Street, just off the FDR. Meet him at the food court. Five o'clock." Lonnie turned and headed down the steps.

"Tell your partner not to hold his breath," Hunter yelled.

Lonnie stopped and turned back. "He said you might say that too, and if you did, I'm supposed to give you one more message. If you're not there by 5:01, he's calling the *Wall Street Journal*. Have a nice day, and don't forget your access pass."

He bounded down the steps, breezed through the gate, and headed east on 81st Street.

Hunter could feel the .38 on his left ankle. For a

brief moment he wanted to grab the gun and open fire on the smug Puerto Rican bastard. But Lonnie Martinez wasn't the problem. Tripp was.

He shut the door. Why shoot the messenger?

Chapter 62

THE FIRST FEW snowflakes hit the windshield as I pulled the car onto the Henry Hudson Parkway.

"Wipers," Kylie said, running the show from the passenger seat.

"Gosh, thanks," I said, turning them on. "I knew I should have taken driver's ed in high school. Anything else?"

"Yeah, I know this is going to sound terrible," Kylie said, "but I have to say it. I love this case."

"Me too. I mean, two dead guys, serious sleep deprivation, the Alden family blocking us at every turn—what's not to love?"

"Come on, Zach. We started out Thursday with a headless body in a million-dollar car. And then it spins out of control. A kidnapping, extortion, a second murder—"

"Stolen pearls," I said.

"This is the kind of stuff we dreamed of when we were at the academy."

"Remind me. Did we dream about how to solve it?"

"Oh, we'll solve it," she said. "I think we should start by visiting Irwin."

Until New Year's Day, Irwin Diamond was the smartest person in city government. He was the previous mayor's right-hand man and a big supporter of Red. But then Muriel Sykes moved into Gracie Mansion, and Irwin went back to his first career: investment banking.

"Do you think Irwin can help us with Gutenberg?" I said.

"I don't know, but every cop in the city is looking for Madison and Tripp. We're the only ones who know about Gutenberg. We have to start somewhere."

"Somewhere" was Irwin's five-bedroom penthouse at 1 Morton Square, one of the city's most exclusive addresses. The three of us sat down in a cozy little area in the middle of a thirty-foot expanse of floor-to-ceiling windows. On a clear day you could probably see across the Hudson, but now the horizon was nothing but a frenzy of swirling snow.

"They predict ten inches," Irwin said, "which

means no matter how Muriel Sykes handles the storm, by tomorrow at this time, four out of the five boroughs will be pissed at her. I'm so glad I'm out of politics. How can I help?"

We filled him in. He had never heard of Project Gutenberg.

"But it sounds dirty," he said, "and the fact that the code name references the Bible makes me think it's extra dirty. White-collar criminals love irony."

"Is Hunter Alden a criminal?" I asked.

He peered at us over rimless glasses. "Alleged. Never convicted."

"What can you tell us about him?"

"Do you know much about investing?"

"It's easy," I said. "You give your broker money, he puts it in something that doesn't pan out the way he expected, and a year later you're lucky if you get back a third."

"You're already smarter than most investors, but let me give you a little tutorial." He stood up and went to the window. "You see these two drops of water? I'll bet you a dollar the one on the left gets to the windowsill before the one on the right. You in?"

"Sure."

We watched the droplets trickle down the glass. Ten seconds later, the one on the right hit the sill.

Irwin reached into his wallet and gave me a dollar. "You ready for something a little riskier?"

"I'm playing with the house's money, so go for it."

He looked at his watch. "I'll bet you fifty dollars that in the next ten minutes my neighbor's cat will jump down onto my terrace, scratch at the door, wait for me to bring him a saucer of milk, drink it, and leave. You in?"

"Hell, no," I said. "Why not?"

"Irwin, I don't know if you and the cat are running some kind of scam together, but I do know that you're too smart to make a crazy bet like that unless you know something that I don't."

"Reliable information is how I make money," he said, "but the difference between me and Alden is that my information comes from meticulous research. He taps phones, hacks email, plants bugs, bribes corporate executives, and gives kickbacks to government officials."

"So he's a crook. But what did Irene mean when she said they made money in the wake of all that suffering?"

"I don't know, but I could give you a hypothetical. Let's say there's a new diet pill that lets you eat all you want and still lose weight. The FDA approves it, and the smart money says the drug company's stock will go up. But Hunter Alden bets millions that it will go down."

"Why?"

"Because he found out that the drug company rigged their clinical trials. But he doesn't blow the whistle. The pill hits the market, hundreds of people who took it die, and the stock goes in the toilet."

"And Hunter makes a lot of money in the wake of a lot of suffering," I said.

"But wouldn't the SEC check all the drug company's stock transactions and realize he had insider information?" Kylie said.

"His name would never show up. He'd do it all through phone calls to a Swiss lawyer and wire transfers to an offshore bank," Irwin said.

"I think now we know what's on that missing flash drive," Kylie said.

I stood up and walked to the window. "Maybe I should have taken your bet. It looks like that cat doesn't want to come out in the snow."

"Oh, my neighbor doesn't have a cat," Irwin said. "I just wanted to show you the power of information, even when it's a lie."

"Thanks," I said. "I don't know if any of this will help us crack the case, but it helps me understand why the 99 percent hate the 1 percent."

Irwin laughed. "Don't hate us too much. Just remember that without the 1 percent, NYPD Red would just be NYPD Blue."

Chapter 63

THE TAXI SKIDDED across Third Avenue, barely missing the M101 bus. Hunter banged on the partition. "Are you trying to get us killed?"

The driver laughed. "Sorry. Not so much snow in Bangladesh."

"Well, maybe you should think about going back where you—" Hunter's phone rang. "Hello," he barked.

"Mr. Alden, this is Sergeant McGrath at the Nineteenth Precinct. Your car's been released. You can send someone to pick it up anytime."

"Send someone? No, Sergeant. You hauled it away, you bring it back. Just use the garage door opener in the car, then exit through the side door of the garage. Can you handle that, or do I have to call the police commissioner?"

"No, sir. I'll find someone to drop it off at your house."

"Just make sure they know what they're driving. That car costs more money than ten cops make in a year. I don't want to see any dings or dents."

"Yes, sir," McGrath said.

The cab stopped at the 117th Street entrance to the East River Plaza, and Hunter entered the massive retail complex for the first and, he hoped, only time in his life.

He followed the signs to Costco, and produced the official access document for a cheery greeter at the front entrance.

"Where's the food court?" he said.

She pointed, and Hunter headed toward it. Tripp was sitting at a table off to the side, a slice of pizza and a soft drink in front of him.

"Stand up," Hunter ordered.

"In case you forgot, I'm running this meeting," Tripp said. "Sit down."

"Not until I make sure you're not wired. Stand up."

"Wired? You must think everyone is as sick as you." Tripp stood, and for the second time that day he let himself be frisked.

"What do you want?" Hunter said when they both sat down.

"You're a negotiator. I thought we'd negotiate."

"Okay, here's my final offer," Hunter said. "You're not getting a penny, and I'm completely restructuring my estate so that when I die, you wind up with nothing."

"*When* you die?" Tripp said. "You're going to prison. Once the world knows what you did, I doubt if you'll live through the first night. And even if they put you in solitary, I wouldn't be surprised if one of the guards kills you."

"You don't have the proof to send me to prison."

"Don't I? How about every single phone call you made to your Swiss lawyer, Mr. Joost? I listened to them. At first I thought you were making some crazy high-flying, high-risk investments, but you sounded so cocksure of yourself—it's like you knew in advance what would happen. Turns out you did."

"Overconfidence is not a crime," Hunter said.

"There's more. It took me weeks of searching through your archives, but I finally found the mother lode—the meeting in Turks and Caicos. You actually taped it. Dumb move, *Leviticus*. And then you *kept* the tape. Even dumber. But I understand why you did it. You hate to lose. Even more, you hate when somebody else wins. That tape was your insurance. You figured if you got caught, you could use it to bargain with. If

Homeland could track down the guy who set up the Gutenberg deal, you might be able to avoid the death penalty."

Hunter laughed. "I don't know what you think you found," Hunter said, "but I'll be sure to look for this so-called mother lode myself as soon as I get home. This meeting is over." He stood up.

"Do you think I'm stupid?" Tripp said. "Do you think you can just run home and erase the evidence? I've got it all, Dad. The phone calls to the lawyer, the meeting in Turks and Caicos—they're all on one flash drive."

"Which you and your partner, Mr. Cain, intend to share with the world, whether I pay you or not."

"There is no more Mr. Cain," Tripp said. "He's been out of the loop for a while. And I've changed my mind about going public."

Hunter sat back down. "Meaning what?"

"Meaning that as much as I want to punish you, I love my grandfather too much to destroy his name, his legacy, and everything he ever worked for. I'm willing to keep the secret a secret. But it will cost you."

"How much?"

Tripp pounded his fist on the table. "How much do you think, asshole? You knew exactly what was going to happen. But you didn't warn anyone. You stood by and let it happen. How much?" he said, dropping his voice to a harsh whisper. "A billion fucking dollars. Every cent you made cashing in on everyone else's misery."

"You're crazy."

"Oh no, Dad. I'm damaged, but I'm not crazy. Monday morning I want you to create a foundation in Mom's name. And then, in a magnanimous philanthropic gesture, you will fund the Marjorie Alden Foundation with a billion dollars in memory of your late wife, and you will appoint your son chairman of the board."

"And what's your grand plan, Mr. Chairman?"

"I'll use the money to repair the damage you've done."

"I bet you will. And what happens to me?"

"You? You'll be a hero. Your picture will be on every front page in America. The benevolent Hunter Alden, a kind and generous global humanitarian. And only I will know what a vile and despicable scumbag you really are."

Chapter 64

TRIPP'S HEART WAS racing as he left Costco and walked through the parking lot to his van. He'd had his father on the ropes, but then he blew it.

"Never let the other guy see your cards," his grandfather had taught him years ago. But Tripp had played a card he didn't even have in his hand. The flash drive.

And now that Hunter knew it existed he'd be scouring the house trying to find it. Sooner or later he'd get to Peter's room, and that would be it.

Tripp got behind the wheel of the van and dialed Patrice.

"Tripp, I'm relieved to hear from you," Patrice said. "Are you all right?"

"I'm okay, but I really need that flash drive I told you about. Did you find it yet?"

"I've looked, and it's nowhere to be seen, but right now I'm more concerned about you than a flash drive."

"Don't worry about me. I just need you to keep looking. I'm sure it's somewhere mixed in with all of Peter's stuff."

"Most of which is still at your house."

"Patrice, you're his brother. It's all yours now. You don't even have to ask anyone. Just go to the house and take it. I'll give you the key code to the garage."

"I think you and I should sit down and talk first," Patrice said. "Can we meet somewhere?"

Tripp felt the cold steel of a gun barrel at the back of his neck. He lifted his head slowly and looked in the rearview mirror.

Madison.

"I can't meet right now," Tripp said. "I'll get back to you soon." He hung up the phone and focused on the man in the mirror.

The hot coffee had left Madison's face red and blotchy. There were blisters on the right side below his ear and a welt on his neck from the stun gun.

"Dude," Tripp said, "you really ought to see a dermatologist, or nobody's going to want to go with you to the prom."

Madison raised the gun and brought it down hard on Tripp's shoulder blade. The pain radiated up to his brain, but Tripp bit down hard, determined not to scream.

"I heard your desperate phone call to Peter's brother. It sounds like you lost your proof. I knew you could never pull this off on your own."

"Maybe not, but after you killed Peter and Silas, and locked me up on that boat, I decided it was safer to go solo. How did you find me, anyway?"

"I never bothered looking for you. I knew you'd contact your father—all I had to do was follow him. I watched the two of you from behind a couple of pallets of paper towels. I couldn't hear anything, but from the body language it looks to me like you cut a deal with him. How much did you ask for?"

"It doesn't matter," Tripp said. "I'll still give you your share."

"*You'll* give me?" Madison drove the gun down on the same shoulder blade.

This time Tripp let out a yelp. "What was that for? I told you you'll get your money—all ten million."

"And how much do you get?" Madison said, readying the gun to come down again.

"The whole billion," Tripp said, grabbing on to his battered shoulder. "Every penny he made from Gutenberg."

Madison laughed. "And why would he give you a

billion if he turned me down for a fraction of that?"

"Because he'll pay whatever it takes to keep me quiet!" Tripp yelled, spinning around to face Madison. "And he's not giving it to *me*. I'm starting a foundation in my mother's name. Once I do that, he knows I'll never say a word about Gutenberg. It would disgrace her memory."

"Was your mom an idealist, Tripp? Is that who you take after? Because clearly you didn't inherit your father's killer instincts for business. Ideals don't mean jack shit to him when there's money on the table. Let's go for a ride."

Tripp turned around and put the key in the ignition. "Where are we going?" he said.

Madison leaned forward. "East 81st Street. I'm going to make a deal with the devil."

"Why? I told you—he agreed to pay. You'll screw up the whole deal."

"You don't get it, do you, Tripp? Dealing is what Hunter Alden lives for. And do you know what he likes best?" Madison whispered, his warm breath in Tripp's ear.

"What?" Tripp said, starting the engine.

"Getting what he wants from the lowest bidder."

Chapter 65

THE TEMPERATURE WAS just on the cusp of freezing, so the roads were covered with what forecasters call a wintry mix, which is a euphemism for the unholy mess of snow, sleet, and icy rain that can cripple the city.

I inched the car along Third Avenue past the usual log-jam in front of Bloomingdale's, where half a dozen overly optimistic shoppers craned their necks, looking for cabs. I saw daylight at 60th Street and picked up speed.

"Do you think we have a shot at getting a search warrant?" Kylie asked.

"You already know the answer to that one, which is why you didn't ask Irwin Diamond," I said. "And don't bother asking Cates again. She gave us a flat-out no yesterday."

"That was different. We were talking about tossing Alden's entire house, looking for a severed head. Now all we want is a tiny little peek inside the garage, where Peter's room is. How long could it take us to find the flash drive?"

"It wouldn't matter if we found Peter's head on Alden's dining room table," I said. "We don't have cause to search. All we have is a doddering old woman talking about what *might* be a white-collar crime."

I made a left onto 67th Street. There's a fire station next to the precinct, so parking on our block is at a premium, even for cops. But there in front of the One Nine was a familiar vehicle taking up twenty feet of NYPD's valuable real estate.

"Looks like Hunter Alden is finally getting his car back," I said.

"Perfect," Kylie said.

I had no clue what she meant, but then I realized she wasn't talking to me. She had that look in her eyes that cartoonists use when one of their characters has a really bad idea. And I knew my partner well enough to know what Kylie's bad idea was.

"I'm going inside," she said, getting out of the car. "Can you bring me back some coffee from Gerri's?"

"No," I said, following her up the stairs and through the precinct door. "They deliver."

She headed straight for Sergeant McGrath at the front desk.

"And where have you been, Detective MacDonald?" he said.

"Fighting crime, and doing a damn fine job of it," she said, shaking the snow out of her hair. "Why do you ask?"

He leaned forward and looked down at her. "Did you get a call this morning from the One Oh Five garage about a crime scene vehicle that was ready to be released to its owner, a Mr. Hunter Alden?"

Kylie looked at me and shrugged. "I did."

"Then why didn't you call Mr. Alden and tell him?" McGrath said.

"The truth?"

"That would be refreshing."

"I didn't call Alden because he's a dick," she said. "Also, I had a dentist's appointment, but mainly because he's done everything he can to obstruct a double homicide investigation, so I figured I'd let him stew."

"The problem, Detective, is that instead of stewing, Alden got on my case. I have enough to do around here dealing with regular folks without having to play Country Club Cop like the two of you."

"For the record," Kylie said, "my partner, Detective

Straight Arrow, didn't know that the car was ready to be picked up."

"Not picked up," McGrath said. "Delivered. In my twenty-two years I've never released anything from the chain of evidence without the owner coming in and signing for it. But it seems your Mr. Alden is exempt from the rules. So now I have to send two of my officers to take it back."

"No you don't. It's my fault this got dumped on you. I'll take the car back." She lowered her eyes. "I'm really, really sorry, Sergeant," said the woman, who really, really never apologizes for anything.

McGrath bought it. "Apology accepted," he said, handing her a packet of papers. "Put it in the garage. If Alden's there, get him to sign for it. If he's not, leave the paperwork on the front seat, and he'll fax me back a signed copy."

He held up a key ring. It had a small black fob and a gold crucifix dangling from it. "Your basic smart key," McGrath said, tapping the Maybach logo on the fob. "Just put it in your pocket, and it does the rest. I don't think Jesus on the cross is original factory equipment, but it couldn't hurt." He tossed her the key ring. "Go with God."

"I'm driving," Kylie said as soon as we were outside. "You can follow." She got behind the wheel.

"One car," I said, getting in the passenger side. "We have a few things to talk about."

The electronic ignition picked up a signal from the key ring, and she started the car with the push of a button. "You sure you don't want to ride in the back and pour yourself a drink? Because the last thing I need is a lecture."

"'You can't search the garage without a warrant' is not a lecture."

"What am I—a rookie?" she said, turning on the wipers. "I know the law. But now that we have permission to enter the garage, anything we see in plain sight is fair game."

"And what's your definition of 'in plain sight'?" I said.

"Anything that is left out in the open, or is unconcealed," she said, pulling the million-dollar car out onto the slushy street. "Or in the case of assholes like Hunter Alden," she added, grinning, "anything in a drawer that I can open without a crowbar."

Chapter 66

HUNTER ALDEN WAS used to being the most important person in the room. But sitting at a table in the food court at Costco, he was nobody. He wanted to stand up and shout, "Don't you people know who I am? I have more money than all of you put together."

He looked at his watch. Seven minutes had passed since Tripp left, *ordering* him to wait five minutes. It only proved how little his son understood him. Did Tripp actually think Hunter would try to follow him? Hunter had people for that. *Had* people. Blackstone was dead, and Wheeler was a ghost he'd never met.

So he'd gone with the only option he could. He had agreed to create the foundation in Marjorie's name. He had promised to hold a press conference on Monday morning, which gave him less than forty-eight hours to find a cheaper way to silence Tripp.

He finally stood up, left the East River Plaza complex, and headed west on 117th Street. Walking through the swirling snow helped clear his head, but he hadn't dressed for the weather, and when he reached Second Avenue, he knocked on the window of an off-duty cab that had stopped at a light.

For two hundred bucks the man was happy to go on duty and drive him to 81st Street.

The house was warm and welcoming, and since Janelle's keys were not on the foyer table, he knew that he had it to himself. He went straight to his study.

He heard the intruder before he saw him.

"Mr. Alden, I've been waiting for you. I took the liberty of making myself at home."

It was Tripp's teacher. He was seated in an armchair, sipping a drink. His face had been burned, but Hunter had no interest in the details.

"How the hell did you get in my house?" he demanded. "Did my wife let you in?"

"I don't believe she's home," Madison said. "Your son let me in."

"Tripp is here? Where?"

"Downstairs in the garage," Madison said.

"Don't move," Hunter said. He went to his desk and pushed the intercom button on his phone. "Tripp. Get your ass up here."

"That's not going to happen," Madison said. "Tripp is . . ." A self-satisfied smile spread across his face. "Tripp is all *tied up* for the moment."

Hunter sat down and crossed his left leg over the right so that his hand was inches from the .38 in his ankle holster. "I don't know what's going on, but you better start talking fast and explain what you're doing here."

"I'm here to let you know that you were right."

"About what?"

"Everyone has his price, Mr. Alden."

"And every generous offer has its expiration date, Mr. Madison. Yesterday I was willing to pay you twenty thousand dollars to let me know when you heard from my—"

"Shut up," Madison snapped. "I'm not talking about the twenty thousand. I'm talking about the hundred million,

Leviticus."

Hunter froze. "You're Cain?"

"I'm done being Cain. All I am now is your son's teacher from Barnaby Prep, and I'm sorry to tell you that Tripp is doing poorly in economics. I understand he's asking a billion dollars, and all he's offering in return is a promise that he won't blow the whistle on you. A *promise*? From a teenage kid who hates everything you stand for? Caveat emptor, Mr. Alden. I, on the other hand, can make you a *guarantee* for a lot less money."

"I've heard your offer. A hundred million."

"That was Tripp's idea. We were going to split it fifty-fifty, but since he's no longer my partner, I'll happily take my fifty. But the sale ends tomorrow night at 9:01—a minute after the Fed opens for wire transfers."

Hunter rested his hand on the cuff of his pants. He could feel the gun on the other side of the fabric.

"Is that your plan?" Madison said. "Shoot me, run downstairs, shoot Tripp, then get rid of two bodies before your wife gets home for dinner? That's not you, Hunter. You're management, not labor."

Hunter moved his hand to the arm of the chair.

"It would be arrogant of someone in my tax bracket to give business advice to someone in yours," Madison said. "But the way I see it, you can give Tripp his billion and hope he doesn't change his mind once he's given it all away. Or pay me fifty million and get a lifetime guarantee. Tripp's lifetime."

Hunter reached over and picked up the picture of Marjorie and Tripp that had sat on his desk for fifteen years. He pondered it briefly, set it back down, and then looked up at Madison.

"I will give you twenty million dollars," he said. "That's my final offer. It expires in ten seconds."

"You drive a hard bargain, Mr. Alden," Madison said. "I accept your offer." He stood up and reached out to shake Hunter's hand.

"Fuck you," Hunter said.

A smile—more like a smirk of victory—spread across Madison's face. He withdrew his hand, took a step back, and exited the room.

Hunter sat in silence until he heard Madison leave through the front door. His eyes were still locked on the picture of Marjorie and Tripp. And then, without warning, it came. A flood of emotions that had been buried under years of cynicism and callousness welled up inside of him. Remorse. Regret. And, most of all, grief over the loss of his only child.

He stood, walked to the bar, grabbed the three-thousand-dollar bottle of Richard Hennessy, and returned to his chair.

Still staring at the picture, he tilted the bottle to his lips and took a long swallow. And another. And another, until he finally reached out to turn the photograph facedown on his desk.

But he couldn't.

All he could do was drain the bottle dry . . . until the only thing he felt was numb.

Chapter 67

"IT WAS A dark and stormy night," Kylie said as she navigated the Maybach uptown.

"How about knocking off the comedy and focusing on your driving?" I said.

"For God's sake, Zach, lighten up. And how about you focus on the fact that I *am* focusing on my driving?"

To her credit, she was. The snow, light and feathery a few hours ago, was now wet and nasty. Patches of black ice collected on the roadway like so many land mines, but for once Kylie was managing to keep her *Smokey and the Bandit* gene under control.

She stopped for a red light at 79th Street and Madison. "Taking one car was stupid," she said. "Did you think about how we're going to get back from Alden's house?"

"I'm a policeman," I said. "I'll call 911. I'm riding with you because I had visions of you pulling into the garage, shutting the door, and ransacking the place while I'm outside in the chase car kicking myself for trusting you."

"You really think I'd do that?"

"Not usually, but I know you, Kylie. Right now you've got this case between your teeth like a dog on a porterhouse, and you're already on shaky ground with Cates. I'm just trying to protect you from yourself."

The light turned green. She drove to 81st Street, turned left, and stopped a few doors away from Alden's town house.

"Which one of these buttons do you think opens the garage door?" she said, looking up at a control panel above the rearview mirror.

Before I could say "I have no idea," the garage door started to go up. "You got it," I said.

"What do you mean 'You got it'? I haven't pushed anything yet."

The garage door opened wide, and light flooded the interior.

"Holy shit," Kylie said.

"Holy shit" was an understatement. There, sitting in the spot reserved for Alden's dream car, was a beat-up old clunker, a blue van—*the* blue van. And standing behind it, lashing the rear doors together with a bungee cord, was our kidnapper-killer, Ryan Madison.

I bolted from the car, drew my gun, and started running toward him, yelling as loud as I could. "NYP—" Before I could get to the "D," my left foot hit metal. Maybe a manhole, maybe a road plate—all I know is it was as slick as a brass fire pole, and half a second later I was on my ass in a pile of snow and road grime.

It may have been the luckiest accident of my life, because as soon as I hit the ground, Madison fired a shot directly at where I had been standing.

I crawled through the slush and got behind a parked car. My gun was in my hand, and I could see Madison standing in a pool of light, but I knew better than to fire. One mistake and the first question they'd ask at the inquiry would be, "Why would you discharge your weapon at a private home in a howling snowstorm?"

Kylie was out of the car and crouched behind the open door. She also had a gun in her hand that I knew she was too smart to use. "NYPD," she yelled. "You're surrounded. Don't move."

He moved. Fast.

He scrambled into the van, threw it in reverse, and skidded onto the street. He turned the wheel hard, hit the gas again, bounced off a parked car, and fishtailed toward Fifth Avenue.

"Get in," Kylie screamed, diving behind the wheel. I slogged my way back into the Maybach.

"Hang on," she said, giving it gas. The tires spun, then caught, and we pitched forward. The van turned left on Fifth Avenue just as the light went from yellow to red.

Kylie hit the horn, ran the light, skidded into the turn, and managed to get the car under control just before we hopped the curb and plowed into the Metropolitan Museum of Art.

"This is definitely not an all-weather car," she said. "Don't worry. I'll get the hang of it."

I grabbed my radio. "This is Detective Zach Jordan. My partner and I just took fire from a private residence at Two Eight East Eight One. Send units to secure the building. Shooter is on the run in a blue Dodge van heading south on Fifth Avenue at Eight Zero Street. Need all available units to cut him off south- and eastbound. Advise responders that officers in pursuit of shooter are in a civilian vehicle, a black limo."

"Damn it, Zach," Kylie said. "Why did you have to call it in so fast?"

"If we're lucky, there's a unit that can stop him before he gets to the transverse. Why wouldn't I call it in?"

"Because the last thing we need is a bunch of cowboys in blue uniforms slipping and sliding all over the place like they're chasing O.J. down the 405. We'll be lucky if they don't all pile up like a demolition derby at a county fair."

"I'm soaking wet from my ass to my elbow, and the last thing *I* need is a partner who wants to do it all on her own and second-guesses every goddamn decision I make. So why don't you back off and take out some of that pent-up hostility on the son of a bitch who just tried to kill me?"

"Sorry," she mumbled. And even though I could barely hear it, I was pretty sure she meant it.

She gunned the engine, and the custom-built limo lurched forward in hot pursuit of the junkyard van.

Smokey and the Bandit rides again.

Chapter 68

"THIS BEAST IS like the world's most expensive toboggan," Kylie yelled as we went slip-sliding through one of the most expensive zip codes in the city. "For a million bucks you'd think they'd include four-wheel drive."

We were less than a block behind the van, but I could barely make out the taillights through the snow. And then at 76th Street they disappeared.

"Son of a bitch killed his lights and pulled in front of that bus," Kylie said.

"Get in front of him," I said. "Cut him off."

"This damn car doesn't have lights or sirens either," Kylie said. She sped up to pass the bus and leaned on the horn. Big mistake. New York City bus drivers don't appreciate horn blowers—especially assholes driving limos.

The bus went faster, and the driver looked down and gave us the finger. We were side by side, and I rolled down my window to flash my badge. But it's hard to imagine that the maniac in the rich-boy car is a cop, and the driver must have figured I was going to reciprocate with my own finger, so he steered the bus into our lane.

Kylie pulled to the left, and just as we sailed past the intersection of 72nd and Fifth, we heard the crash. It took only a second to process that it wasn't us, and it wasn't the bus. It was the van.

Madison had turned right, smashed through a sawhorse, and was heading west through Central Park.

Kylie hit the brakes, and the car did a complete 360. She threw it in reverse, backed up half a block, and barreled through the 72nd Street Inventor's Gate entrance to the park, maneuvering around the chunks of sawhorse that were scattered across the roadway.

The van was still moving, but the bungee cord hadn't survived the crash through the barrier. The rear doors were open.

With our high beams on, all we could see in front of us were the two doors swinging wildly in the swirling snow. Then Kylie dimmed the lights, and we had a clear view inside the van. Tripp Alden, arms and legs tied, was struggling to work his way to the open doors.

She moved into the left lane and pulled alongside the van.

"What are you doing?" I said.

"I was going to ram him from behind," she said, "but if the kid falls out, I'll run right over him."

We took the curve onto the East Drive, and we were only inches from the van when Madison pulled his wheel to the left and smashed into the Maybach's right fender.

"Back off him," I yelled as Kylie managed to steer through the impact. "I'm calling it in. We can have every exit to the park shut down in thirty seconds."

"You can close off the vehicle exits," she said, "but if we lose him, he'll abandon the car and hop over any wall from here to 110th Street."

She pulled alongside the van again, and this time Madison turned hard to the right, jumped the curb, and hopped onto the lawn, which in July is lush and green, but in the dead of January glistened like glass in the headlights.

The van spun out of control and went fishtailing down a rolling hill. The Maybach didn't do any better. Kylie hit the brake, but there was nothing for the tires to grab on to, and we whizzed down the icy slope like a million-dollar hockey puck.

Our car was heavier than the van, and we were gaining ground as we moved downhill faster. We could see Tripp clearly now. He had twisted his body sideways and inched his way to the rear. The doors had stopped swinging. With gravity pulling them one way and the wind blowing them the other, they were sticking straight out like fins.

Tripp rolled to his right, then left, then right again trying to build up momentum.

"He's coming out," I yelled.

And out he came. With one final roll, he toppled out of the van directly into the path of his father's car.

Kylie pulled the wheel to the left, missing him by inches. As far as I could tell he'd be all right. But the Maybach wouldn't.

As a kid I'd been to this section of the park hundreds of times. It's the best place in the city to sail model boats.

"We're headed for the drink," I yelled as we bore down on Conservatory Water, the landmark oval boat pond inspired by those that grace the parks of Paris.

"It's January," Kylie said. "They drain it for the winter. There is no water."

The van, only twenty feet ahead of us, disappeared

into the empty boat pond. Seconds later, the Maybach followed, and we nose-dived into the pitch-black concrete hole.

We hit hard. The front bumper took the impact, and in a nanosecond the air bags exploded.

On the plus side, the nylon bag that exploded from the dashboard kept my skull from crashing through the windshield. But I felt like I'd been kicked in the face by a mule. My ears were ringing from the blast, my lungs were filled with chemical dust, and my brain was still reeling.

But I was alive. And so was Kylie.

"Zach," she said, her nose bloodied, her breathing labored. "Madison at eleven o'clock."

Our headlights were still working, and I could make out the van on its side to our left. Madison was pulling himself up out of the passenger window.

"He's getting away," she said, fumbling to find her seat belt button release.

She was wrong. Madison wasn't trying to escape. He jumped off the van and charged toward us, gun in hand.

He was enraged, his face bloodied as he staggered up to Kylie's window, and pointed the gun directly at her head.

As a cop I can think of no greater failure than

watching helplessly as someone murders your partner in cold blood. Neither of us was wearing a vest, but had I been on my feet I know I'd have thrown myself between Kylie and the bullet without giving it a second thought.

But I was still harnessed to my seat, unable to move. The deflated air bag clung to my chest, and I shoved my hand under it, desperately grabbing for my own gun. It was too little too late. Kylie was trapped.

She couldn't move, and Madison couldn't miss.

He took one step back, screamed something unintelligible into the wind, and pulled the trigger.

Chapter 69

I BRACED MYSELF for the explosion, knowing that there were only two possible outcomes. Either Madison would kill us both with a single shot, or he'd take Kylie down and use his next bullet on me.

But there was a third possibility I'd never even considered.

Madison fired, and the window blossomed into a giant spiderweb pattern. But the glass didn't shatter. He fired two more times, but the bullets didn't penetrate.

And then I remembered the casual remark Silas Blackstone had dropped when he was trying to impress us with how rich his client was. This was no run-of-the-mill four-hundred-thousand-dollar set of wheels. This one was tricked out with armor plate and bulletproof windows.

Hunter Alden's Maybach had saved our lives.

Ryan Madison was as surprised as we were. Realizing he now had two very pissed off cops on his hands, he did the only thing he could do.

He ran.

There was a set of stairs on the east side of the pond, but it was at least two hundred feet away, and the pond floor was patched with ice. So he opted for the same spot where his van had gone airborne, firing over his shoulder as he ran.

I radioed for backup, and the two of us got out of the car and crouched behind our steel-plated doors.

"He needs both hands to get up and over the side of the pond," I said. "As soon as he holsters his gun, I'm going after him. You cover me."

Madison fired another shot in our direction.

"And if possible, I'm going to try to take him alive," I said.

"Now," she said.

Madison had reached the western edge of the concrete pond, tucked his gun into his jacket, and put his hands on the stone wall.

I darted out from behind the door and ran toward him.

I thought he'd have trouble getting over the wall,

but he pushed up, threw one leg over the side, and within seconds he was standing on the edge of the pond, pointing his gun right at me.

I hit the ground, and a bullet splintered the concrete less than a foot from my head.

Kylie fired at him, and the shot went wide.

"You missed, bitch," he screamed.

I knew better. Kylie was the best shot in our class at the academy. Her shot hadn't missed. She was trying to draw his fire so I could get to him.

I could hear the sirens and see the flashing lights making their way into the park from East 72nd Street.

"Madison," I yelled. "You're surrounded. Throw down the gun."

"I've seen too many movies, Jordan," he yelled. "Throwing down the gun makes for a piss-poor ending."

He fired at me. Once again the bullet missed by inches. I rolled.

"Zach?" Kylie yelled.

All she said was my name, but we'd been partners long enough for me to put it in context.

"Do it," I screamed.

Kylie stood up and fired over the door of the Maybach. The bullet made a neat little hole directly under Madison's jaw, and a much bigger, much messier one in the back of his skull.

A gurgling growl came from his throat, and for an instant he remained frozen, arms in the air. Then his body pitched forward over the side of the boat pond and landed facedown on the cold stone bottom.

It reminded me of the very first time I'd seen Ryan Madison. He'd been jumping up and down on a desk in his classroom, fighting off imaginary airplanes. Then, mortally wounded, the great King Kong had gently set his captive Barbie doll on the desk, and fallen to the floor.

I looked over at Kylie. She was walking toward me, the flashing strobes of an army of cop cars bouncing off her blonde hair. Once again it was beauty killed the beast.

"Let's go," she said.

"Go? Kylie, you just killed a man. It was a clean shoot, but you can't walk out and—"

"Zach, listen to me. I'm going to be doing paperwork on this mess for a week and a half, but I'll be damned if I'm starting now. Tripp Alden is still on the run. As far as I'm concerned, he's a fugitive, and we're bringing him in." She headed for the edge of the pond. "You're either with me, or you're not," she yelled over her shoulder. "You decide."

I followed. "One question," I yelled back. "How do you propose we find him?"

"First thing I'm going to need," she said, hoisting herself over the side of the pond, "is a car."

Chapter 70

"WE'RE NOT MAKING the same mistake twice," Kylie said, passing up three sedans until she spotted an empty SUV with the motor running. "Get in."

We were moving before I had the door closed. Two cops were standing in the cold, waiting for orders. Kylie hit the brakes and rolled down the window. "Is this your vehicle?" she asked.

"No, ma'am," one said.

"Detective MacDonald. Find out who this belongs to and tell them I swapped cars with them. Mine's at the bottom of the pond."

She made a U-turn while I put out a BOLO on Tripp Alden and dispatched units to Hutch's apartment and Lonnie's.

"I don't care how many politicians Hunter Alden has in his back pocket," Kylie said. "He's hid behind all that power and privilege long enough. I'm not taking his shit anymore."

"Damn it, Kylie, who did you think you'd serve and protect when you signed on to Red? Boy Scouts? Kidney donors? Hunter Alden is a despicable human being, but he makes more money, pays more taxes, and generates more jobs than Joe Six-Pack. If you can't handle him, you're in the wrong outfit."

She stopped at a light. Some people cry when they're in pain. Kylie MacDonald breathes fire. "Ryan Madison put a gun six inches from my head and pulled the trigger. That wouldn't have happened if Hunter Alden hadn't lied to us. I'll get him, Zach. I swear to God I'll get him."

"I want to nail him for something as much as you do, but coming on like a storm trooper and 'not taking his shit' is not an option."

We drove the rest of the way in silence. There were two units from the One Nine parked outside Alden's town house. The senior cop approached us.

"He's in there, Zach. He says his kid's not home, and I can't search the place."

I leaned on the intercom button until the gate opened. By the time Kylie and I got to the top of the stairs, Alden had stepped out and was sneering at us like we'd breached the perimeter and were planning to shove takeout menus under his door. "Where's my son?" he demanded.

"We were about to ask you the same thing," Kylie said.

"How the hell would I know?"

"He was in your garage a half hour ago," she said.

"And I was upstairs with a goddamn murderer trying to keep Tripp from being his next victim. I was doing what I had to do to keep my son alive. If the two of you had done your job, I wouldn't be in that situation."

Kylie didn't back off. "Our job? You mean like find your son's kidnapper? We might have had better luck if you'd have bothered to report him kidnapped."

"Don't make me the heavy, Detective. *'Call the cops, and we kill your kid.'* What was I supposed to do? I thought I might be dealing with the Russian Mafia, but it turns out to be his pissant teacher, Madison. When he finally showed up, I did what I do best. I closed a deal with him. The plan is for him to come back tomorrow, and I'll wire him the money."

"Mr. Madison's plans have been changed," Kylie said. "He won't be coming back."

"You have him in custody?"

"He's on his way to the morgue. Your car was

involved in the police action. It's going to take a few more days before you get it back."

"Screw my car. Where is Tripp?"

"I believe that question has been asked and answered," Kylie said.

Clearly my attempt at sensitivity training with Kylie had failed. I decided to step in.

"Mr. Alden," I said, "we did our best to apprehend Madison alive, but he opened fire on us. First from your garage, and again when we followed him to the park. In the middle of it all, Tripp managed to escape. He took off. We were hoping he came home."

"He didn't. Now you can stop hoping, get out, and take your friends with you," he said, pointing at the two squad cars in front of the house. "They're blocking my driveway."

He took a step back and slammed the door.

My cell rang, and I checked the caller ID. "Cates," I said.

Kylie threw her hands up, and I took the call. "Yes, boss."

"I'm standing here with a dead prep school teacher, a private automobile that will probably cost the taxpayers half a million dollars to restore, and a hundred reporters behind the yellow tape all clamoring to know who gets credit for this mess."

"Captain—"

"I'm not finished, Jordan. What if the PC shows up and asks me why two officers under my command shot a suspect and went AWOL?"

"Captain, you can tell the PC that we were in pursuit of two suspects. We caught one, but we couldn't stop to file a report. We had to keep going."

"*You* tell him. Because if he shows up and you're not here, I'm telling him you left the scene so you could look for a better job with Traffic Enforcement."

"We're on the way, Captain."

"One more thing, Jordan. Did you search the blue van after you ran it into the pond?"

No. We raced out of the park because my partner was still reeling from having a gun to her head, and she was hell-bent on confronting Hunter Alden.

"No, ma'am," I said. "The first responders were almost on the scene, so we left the van to them. Can you tell me what was in there, or do I have to wait to read about it in tomorrow's paper?"

"I'd rather wait till you and your partner get here," Cates said. "I want to see the look on your faces when you find out what you missed."

Chapter 71

NOTHING ATTRACTS A crowd like a shoot-out, and by the time we got back to the park, it was lit up like a movie set and filled up with cop cars, fire engines, EMS wagons, news crews, and a mammoth Ford 4400 Jerr-Dan tow truck.

And Cates.

"IO 52," she barked as soon as she saw us coming. "Or is that another departmental regulation you'd like to break?"

Interim Order 52 requires every officer who discharges a weapon resulting in injury or death to take a sobriety test. No cop has ever flunked it, and most cops find it demeaning, which is probably why Cates yelled it loud enough for at least a dozen cops to hear it.

"She's more pissed at me than she is at you," Kylie

mumbled as we took NYPD's version of a perp walk to a van, where someone from Internal Affairs was waiting to give us each a Breathalyzer test.

We were declared alcohol-free and reported back to Cates, who was with Chuck Dryden behind a screen he used as a paparazzi deterrent.

"This was in the van," he said, pointing at a yellow polyethylene case that was crusted with frost. "It's Tripp Alden's camera case."

As soon as he said it, I knew the box wouldn't contain camera equipment. "Peter Chevalier," I said, more statement than question.

Dryden snapped the latches and opened the top, and my eyes locked on the severed head.

"It's been stored at below-zero temperatures for days and had only recently been removed from the deep freeze," Dryden said.

"And I'll bet Hunter Alden was the one who kept it on ice," Kylie said. "Madison was pulling out of his garage when we spotted him."

"I know where you're going with this," Cates said, "but unless you saw Alden hand him the head, there's no way you can tie him to it."

"Were there any prints on the box?" I asked.

"Wiped clean."

"Doc, we've got the killer, and you've already

autopsied Chevalier's body," Cates said. "How long until we can get this to the family so they can make funeral arrangements?"

"Not long. I can release it in a few hours."

Dryden started to leave, then turned back and looked at Cates. "For what it's worth, my team inspected the terrain," he said, pointing at the area where Kylie had lost control of the Maybach. "It's like a luge track. Once that car came over the hill, there was nothing the detectives could have done. They were at the mercy of Mother Nature."

"And now they're at the mercy of Mama Cates. This goes way beyond forensics, Dr. Dryden, but I'm sure the detectives appreciate the fact that you tried to cover their asses."

Chuck gave us a shrug and left.

"Captain," I said.

"Save the explanations for another day," Cates said. "I've learned my lesson with you two. Let the infractions pile up until we close the case. Then I can waste my time trying to figure out how to get you two to play by the rules."

Her cell phone rang, and she jumped into her car so she could be heard over the howling wind.

Kylie and I just stood there.

"I have no regrets," she said.

"You never do."

"What's your problem?" she demanded.

"Nothing."

"Zach, there's only one person who can tell us what we need to know to charge Hunter Alden with a crime, and that's Tripp. So, yeah, I made the call to chase after him instead of hanging around here until some asshole from IA could tell me that I haven't been drinking. I didn't twist your arm to go with me, so don't give me the same old thou-shalt-not-break-the-rules crap I've heard a dozen times from Cates and every CO I ever worked for."

"Kylie, I'm cold, I'm wet, and I feel like shit because I left the scene to chase a ghost instead of staying behind and finding that camera case. But seeing as you saved my life tonight, I'll spare you the sermon, and just say thank you for shooting Madison before he shot me."

She was quiet for a few seconds, and then a small smile crept across her face. "All that wind and snow . . . It was a hell of a shot," she said. "Did I ever mention I was first in my class at the academy?"

I couldn't stop myself from smiling back. "Not since last night."

The car door opened, and Cates leaned out. "Get in," she said.

We did, and her driver headed out of the park.

"That was Patrice Chevalier," Cates said. "I had left him a message that we found Peter, and he called back to thank me."

"Where are we going now?" Kylie said.

"Back to the house."

"Captain, with all due respect, we're trying to find Tripp Alden. Sitting around the office isn't the best way to get that done."

"Tripp Alden is meeting us there," Cates said. "Dr. Chevalier is bringing him in."

In a rare moment of self-restraint, Kylie sat there and didn't say another word for the rest of the ride.

Chapter 72

I READ TRIPP Alden his Miranda rights, and as soon as I got to "You have the right to consult an attorney," he cut me off.

"Yeah, I want one. I called my grandfather before I turned myself in. He's sending a guy."

The *guy* turned out to be Dennis Woloch, known in legal circles as the Warlock because of his uncanny ability to cast a spell over juries. Woloch only took on two types of clients: the filthy rich, who could afford his astronomical fees, and the dirt poor, for whom he'd work pro bono just so he could dominate the six o'clock news with his litigating brilliance.

Grandpa Alden wasn't taking any chances. He'd sent a flamethrower to a marshmallow roast.

"Detectives," Woloch said, "are you charging my client with anything?"

"Your client was the victim of a crime," I said. "One which we believe we've resolved. But we have a few questions about the kidnapping."

Woloch nodded and allowed Tripp to recount what we'd already heard from Gittleman and Lonnie. When he got to the part where Augie showed up, I asked the obvious. "Why would you stun-gun your rescuer and then take off?"

"Don't answer that," Woloch said. "And you, Detective, should not be asking a boy who was traumatized by a madman to explain his reaction when a total stranger walked into his prison cell and *supposedly* rescued him. At that point my client trusted no one. Move along."

"After you left the school, you didn't call your family," I said. "Instead you decided to call your kidnapper. Then you met him at a diner, where he killed Silas Blackstone."

"That's not a question," Woloch said. "And even if it could ever lead to one, it's irrelevant, because you have your facts wrong. My client did not *call his kidnapper*. The man who abducted him wore several disguises and only spoke through a voice modifier. That is not who Tripp called. No, in his fear and desperation he reached out to the one person he felt he could turn to: his mentor, Ryan Madison."

"Do you know anything about the murder of Peter Chevalier?" Kylie asked.

Tripp shook his head.

"Tell us about the flash drive you gave him."

Warlock slapped both palms on the table. "This interview is over."

"Not if we charge him with assault on a school employee engaged in the performance of his duties," Kylie said, lobbing her last marshmallow at the roaring flamethrower.

The Warlock laughed loud and hard. "I thought I was talking to the Red team—an elite unit trained to resolve issues for people of wealth and influence," he said. "And you plan to slap the heir to the Alden fortune with a misdemeanor? That smells like the Brown team to me. Write the boy an appearance ticket, Detective, and we'll be on our way."

He stood up. Tripp didn't move.

"Come on," Woloch said. "I'll drop you at your grandfather's house."

"Just a minute," Tripp said. He looked at us. "You caught him, right? Madison—is he . . . ?"

"We tried to take him alive," I said. "But we couldn't."

"Thank you," he said. "He killed Peter, and I know I was next. Thanks."

He stood up and followed Woloch out of the room.

Cates had watched it all from behind the two-way. She walked in as soon as they left. "Dr. Chevalier asked me to thank you as well. He's flying back to Haiti as soon as the snow lifts in the morning."

"Did you hear the last thing Tripp said?" Kylie asked.

"He thanked you for saving his life," Cates said.

"Hunter Alden told us that he agreed to pay Madison. The plan was to wire the money to him tomorrow."

"So?"

"So why would Tripp think Madison was going to kill him if his father was a day away from paying the ransom?"

"I don't know," Cates said. "What I do know is that you wrecked a million-dollar car and you caught a murderer. On balance I'd say you had a good day."

"Not good enough," Kylie said. "Hunter Alden is dirty, and we're trying to figure out at what."

"Welcome to Red," Cates said. "Some of our best customers are dirty, but your job is to be there for them when they're victimized, not spend your time trying to figure out what felonious and immoral shit they're doing under the radar."

"Wow," Kylie said. "That's . . ."

"Cynical?" Cates said. "Yeah, that happens to a lot of cops. The system has a way of beating you down. But don't worry, MacDonald. You're immune."

"Why's that?"

"You can't get frustrated by the rules if you refuse to play by them."

Chapter 73

"I NEED FOOD and alcohol, not necessarily in that order," Kylie said as soon as Cates left. "You game?"

I've arrested a lot of smart people for doing stupid things, and sometimes I want to grab them and say, "What the hell were you thinking?" But I already know the answer. People don't always think.

Which is why twenty-four hours after Cheryl walked out of my apartment, and fifteen hours after Gerri warned me that Kylie was playing fast and loose with her marriage and my libido, I decided that a third night of drinking with my ex-girlfriend was just what the doctor ordered.

"Hell yeah," I said.

I took a hot shower, found some dry clothes in my locker, and we got a patrol car to run us over to T-Bar Steak and Lounge on Third Avenue.

"I've never worked a kidnapping case," Kylie said once we had ordered our food and had drinks in our hands. "But I've seen a lot of kidnapping movies. You know the difference between cinema and the real thing?"

"I'm going to take a wild guess and say popcorn."

"I'm serious, Zach. In a film, when the family gets their kid back, there's always all this hugging and kissing and crying, but Hunter and Janelle Alden didn't even show up at the station to say hello. Two people were murdered. Their son escaped alive. Where was the tearful reunion?"

"Janelle wasn't home when we were there, so she might not even know yet. And Hunter's version of a happy ending may be hugging and kissing the money he wound up not paying the kidnapper."

"Or it's not a happy ending for Hunter, because whether Tripp was part of Madison's blackmail scheme or not, he still has plenty on his old man."

"I thought we had a deal," I said. "No cop talk at the dinner table."

"No problem," she said, taking a generous swallow of her Jack and Coke. "What else can we talk about? Have you heard from Cheryl today? How about that madcap husband of mine showing up unannounced? The divorce lawyer asked for a fifteen-thousand-dollar retainer. Do you think I should—"

"You win. Let's talk about the case."

"Cates thinks it's closed," Kylie said.

"She's right. It was a double homicide, and we nailed it. In the process, we broke up the very kidnapping we were told to stay away from."

"And Tripp Alden was damn lucky that we didn't listen."

"Unfortunately, they don't give out medals for not listening, or you'd have a closet full. Kylie, I know you. You don't want to *talk* about the case. You have a theory, and you're trying to lead me down the path so I can get there on my own, but my brain is fried, so lay it on me before I add alcohol."

"Okay. I think Tripp Alden was right. Madison was going to kill him, and I think his life is still at risk."

I set my drink on the table. She had my undivided attention.

"Track with me," she said. "Madison goes to the house, and Hunter agrees to pay the ransom. His son is tied up in the van. Why doesn't he go downstairs and give the kid some peace of mind that he's going to be set free?"

"Because he sucks as a dad."

"Right, so here's a different spin on the same question. He's just coughed up millions to save Tripp's life. The last thing he needs is for the kid to try something stupid and get himself killed. So why didn't Hunter go downstairs to the garage and tell Tripp to chill for twenty-four hours? He's a smart businessman. Wouldn't that have been the smart way to protect his investment?"

She'd led me down the path, and I hated where it was headed. "Are you saying that the kid knows too much, and Hunter wanted him dead?"

"Not only wanted him dead, but was willing to pay Madison to do it. And he'd have gotten away with it. *Desperate father pays ransom, only to have the kidnapper renege on the deal and murder his son.*"

Before I could process her theory, my cell rang. It was Sergeant McGrath.

"Zach, it's Bob."

"If we're on a first-name basis, you need a favor. What do you want?"

"The key to Alden's car. They flatbedded it to the One Oh Five garage, but they can't start it without that little fob I gave you."

"Actually, you gave it to my partner."

"That's the favor. Make my life easy. You ask her for it."

"It's McGrath," I said to Kylie. "Do you still have the key to the Maybach?"

She dug into her pocket and dropped it on the table.

"Got it," I said. "And the good news is there's not a scratch on it. Send a uniform to T-Bar at Seven Three and Three, and it's all yours . . . Bob."

I picked up the key ring. It still had Peter's gold crucifix on it. "I think we should take this off and get it back to Patrice," I said.

I grabbed the cross and started to slide it off the ring. It was tight, so I put a little pressure on it. Too much pressure, and it broke into two pieces.

"Klutz," Kylie said.

"No, I think it's supposed to come apart," I said, holding it close to the flickering candlelight to get a better look.

The bottom leg of the cross had slid off like the sheath to a sword. Except that instead of there being a blade inside the sheath, there was a USB port.

"It's not your average crucifix," I said, handing it to Kylie. "This one's also a flash drive."

Chapter 74

"HALLELUJAH," KYLIE SAID, holding up the cross. "And I swear to God we're going to do this one by the book."

"Not a hundred percent," I said. "The book says we have to clear it with the captain and an ADA before we chase down a judge to sign a search warrant."

"I believe that rule is flexible," Kylie said, looking at me with a straight face. "Especially if it's a Saturday night, it's snowing, and you know that Cates will tear you a new one if she thinks you're making Alden the target of a witch hunt."

We wolfed down our dinner, returned the fob to McGrath, and made our way to West End Avenue, where Leah LaBreche, the on-call judge, was waiting for us.

"Sober as a judge" does not always apply at ten

o'clock on a Saturday night, but Judge LaBreche was a new mom, so she was awake, alert, and had a few questions before she'd sign.

"A flash drive?" she said. "At this hour? Why couldn't this wait till morning?"

Kylie launched into a rapid-fire explanation, throwing around phrases like "double homicide," "high-profile kidnapping," and "close friends of the new mayor," and ending with "Our commanding officer thought it was important enough to drive through a snowstorm to get your signature."

If Judge LaBreche had any further questions, she didn't get to them. A baby started crying, and her focus shifted immediately.

"It's my son Landon. He's teething," she said, taking the pen from Kylie.

She signed, and we left.

Lying about Cates could get us disciplined, but the search was now legal. Nothing we found could be suppressed.

"My place or yours?" Kylie asked as soon as the judge closed her door.

We had no idea what we were looking for, and we didn't know if we'd recognize it if we found it, but we knew we wanted someplace private if we did. We decided on my apartment.

I plugged the flash drive into my computer and double-clicked on it. None of the folders were locked. "God bless Irene Gerrity," I said. "She doesn't believe in passwords."

"Or she did," Kylie said, "but somewhere along the line she realized she'd never be able to remember them."

Irene had it all perfectly organized. Eight folders, each one labeled. I clicked on the one marked Phone Calls, and dozens of MP3 file icons popped up.

I played one.

"Mr. Joost. This is Leviticus."

I had no idea who Joost was, but Leviticus's voice was unmistakable. Hunter Alden. We listened to the rest of the call.

"It seems like an everyday stock deal," Kylie said, "but based on what Irwin Diamond taught us about insider trading, I'll bet Mr. Joost is somewhere in Switzerland, and the SEC will have no record of Leviticus or the transaction."

We played three more, but it was like looking at the ticker tape crawling along the bottom of the screen on CNBC. All the information is right there, but I didn't have the chops to make sense of it.

"Refresh my memory," I said. "Do you remember

the difference between puts and calls, or do I have to get Warren Buffett on the phone?"

"If you buy a put option, you're betting that the stock is going to go down," Kylie said. "If it does, you make money. A call option is the opposite. You bet on a stock you think will go up."

We listened to six more phone calls, but they only made things murkier. Alden wasn't betting on one stock. He was buying puts on a dozen different companies, and calls on a bunch of others.

I opened the folder marked Puts and clicked on a spreadsheet. Irene had it all organized—dates, prices, profits.

"Talk about the rich getting richer," Kylie said. "He made fifty-seven million dollars."

"Look closer," I said. "It's five hundred and seventy million. Every single stock he said would go down tanked."

"It has to be insider trading, but how did he know the inside dope about so many different companies?"

I opened the Calls spreadsheet. Sure enough, every stock Alden had bet on to go up had taken off, and he'd made another four hundred and forty-two million.

"It adds up to over a billion dollars profit," Kylie said. "In what—a month?"

I went back to the Phone Calls folder and organized the icons by date. The first one was time-stamped September 4, 2001, at 8:11 a.m. The last was October 12 at 11:09 a.m.

"It took him all of five weeks," I said. "Except . . ."

The words wouldn't come out. In fact, I was afraid if I opened my mouth I would throw up.

I tapped the computer screen. "Look at the dates," I managed to say.

Kylie followed my finger. "Oh God," she said.

Alden had bought furiously from the fourth through the tenth and started selling everything off on the seventeenth.

And, of course, there were no transactions on September eleventh or the entire week that followed. *America had been closed for business.*

We went back and looked at all the stocks Hunter had bet against. American Airlines, United, Merrill Lynch, Morgan Stanley, AXA—all the stocks that had plummeted after the towers came down. And then we looked at the list of stocks he had bet on. Raytheon, United Technologies, Northrop Grumman—and a list of other companies that America turns to when it gears up for war.

"Hunter Alden knew about 9/11 a week before it happened," Kylie said.

I put my hand to my mouth and nodded.

"Zach, it's beyond evil. He made a billion dollars exploiting what he knew, and then he was willing to let his son die to cover his tracks."

I still couldn't speak. I ran to the bathroom and managed to get there just in time to blow my T-Bar steak into the toilet.

Chapter 75

"EVERYONE WANTS TO get rich," Hutch Alden had told Hunter when the boy was only ten years old. "They start out poor, they reach for the moon, and if they fall on their asses, what the hell? They go back to being poor. You're different. You're starting out rich. Your job is to stay that way."

"How do I do that?" Hunter had asked.

"I've got twenty-six rules. I'll teach them to you."

Three decades later, Hunter Alden was finally putting rule number eighteen to the test. *Always have an exit strategy.*

He first started planning an escape route on September 12, 2001. He knew there would be an attack on American soil, but even he had been shocked by the magnitude. He knew if the day ever came when his connection to 9/11 was at risk of being leaked, he'd have to leave the country.

Today was that day, and as soon as the storm lifted, he was flying to Cuba. Permanently. The U.S. and Cuba had an extradition treaty that was over a century old, but with no diplomatic relations, it was as intimidating as a jaywalking ticket.

Hunter filled two suitcases with bare essentials. It was wrenching, but the alternative was unthinkable. Robert Vesco and Marc Rich had been smart enough to get out while they could. Bernie Madoff stuck around and got 150 years in prison. Hunter knew he had only two choices: spend his days on the beach in Playa Varadero, or in a cell in Otisville.

The doorbell rang. It was Findley.

"Crazy night to be going to the airport," he said.

"Did you tell my father I'm borrowing his car and driver?" Hunter said.

"Come on, sport," Findley said. "How far do you and me go back? I been covering your ass since before you figured out how to wipe it. You said keep it on the down low, so that's what I done. I didn't tell Mr. Hutch, I didn't tell Lorna, I didn't tell nobody. Like usual, it's just between us chickens."

He picked up the two suitcases that were sitting at the front door and put them in the trunk of the

Cadillac. Then he came back and walked Hunter to the car.

"And what's with the hush-hush, anyway?" Findley asked once he got behind the wheel. "You know your father would give you the shirt off his back. He don't care if I give you a ride to the airport."

"Hutch and I don't see eye to eye on this deal I'm going to close. It's just going to upset him if I tell him I'm going."

"Your secret's safe with me, sport," Findley said. "It's going to take us a good hour to get to HPN. Even then, you'll be lucky if they got a working runway. Why don't you take a load off and pour yourself a drink? I got a fresh supply of your favorite."

Hunter opened the bar and took out a bottle of Johnnie Walker Blue. "It's not as fresh as you think," he said. "Somebody's been at it."

Findley laughed. "That somebody was me. All I had was one lousy shot, and that was two days ago, so I'm safe to drive. But if you run out of booze before we get to Westchester, I'll find a liquor store and pick you up another one."

Hunter unscrewed the cap and poured the Scotch into a crystal rocks glass. He leaned back in his seat and tipped the glass, letting the whiskey slide down his throat and warm him from the inside.

Findley watched him through the rearview mirror. "From the expression on your face, it looks like I have me another satisfied customer."

Hunter took another swallow and felt the Blue magic working on his brain. "That's what I always liked about you, Findley," Hunter said. "You always took good care of me."

"That I did, sport. And we had a lot of good times together," Findley said, keeping one eye on the road and the other on the mirror. His mind flashed back to the six-year-old Hunter, laughing and singing as they drove off to kindergarten.

Hunter downed his drink, grabbed the bottle, and tried to refill his glass. His hand dropped to his side, and the bottle crashed to the floor.

Findley pulled the car over and turned around. Hunter Alden was unconscious on the backseat. The booze and the drugs had worked fast.

"I'm sorry, sport," Findley said, tears streaming down his cheeks. "You been like family to me. Always have. But not anymore."

Chapter 76

HUNTER ALDEN OPENED his eyes and strained to sit up, but a dozen thick rubber tarp straps lashed him to the table.

"Findley," he screamed.

No answer.

He stared straight up, turning his head left, and then right, as much as he could. The room was so big and the straps were so tight that he couldn't twist far enough to see the walls. Just a few recessed lights, set on dim. He tilted his chin to the ceiling and rolled his eyes back so he could look behind him.

And there, fifteen feet over his head, was a disco ball. It wasn't moving, but by shifting his gaze, he could watch the light reflect off the thousands of tiny mirrored facets. *Where the hell was he?*

"Findley," he called out again.

"Findley is not here," a voice said.

"Whoever you are, untie me," Hunter bellowed. "Now."

"I can't do that, Mr. Alden," the voice said.

"Show your goddamn face."

A tall figure wearing scrubs and a surgical mask stepped up and leaned over the table just enough so Hunter could look straight up at him. The man lowered his mask.

"You're Peter's brother," Hunter said.

"Patrice Chevalier. *Doctor* Patrice Chevalier."

"I don't know where I am, and I don't know how I got here, but get me the hell out of here."

"You're in a hospital in Brooklyn."

"A hospital?" Hunter said, jerking his eyes upward to the glitter ball.

"A makeshift hospital," Chevalier said. "Most of the time it is Klib Zanmi Ayisyen, a Haitian friendship club."

"Well, it's not coming off very freaking friendly. Cut me loose, you son of a bitch. I don't know what you want from me, but tying me down is not the smartest way to negotiate."

"My brother spent so many joyful nights here," Patrice said. "It's one of the few places in the city where people of the Haitian diaspora can come together and connect with their roots, their traditions, their culture."

"I was good to your brother," Hunter said. "I put a roof over his head, food in his belly, money in his pocket, and every time he had his hand out because there was a flood, an earthquake, or a goddamn cholera epidemic, I wrote him a check."

"Did you love him?" Patrice asked softly.

"What kind of a dumbass question is that?" Hunter said, pressing his body hard against the rubber bonds. "He was an employee. I treated him fair, paid him well—did he ever complain about me?"

"Tripp loved him."

"Is that why you're doing this? Madison is dead, so now Tripp recruited you to bleed money out of me?"

"I don't want your money."

"Then what do you want?"

"*Limyè!*" Patrice called out.

The room flooded with bright light, and two more people in full operating room attire entered. One man, one woman, both black.

"Oh Jesus, what are you doing?" Hunter said.

"I'm doing what I'm trained to do. Did you know that Peter paid for my medical school education?"

"Listen to me. I didn't have anything to do with his death. I swear."

"Of course you did. A single butterfly flapping its wings in one part of the world might ultimately cause a hurricane in another part of the world. It's called the butterfly effect. But you are not a butterfly, Mr. Alden. You are a bull. And the evil you do wreaks havoc and destroys lives around the globe."

"You're a goddamn doctor," Hunter screamed. "You're supposed to save lives, not kill people out of revenge."

"I abhor revenge, Mr. Alden. I believe as Gandhi said, 'An eye for an eye only ends up making the whole world blind.' But you are right about one thing. I am a doctor. My mission is to save lives."

"Now you're talking," Hunter said. "That's where I can help you. I can give you enough money to build a hundred clinics, save a million lives. I'll do whatever it takes to help."

"No you won't," Patrice said, his jaw tightening, his lips taut. "The world is filled with humanitarians. You are not one of them. You're a profiteer, Mr. Alden. Every disaster unleashed on humanity, natural or man-made, is just another opportunity for you to amass more money. You profited from New Orleans, Iraq, Indonesia, Fukushima, and, yes, Haiti. Project Gutenberg is not the only time you've capitalized on other people's misery. It's just the most horrific."

"Tell me what you want. Just name your price."

"I'm a physician, Mr. Alden, and when I see a cancer about to metastasize into vital, healthy organs, my job is to eradicate it." He pulled the surgical mask back over his face.

The nurse stood ready with three syringes: sodium thiopental, pancuronium bromide, and potassium chloride.

"As for your offer to subsidize our efforts in Haiti," Chevalier said as he administered the first of the three injections, "thank you, but we already have a benefactor."

Hunter's eyes drooped as the barbiturate slowed his heart and shut down his central nervous system.

"His name is Hunter Hutchinson Alden III. His friends call him Tripp," Patrice said, reaching for the second syringe, "but my brother was the only one who had any right to call him son."

Chapter 77

I WAS JOLTED from my sleep by the nerve-jangling sound of my cell phone and the life-affirming smell of fresh-brewed coffee. I looked at the clock: 5:27. I'm used to predawn phone calls, so another one didn't faze me, but the smell of coffee coming from my kitchen scared the crap out of me.

I answered the phone.

It was Cates. It took her less than fifteen seconds to tell me what I'd missed since I went to bed. I hung up and followed the aroma of dark roast. I desperately needed caffeine, but even more important, I needed to know who was in my kitchen.

"Good morning," Kylie said, standing at the counter, cracking eggs into a bowl. "Coffee's up."

"Thanks. Not to sound ungrateful," I said, pouring a cup, "but what are you doing here?"

"I spent the night here."

My brain was stuck somewhere between REM sleep and the rude-awakening phone call from Cates, and it struggled to put together the pieces of the puzzle that equaled last night. At 2:00 a.m., after twenty straight hours of chasing bad guys, dodging bullets, and getting smashed in the face by an air bag, I had crashed from exhaustion. That's all I remembered.

"I thought we had wrapped it up last night, and you were going home," I said.

"I didn't. I decided to spend the night here."

"Don't take this the wrong way, but . . ." I held back. My head wasn't clear enough to ask the question or deal with the answer.

"But what?" Kylie demanded. "Spit it out."

"Just wondering," I said. "Where did you sleep?"

"Oh, for God's sake, Zach, get over yourself. I'm still married, and even if I weren't, I'm not in the habit of crawling into bed with guys who smell of vomit. But if your girlfriend asks, you can tell her I slept on the couch for a couple of hours. The rest of the time I was on the Web, trying to figure out how we can hang Hunter Alden for what he did."

"I hate to tell you this," I said, "but we can't hang him."

"I know *we* can't. We have to bring in the Feds. What I was trying to scope out is which agency would be the best one to talk to: the SEC, FBI, Homeland. But I'm starting to lean toward the NYPD JTTF."

"Kylie, nobody can hang Hunter Alden. He's dead."

That stopped her in her tracks.

"Cates just called," I said. "He was murdered. They found his body covered with snow under the statue of the charging bull near Wall Street."

"*Wall Street?* Holy symbolism, Batman."

"I need a quick shower," I said. "Then we should head downtown."

"Do we have time for breakfast?" she said. "I was just about to scramble some eggs."

"I wouldn't eat anything if I were you."

"Why not?"

"Like I said, Alden's body was dumped under the statue. But his head is nowhere to be seen."

Kylie stared at me, wide-eyed. "Decapitated?"

"Cut off clean."

"Wow," she said. "Now we really can't hang him."

Chapter 78

ON ANY GIVEN summer day, the bronze sculpture of the charging bull is a magnet for thousands of tourists, most of whom commemorate their visit by posing next to it for a photo to show the folks back home.

But on this frigid Sunday morning, NYPD had cordoned off the seven-thousand-pound symbol of capitalism, and the only one snapping pictures was Chuck Dryden.

"Four bodies in four days," Kylie said when we got there.

"But only two heads," Dr. Cut And Dryden said, clicking off a few more shots of what remained of Hunter Alden. "If this keeps up, we're going to need a new category in the crime stats."

We knew him well enough to know he wasn't joking.

"TOD was between ten p.m. and two a.m.," Dryden reported. "Like the previous victim, he was decapitated postmortem, but Chevalier was jumped in a parking lot, and his head was hacked off with a rope saw. Alden was taken someplace where the killer wouldn't be rushed, and the head was removed with surgical precision."

I made a mental list of people who had motive and surgical skills. One name was all I could come up with.

"Have you recovered the head?" Kylie asked.

"No. The victim's wallet was still in his pocket, cash intact. I confirmed his ID with prints. But you located the last one. I'm sure you'll do it again."

I wasn't so sure.

The snow had stopped, and because commerce is a priority in our city, the roads in the financial district were plowed and ready for the opening bell Monday morning. We walked down Broadway, found a Starbucks, and solved Alden's murder before our coffee was ready.

"Patrice killed him," Kylie said.

"Unless there was an eyewitness, or he left damning forensic evidence, we'll never prove it," I said. "Let's bring him in and question him."

"Or at least shake his hand," Kylie said. "Although I doubt if he's still in this country."

"He's not going anywhere till the airports open. Let's find him."

We couldn't. Patrice didn't answer his phone, and his hotel said he had checked out the day before. There was only one other way to track him down.

We went back to Hunter Alden's house. Tripp answered the door.

"My mom and my grandfather are at the funeral home making arrangements," he said.

"Then we'll talk to you," I said.

He shrugged. "Let's go to my room," he said.

We followed him up to the third floor. It was a typical rich teenager's room. Just as unkempt and disorganized as you'd expect, only a hell of a lot bigger. We sat down in a cluster of director's chairs.

"We're sorry for your loss," I said.

"I'm not," Tripp said. "He was a really bad dude. Take my word for it."

"We're not here to judge the victim," I said. "We're here to catch his killer."

"I hope you're not going to ask me if he had any enemies."

"The first thing we have to do is fill out our report on how you wound up at the precinct safe and sound last night. Dr. Chevalier brought you in, and we'd like to ask him a few questions. Do you know where we can find him?"

"He's on his way back to Haiti."

"The airports are closed," I said. "All flights are grounded till noon."

"Commercial flights, yeah, but private aircraft have been flying out of Westchester since dawn," Tripp said. "I let Patrice use the family jet so he could take Peter's body back home."

So much for questioning anyone with surgical skills.

"Peter's funeral is Thursday," he said. "Patrice asked me to do the eulogy. I can go, can't I? I mean my lawyer said not to worry about the stun gun thing."

"Augie Hoffman isn't pressing charges, and after all you've been through the DA's office won't pursue it either," I said. "You can definitely go to Peter's funeral. And we're sorry for your loss—we know how much he meant to you."

"Thanks. At least I still have Patrice. After graduation I'm going down to Haiti and live with him."

"What about college?"

"You think any of the film schools I applied to are going to take me once they find out that my letter of recommendation came from a homicidal maniac?"

"Hell yeah," Kylie said. "They might even want to make a movie out of it."

"I've got a better movie idea," he said. "Teenager suddenly inherits billions of dollars and starts giving it away."

"Is that your plan?" I said.

"The only plan I have is to not be anything like my father. He dedicated his life to making money, and he didn't care who got hurt along the way. Now that it's mine, I'm going to try to use it to make up for the damage he did."

"That's very generous of you," Kylie said.

She forced a smile, but I could see by the look in her eyes that Tripp Alden had completely ruined her day.

Chapter 79

"NOW WHAT DO we do?" Kylie said as soon as we were back in the car.

"I don't know, but the best I can come up with is we think long and hard about turning that flash drive over to the Feds."

"Zach, do you have any idea how many cops I know who died on that day?"

"We all lost someone, Kylie, but crucifying Hunter Alden won't bring any of them back."

"So are we just supposed to keep our mouths shut? Not only did the man fail to prevent one of the most heinous crimes in the history of the world: he profited from it."

"What do you want to do? Prosecute him from the neck down?"

"He made over a billion dollars in blood money."

"You know that, I know that, and Tripp knows it. He's ready to start making reparations. The only thing we can do is blow the whistle, and if we do, I guarantee you the government will freeze every nickel Hunter Alden ever made. Tripp Alden won't have enough money to buy a cup of coffee."

"You don't know that for sure."

"Kylie, I am in uncharted waters. I don't even know if what we found on the flash drive is admissible evidence. We got the warrant without authorization, and the search wasn't connected to the case we were investigating. How long do you think it would take the Warlock to have it suppressed?"

"So we send it off to the Feds anonymously," she said. "I don't care if we get credit. Our job is to report a crime when we see it."

"It sounds like you suddenly decided to go by the book. You must have read it sometime after you lied your ass off to Judge LaBreche."

My phone rang. Cates.

"Mayor Sykes is looking for you," she said. "Drop what you're doing and meet her at Gracie Mansion."

"Do you know what it's about?"

"She didn't say, but the son of her biggest contributor was murdered five days into her term, so I'm guessing it's not a medal-pinning ceremony."

Mayor Sykes was downstairs when we got there, surrounded by at least a dozen happy, hyper kids who were running around, having the time of their young lives.

"It's not usually this crazy," Sykes said, "but it's my first Sunday in my new home, so I invited the whole family over for a mansion-warming party."

We followed her upstairs to her office. She closed the door, but she didn't sit down. It was going to be a short meeting.

"Thank you for solving a double homicide and for getting Tripp Alden out of it alive," she said. "Now I need to know how to deal with this Hunter Alden fiasco."

"Madam Mayor," I said, "there are a lot of people better qualified to give you political advice than we are."

"But you're the only two people I trust to tell me if NYPD has a shot at catching Hunter's killer. I have a press conference tomorrow, and I don't want to stand up there promising something you don't think we can deliver."

For the past six years, Muriel Sykes had been U.S. attorney for the Southern District of New York—the same job Rudy Giuliani held before he was elected mayor. Nobody knew the realities and the limitations of the criminal justice system better than she did.

"We have an idea of what went down, but nothing we could take to the DA to charge anyone," Kylie said. "Not now and probably not ever."

"In that case, I'll focus on the fact that we have tragically lost one of the giants who drive the financial engine of the city of New York, a pillar of the community, and a loving husband and father," she said. "I'll just leave out the fact that everyone hated the bastard's guts."

She opened the door. "Thank you for coming, Detectives. Grandma Muriel has to get back to her party."

"Madam Mayor," Kylie said. "One more question. In private."

Sykes shut the door. "Go ahead."

"We have a witness who says Hunter made a lot of money on some egregious insider trading," Kylie said. "She's suffering from Alzheimer's, but she claims there's a flash drive floating around somewhere that might have hard evidence."

"What's the question?" Sykes said.

"What if she's right, and what would we do if we found it?"

"Why the hell would you look? Hunter was a scumbag. I'd be surprised if he *weren't* involved in insider trading. But he's dead. Anything you found would only hurt Hutch Alden, and while you may be unqualified to give political advice, you're smart enough to know that politicians don't bite the hand that feeds them. They kiss ass."

There was a knock on the door, and Sykes opened it.

"I'm coming," she said to the two boys who were standing outside.

She turned back to us. "Let's just hope that if that flash drive really does exist, nobody ever gets their hands on it."

She and the kids headed down the stairs and left Kylie and me standing in the doorway.

"I'm still not sure what to do," Kylie said.

"We don't have to do anything today," I said. "Let's both sleep on it."

Kylie looked at me with a devilish grin.

I smiled back. "Separate apartments," I said.

Chapter 80

I DIDN'T SLEEP well. As much as I would have liked to expose Hunter Alden to the world, I knew in my heart that Tripp could do more good with the family fortune if I kept quiet. But I wasn't sure I could convince Kylie.

So when I walked into Gerri's Diner on Monday morning, all I wanted was a cup of coffee, a bowl of oatmeal, and a quiet place to sit and think. But that doesn't happen when everything you've been involved in over the past few days explodes across every media outlet in the city.

Prep school teacher kidnaps student, cop drives million-dollar car into the boat pond, decapitated billionaire's body left under the icon of prosperity—it all makes for spellbinding journalism.

As soon as I stepped through the door, a dozen

cops shouted my name, stood up and applauded, or came over to shake my hand.

Gerri handed me the *Times,* the *News,* and the *Post,* and escorted me to a booth in the rear. "You may be a jerk in your personal life," she said, "but you are one hell of a good cop."

I scanned the papers, and five minutes later Kylie walked into the same reception. But as soon as the applause died down, somebody with a sound effects app on his phone tapped a button, and we heard the screeching of brakes and a loud crash. Cop humor.

Kylie sat down across from me. "What's new in the papers?" she said.

"Apparently, we're not the only heroes," I said. "Hutch Alden really knows how to spin the facts to the family's advantage."

I slid the *Post* across the table and pointed to a headline on page three. "'Billionaire Gives Life to Save Son.' Read all about it."

She read the first paragraph and shoved it aside. "Why would you show me this? It only makes me want to crucify the bastard even more."

"Because I know you. Your mind is already made up. Where did you net out?"

She dug into her pocket and put the flash drive on

the table. "I'll go with the majority. We can't show this to anyone."

"Thanks," I said. "I was hoping that the mayor's little 'bite the hand that feeds them' speech would change your mind."

"Oh, I didn't buy that crap," Kylie said. "Spence is the one who changed my mind."

"You discussed this with Spence?"

"Relax. I didn't give him any of the details. Just the big picture. We had dinner last night. He may be an addict, but he's clean right now, and I've always trusted his moral compass."

"What did he say that convinced you?"

"He said, 'If you're going to turn Hunter Alden over to the Feds, then you may as well turn me in to NYPD. I was buying drugs illegally for months. You knew about it, and you were willing to look the other way. But a crime is a crime, Kylie. Arrest me.' Then he held up his hands so I could cuff him."

I laughed out loud. "What did you do?"

"I stuck him with my salad fork and called him an asshole."

"But you didn't arrest him."

"No, I'm too busy trying to rehabilitate him."

"Wow. You're an even bigger hypocrite than I realized."

"Zach, ever since we discovered what was on that flash drive, I wanted to bring Hunter Alden to justice. Even after he was dead, I was still obsessed with making him pay for what he did. But to quote my recovering addict husband, 'Justice doesn't necessarily make the world a better place. Compassion always does.'"

I picked up the flash drive. "We may not be showing this to anyone, but we still have to hold on to it, just to make sure Tripp holds up his end of the bargain."

"I know the perfect hiding place," Kylie said. "No one will ever find it, and we can get to it anytime we want."

A half hour later we were at the property clerk's office. I filled out the paperwork, he tagged and bagged the crucifix–flash drive, and the only evidence of Hunter Alden's crime against humanity left our hands and made the first step in a chain of custody that would transport it to its final resting place, a sprawling warehouse in Long Island City, where it would be stored for decades.

"Any regrets?" I asked Kylie.

"Not about this, but I wish you had never showed me that article in the *Post* about Hunter Alden. It pisses me off that the son of a bitch is going to get a hero's funeral."

"Just his body," I said. "But I'm pretty sure his head will rot in a pauper's grave in Haiti for all eternity."

Epilogue

FUNK

CHAPTER 81

THEY SAY POLICE work is hours of boredom punctuated by moments of sheer terror. The week after we wrapped up the Alden case was the most boring of my career.

And the most depressing.

I remember laughing at breakfast Monday morning when Kylie made the crack about sticking Spence with her salad fork, but it was now Friday afternoon, and I hadn't cracked a smile since.

Nothing felt good. For starters, when the storm hit the city, the Department of Sanitation hooked up plows to all its trucks, and for the next five days snow removal trumped garbage collection.

Within hours, the fresh coat of pristine white flakes turned into gray grunge, and by the time the trucks went back to normal service, the sidewalks were thick with slush, and the curbs were lined with more than fifty thousand tons of ripe garbage. And because it was early January, there were also more than a hundred thousand dried-up Christmas trees waiting to be recycled.

New York is a tough town, but once again, Mother Nature had kicked our ass.

Wednesday was Hunter Alden's funeral, and I slipped quietly into the back row of the Fifth Avenue Presbyterian Church. One by one, people of power and influence, all of whom I'm sure were in some way beholden to Hutch, took the podium to praise Hunter's wisdom, his business acumen, and of course his greatest sacrifice: laying down his life to save his son.

At one point I wanted to jump up and shout, "Look at the timeline, people. Tripp was in police custody six hours before Hunter was executed for his sins." But I figured if Tripp could sit there without saying a word, so could I.

I sat through five eulogies, but when Mayor Sykes got up to speak, I left. She was what she was, but I didn't have to watch.

The string of nightly dinners I'd had with Kylie ended at three. There was a lot of paperwork to do, but nothing to keep us working late, and she was out the door every night before six.

On Thursday I overheard her on the phone with her friend Janet Longobardi, the woman who had set her up with the divorce lawyer.

I couldn't pick up the entire conversation, but I caught enough to bum me out even more.

"He's really responding well to this Better Choices program. No, he's still living in Shelley's apartment, but we're talking about going away together for the weekend. The lawyer's on hold for now, but trust me, I'm keeping all my options open."

I wondered if that's what I'd become. An option Kylie was keeping open.

I hadn't expected to hear from Cheryl before Mildred's funeral on Tuesday, and I didn't. By Friday afternoon I still hadn't heard from her, and she hadn't come back to the office.

At 3:00 p.m. I was at my desk, staring at a half-eaten bagel that had been sitting there since breakfast, wondering how I was going to get through the weekend. And just when I was sure things couldn't get any worse, they did. The text came in from Cheryl.

Short notice. Long drive. Dinner at NWHC?
8 pm.

These days it's easy to end a relationship. You can

text. You can email. You can even do it in 140 characters or less on Twitter. But Cheryl wasn't the type to end things electronically. She's old-school. When she breaks it off with a guy, she has to do it to his face.

That's what the last-minute dinner invitation was. She wanted to meet me at a restaurant in Ulster County, and would I mind making the two-hundred-mile round-trip so she could dump me properly.

I texted her back.

Sure.

It seemed like a fitting way to end a miserable week.

Chapter 82

AS LONG AS I had to drive two hours for my farewell dinner with Cheryl, at least she picked a great restaurant. Her house in Woodstock was only five miles from New World Home Cooking, but having tasted chef Ric Orlando's food before, I knew it was well worth the hundred-mile trip.

I pulled into the NWHC parking lot ten minutes early and went inside. It's a big old rambling barn with art on the walls, music in the air, and a staff that never forgets a face. Liz Corrado, Ric's wife and partner, greeted me with a hug.

"Cheryl's not here yet, but you're in luck," she said, escorting me to the bar. "It's Free Drinks for Heroes Night."

"Just a club soda for now," I said, knowing I had to stay sober for the ride back to New York.

A few minutes later, Cheryl arrived wearing a white parka and a matching ski cap that set off her dark brown eyes, jet-black hair, and glowing caramel skin. She looked spectacular.

Then she spotted me, and her face lit up. She wrapped her arms around me and gave me a lingering kiss. Not what I had expected.

Liz showed us to our table, and Cheryl ordered a bottle of champagne. Also not what I had expected.

"What are we celebrating?" I asked.

"It's New Year's Eve."

"You should call the *New York Times*. Those idiots had January tenth plastered all over today's paper."

And then she said the last thing I ever expected. "I don't care what day it is for the rest of the world. You and I are starting the year all over again. The first ten days are getting a mulligan—like they never happened."

"No penalties?"

"I think we should analyze our game so we don't make the same mistakes again, but no penalties."

"I've already been analyzed by a woman who is as renowned for her psychological insight as she is for her flapjacks."

"Ah yes. And what did Dr. Gerri say?"

"I don't remember it verbatim, but something about me being a jealous asshole."

"Spot-on. And what did she say about me?"

"I believe her exact diagnosis was 'perfect in every way.' "

"I'm not. I've been holding out on you. I'm sorry." Her eyes watered up, and she turned away.

"Hey, whatever it was, it's over. You don't have to talk about it."

"Yes, I do," she said, dabbing at her eyes. "A few months ago Mildred called me. She knew Fred would be devastated when she died, and she asked if I could be there to help him get through it. I couldn't say no."

"Wow. I thought—"

"You thought I dropped everything for Fred," she said, "but I stopped loving him a long time ago. What I did I did for Mildred. I'm sorry. I feel terrible."

"Why? What you did was nothing short of noble."

"I should have told you, but you were under the gun with the Alden case, and once I knew Mildred only had a few days left, I couldn't think straight. I was going to call you after the funeral, but . . ."

"Fred needed you."

"He lost his mother and the baby he thought was his. I did the best I could, but now it's over." She let out a sigh. "I'm ready to move on. Are you?"

"Just tell me where we're going."

"I was thinking my house for the weekend."

"I didn't bring any clothes."

She smiled and let her tongue brush her lip. "What makes you think you'll be needing any?"

The waitress brought the champagne, opened it, and poured two glasses.

"I never congratulated you and Kylie on closing the Alden case," Cheryl said, lifting her glass. "Here's to two of the best cops on the force. What is she doing to celebrate this weekend?"

I reached across the table. "Damned if I know," I said, touching my glass to hers.

Her eyes told me it was the perfect answer.

ACKNOWLEDGMENTS

The authors would like to thank Undersheriff Frank Faluotico and Chief Civil Administrator John McGovern of the Ulster County NY Sheriff's Office, NYPD Detective Sal Catapano, Art McFarland of WABC-TV, Jon Berg, Mike Winfield Danehy, Marie Fleurimond, Gerri Gomperts, Maureen Villante, Suzanne Lorenz, Dr. John Froude, Dan Fennessey, Bob Beatty, Mel Berger, and Jason Wood for their help in making this work of fiction ring true.

14TH

DEADLY SIN

JAMES PATTERSON

THE WORLD'S BESTSELLING THRILLER WRITER

AND MAXINE PAETRO

Turn the page for an excerpt

I WAS BEHIND my desk that morning as light streamed through the Bryant Street windows and slashed across the squad room's linoleum floor.

My partner, Inspector Rich Conklin, was standing behind me to my right, and Chief of Police Warren Jacobi loomed impatiently over my left shoulder.

Jacobi had caught a couple of bullets in his leg and hip a few years ago and the injuries had aged him. He was fifty pounds overweight, his joints crackled and popped when he walked, and the pain had drained the fun from his salty sense of humor.

He grumbled, "Wait till you see this," and handed me a disc; then he sighed loudly as we waited for my "lazy-ass computer" to boot up.

I slid the disc into the drawer. The drive whirred, and then a video, time-dated 3:06 this morning, appeared on my screen. The camera had been positioned under flickering streetlights in a nearly deserted block in the notoriously sketchy Tenderloin. The footage was grainy, shot with a cheap surveillance cam of the type used more as a prop than as a tool for actually identifying people.

"That's Ellis Street," said Jacobi. "And that's what I call crud," he added, stabbing a sausage-like finger at three figures entering the frame. The men wore black billed caps and navy-blue Windbreakers with white letters reading SFPD across the back. They also held automatic handguns as they headed smartly toward an all-night check-cashing store with a yellow sign above the window reading Payday Loans. Checks Cashed.

I straightened in my seat, then turned to shoot a look at Jacobi.

What the hell is this?

"Balls on these bastards," he said. "Boxer. It's hard to make out. Can't you focus that picture?"

"What you see is what you get," I said.

For long, gritty seconds, we watched the cops advance along the dark commercial street lined with low, blocky buildings. Then they converged on the lit-up storefront and went through the door in single file.

A moment later, the lights inside the store went out. The door burst open and one of the "cops" ran out with a satchel under one arm, followed by the other two men, who were carrying similar bags.

Now that they were heading toward the camera, I looked for facial features, something that could be run through facial-recognition software.

But *the faces were all the same*.

Then I got it. The bad guys were wearing latex masks that completely disguised their features. Seconds after leaving the store, the men in the SFPD Windbreakers had run out of camera range.

Jacobi said, "Christ. Someone please tell me that these men are anything but cops."

I FELT SICKENED at what I had just seen on the footage. Like Jacobi, I hoped we were looking at holdup guys with a bad sense of humor, not actual police officers pulling off an armed robbery.

I asked Jacobi, "Were there any fatalities?"

"One," he said. "The owner wouldn't give up the combination to the safe until he was shot to pieces. He managed a few words with the EMTs before he bled out on the floor. He said cops did it. The kid who worked for him was interviewed on scene. He said there had been about sixty grand in the floor safe."

Conklin whistled.

Jacobi went on, "This is the second one like this. A few days ago, three men in SFPD caps and

Windbreakers robbed a Spanish market. A mercado. No one died, but it was another big score. It goes without saying, these guys have to be stopped or every man and woman in uniform is going to take shit for this whether we deserve it or not."

Conklin and I nodded, and Jacobi kept going.

"Robbery squad is already working the case, but I told Brady I want the two of you to work with them now that we've got a homicide.

"Boxer. You know Philip Pikelny, who heads up Robbery? Call him. You and Conklin work with his guys. This is the most important case in the house."

"We've got it, Chief."

Muttering to himself, Jacobi stumped out of the bullpen.

About now, Robbery would be canvassing Ellis Street and Forensics would be taking apart a check-cashing shop called Payday Loans. Checks Cashed. All we could hope for was a snitch or that this professional crew had left evidence behind.

I called Phil Pikelny and repeated Jacobi's instructions. The sergeant told me what he knew about the case so far.

"The scene is still off-limits," Phil said. "CSU

has barred the doors until they're done, which could be later today."

Phil told me he would get us the footage of the first "Windbreaker heist," the armed robbery of a mercado.

"It's with the DA's Office, but I'll put in a request to get a copy to you ASAP."

I called Administration and asked for time sheets for every cop at every rank in the Southern Station, thinking maybe we could at least make a list of cops who were off duty when those heists went down.

And for me, question number one was: Were these robbers really cops? Or just crooks in cops' clothing? Either way, wearing police Windbreakers probably gave the robbers a few seconds' grace before the victims knew they were being hit.

My good-doin' partner made a breakfast burrito run and I put up a fresh pot of coffee in the break room. Then we settled into our facing desks, ready for a roll-up-your-sleeves desktop investigation.

HOURS AFTER TALKING with Phil Pikelny, Conklin and I were still waiting for the DA's Office to send over the video of the Windbreaker cops' first known heist. I checked my watch. I could still make it. I told my partner I'd be back in a couple of hours.

"I have a date and I can't be late."

Richie opened his desk drawer, pulled out a slim, brightly wrapped package with a bow and a gift card, and handed it to me.

"This is for Claire. Try to bring me back some cake." He grinned winningly. He's a handsome guy who has somehow avoided becoming vain.

I took the gift, as well as the one I'd stashed inside my top drawer, then got my car out of the lot across the street. Two twisted streets and ten minutes later, I parked my ancient Explorer at the curb in front of the Bay Club. I put my ID on the dash. Then I walked around the corner to Marlowe, a fabulous eatery housed in a brick building with wine and food quotes etched on the large-paned casement windows.

I peered through the glass and saw Yuki and Claire in the back at a table for four. They seemed intensely involved in conversation, and from the looks on their faces, they were taking opposite sides. I came through the door into the bright, industrial-style interior, and Yuki spotted me right away. It almost looked like she was hoping for rescue.

She called out over the loud conversation that was bouncing off the tile and steel surfaces: "Lindsay, over here."

I headed toward my pals, and Claire stood up for my hug. She looked gorgeous, wearing black pants, a V-neck sweater, and a diamond pendant shaped like a butterfly around her neck. Claire is usually trying to lose a few pounds, but she always looks perfect to me.

I said, "Love you, Butterfly. Happy birthday, girlfriend."

She laughed. "Love you, too, Linds."

She hugged me back, and I swung into a chair

across from her and next to Yuki. Small-boned Yuki was impeccably dressed in a blue suit, her sleek hair falling to her creamy silk collar. A string of pale angel skin coral beads at her throat. When I'd last seen Yuki a week ago, she'd looked a little happier than she did now.

"You OK?" I asked.

"I'm good," she said.

We embraced, and I had just hung my jacket over the back of my chair when Cindy sailed up to the table, glowing like a rose at sunrise.

There was more hugging and kissing all around, Cindy adding a gift to the growing pile of sparkly paper and ribbons in the center of the table. We high-fived each other and I signaled to the waiter.

I was hungry for the specialty of the house: a hamburger made with Niman Ranch beef, topped with caramelized onions, bacon, cheese, and horse-radish aioli, nestled between halves of a hot, buttered bun. With fries. And even more than that upcoming delight, I was very glad to be with my best friends.

It was Cindy who had named our little group the Women's Murder Club. It was kind of a joke, and at the same time entirely for real, because the four of us certainly surrounded the subject of murder: me in Homicide; Claire, San Francisco's medical examiner; Yuki, a rising star in the DA's Office; and Cindy Thomas, a top-tier crime reporter at the *San Francisco Chronicle*.

Cindy was a new author, too. Her nonfiction book, *Fish's Girl: A True Story of Love and Serial Murder,* was grounded in a case Conklin and I had worked and two killers we had both known very well. Cindy had followed up the case and helped bring one of those killers down.

Her book was coming out at the end of the week. I was pretty sure that was why she was glowing.

After we'd ordered drinks, Claire piped up. "Yuki's quitting her job."

Cindy and I both said, "No way!" at the same time.

"I'm *thinking* about it," Yuki said, "just *thinking* about it. It's, like, an idea, you know? Geesh, you guys."

Cindy jumped in with what I was imagining.

"Oh. My. God. I know what's going on with you. You're *pregnant.*"

Yuki was married to my boss, the tough but fair Lieutenant Jackson Brady—but they'd only been married for four *months*. I didn't have a chance to get my mind around the idea of Yuki and Brady having a child, because Yuki was answering Cindy in her typical rapid-fire style.

"No, no, *no,* I'm not pregnant, but if you don't mind, all of you, we have to order lunch *now,* because I absolutely have to be in a deposition in an hour."

And that was when my phone rang.

I looked at the caller ID while everyone stared bullets at me. We had one rule for our no-holds-barred get-togethers.

No phone calls.

"Sorry," I said. "I've got to take this."

And I did.

I LEFT THE girls and found a niche where I could take the call in private.

"What's wrong?" I said to Lieutenant Brady.

"A dead body at Twenty-Fourth and Balmy Alley," he said. "I need you and Conklin to do a preliminary workup. Lock down the scene and sit tight until replacements arrive. Jacobi wants you and Conklin on the check-cashing heist, nothing else."

I rejoined my friends.

I said, "Sorry, guys. That was the boss. I've got to go."

Yuki tossed her napkin a few inches into the air in exasperation.

Cindy said, "What can you tell me?"

You can take the reporter out of the *Chronicle*,

but you can't take the reporter out of Cindy.

"Nothing," I said. "I can't tell you even one little thing."

"How many times do I have to prove I'm trustworthy?" said Cindy. "Plus, you owe me."

Actually, Cindy was right. On both counts. I trusted her. And a few months ago, she'd saved my life.

"I still can't tell you anything. Not a word."

I grabbed for my jacket and had just about secured it when Claire said, "I cannot believe this is happening *again*."

The expression on her face stopped me. She was pissed. Highly.

"*What's* happening again?" I asked her.

"This is almost exactly what happened last year on my birthday," said Claire. "And the year before *that*."

"Are you sure?"

"I'm *damned* sure. Although as I recall, last year we actually ate most of our lunch before you bolted from the table. Check your memory, Lindsay. When was the last time you saw me blow out the candles?"

"I'm sorry. I can't get out of this. I'll make it up to you, Claire. To everyone. Including myself. That's an iron-clad promise."

I apologized some more, blew kisses, and fled the restaurant. I called Rich Conklin from the street, and while I walked to my car, I said, "I'm ten minutes away."

"Same here."

The engine started right up. I peeled out and pointed the Explorer toward a busy intersection in the Mission.

The Thomas Berryman Number

James Patterson

One of the classic novels of suspense by the world's bestselling thriller writer.

It starts with three terrifying murders in the American South. It ends with a relentless and unforgettable manhunt in the North.

In between is the gripping story of a ruthless assassin, the woman he loves, and the beloved leader he is hired to kill.

'*The Thomas Berryman Number* is sure-fire!'
New York Times

CENTURY

Also by James Patterson

ALEX CROSS NOVELS

Along Came a Spider • Kiss the Girls • Jack and Jill •
Cat and Mouse • Pop Goes the Weasel • Roses are Red •
Violets are Blue • Four Blind Mice • The Big Bad Wolf •
London Bridges • Mary, Mary • Cross • Double Cross •
Cross Country • Alex Cross's Trial (*with Richard DiLallo*) •
I, Alex Cross • Cross Fire • Kill Alex Cross • Merry Christmas,
Alex Cross • Alex Cross, Run • Cross My Heart • Hope to Die

THE WOMEN'S MURDER CLUB SERIES

1st to Die • 2nd Chance (*with Andrew Gross*) •
3rd Degree (*with Andrew Gross*) • 4th of July (*with Maxine Paetro*) •
The 5th Horseman (*with Maxine Paetro*) • The 6th Target (*with
Maxine Paetro*) • 7th Heaven (*with Maxine Paetro*) •
8th Confession (*with Maxine Paetro*) • 9th Judgement (*with
Maxine Paetro*) • 10th Anniversary (*with Maxine Paetro*) •
11th Hour (*with Maxine Paetro*) • 12th of Never (*with Maxine
Paetro*) • Unlucky 13 (*with Maxine Paetro*) •
14th Deadly Sin (*with Maxine Paetro*)

DETECTIVE MICHAEL BENNETT SERIES

Step on a Crack (*with Michael Ledwidge*) •
Run for Your Life (*with Michael Ledwidge*) •
Worst Case (*with Michael Ledwidge*) • Tick Tock (*with Michael
Ledwidge*) • I, Michael Bennett (*with Michael Ledwidge*) •
Gone (*with Michael Ledwidge*) • Burn (*with Michael Ledwidge*) •
Alert (*with Michael Ledwidge*)

PRIVATE NOVELS

Private (*with Maxine Paetro*) • Private London (*with Mark
Pearson*) • Private Games (*with Mark Sullivan*) • Private: No. 1
Suspect (*with Maxine Paetro*) • Private Berlin (*with Mark
Sullivan*) • Private Down Under (*with Michael White*) •
Private L.A. (*with Mark Sullivan*) • Private India (*with
Ashwin Sanghi*) • Private Vegas (*with Maxine Paetro*) •
Private Sydney (*with Kathryn Fox, to be published August 2015*)

I FUNNY SERIES

I Funny (*with Chris Grabenstein*) • I Even Funnier (*with Chris Grabenstein*) • I Totally Funniest (*with Chris Grabenstein*)

TREASURE HUNTERS SERIES

Treasure Hunters (*with Chris Grabenstein*) •
Danger Down the Nile (*with Chris Grabenstein*)

HOUSE OF ROBOTS

House of Robots (*with Chris Grabenstein*)

KENNY WRIGHT

Kenny Wright: Superhero (*with Chris Tebbetts*)

HOMEROOM DIARIES

Homeroom Diaries (*with Lisa Papademetriou*)

MAXIMUM RIDE SERIES

The Angel Experiment • School's Out Forever • Saving the World and Other Extreme Sports • The Final Warning • Max • Fang • Angel • Nevermore • Forever

CONFESSIONS SERIES

Confessions of a Murder Suspect (*with Maxine Paetro*) •
The Private School Murders (*with Maxine Paetro*) •
The Paris Mysteries (*with Maxine Paetro*)

For more information about James Patterson's novels, visit www.jamespatterson.co.uk

Or become a fan on Facebook